Poppy at the Front

Jon Wilkins

Brigand
London

Copyright © 2020 by Jon Wilkins

The moral right of the author has been asserted.
All rights reserved. No part of the publication may be reproduced or transmitted in any form or by any means, without permission.
Brigand Press

All contact: info@brigand.london

Cover ©Kurt MISAR / Adobe Stock
Retouching & Artwork layout
www.scottpearce.co.uk

Map Drawn by Leo Zahibi
lezhengai.artstation.com

Poppy Flowers at the Front
Jon Wilkins
Visit my website at www.jonathanwilkins.co.uk
Email: jonwilkins@btinternet.com

British Library Cataloguing-in-Publication Data
A catalogue record for this book is
available from the British Library
Printed and Bound in Great Britain by CPI
Group (UK) Ltd, Croydon CR0 4YY

ISBN: 978-1-912978-17-5

Poppy Flowers at the Front

To Annie my darling wife.
My two wonderful sons David and Charlie.
To my brothers Viv and Joss.
To my parents, who I miss terribly.

Poppy Flowers at the Front

Poppy Flowers at the Front

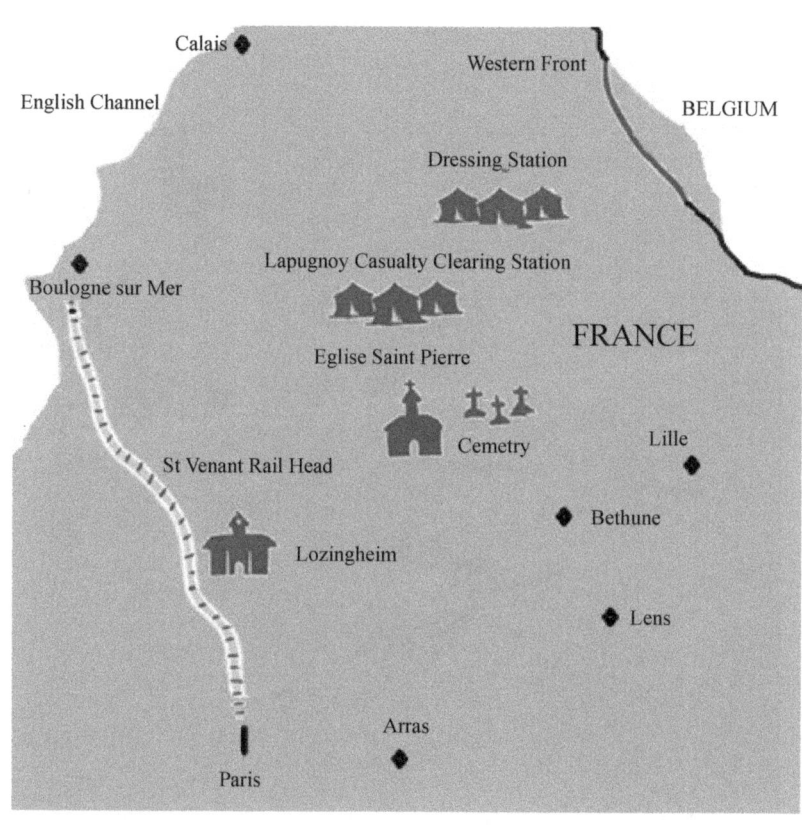

Poppy Flowers at the Front

Chapter 1

"The best thing one can do when it's raining is to let it rain..."

I am Lady Pandora Ophelia Loveday, Poppy to my friends. This is my story.

It was the screaming that really got to me. I could put up with most things and to be honest I had done so these past few months. The sound of the bombs didn't really faze me, nor the constantly falling rain and cloying mud. The fleas I found in my hair or clothes were just a nuisance as long as you caught them early. What I did hate was the screaming. It made my blood run cold, the screaming of men in agony, men who had lost their sight or had lost a limb. It ripped my heart out. Young boys in pain, a pain they did not deserve. Boys who screamed in terror, far from their homes and their mothers. Boys who screamed at things that weren't there, at memories of falling friends. Boys who screamed when they should be at home having fun. The number of times I had lied to a dying boy with the words 'mam's here now son' were countless. I lied to help them, to reassure them, to remind them of their mother's love, the love they would never feel again as they died in this foreign field. I often wanted a hug from my mother, I knew what they were missing. Writing this down seems so easy. Doing it all is rather more difficult. Like I am in two worlds. A world of the reality and nasty business of war and then this calmness seems to envelop me when I write. So, rain and wind, snow, and ice, all this I can put up with. Incessant screaming though is another thing all together. It is unseen. They are behind me in the ambulance. Unless I have to load it up when we are an orderly short, all I do is hear them. Then when I park up at the Clearing Station or at the ambulance train I have the honour of seeing them. Mangled bodies, missing limbs, gas burns, trench foot, gangrene... all the pleasures of this so-called modern warfare. All the pleasures plus the screaming that never seems to end. It's my birthday today. I told them when I enlisted I was nineteen so today should be my twentieth. I'm not sure the commander Lady Greenwood believes me. She can see through quite a lot! On my small up-turned crate are my birthday treats from home. Some toffee, gob stoppers, humbugs and delicious looking soaps. Though what I do need is some carbolic rather than some fancy French stuff. I often scrub myself raw to get rid of the grime. Mother sent me a journal which I will now start to fill in. It will certainly be for my eyes only. She must never see it, or I will have her preaching at me even more not to be here. I think I'll officially start my journal on a fresh page now. It's quiet for a change!

I looked back at what I had just written; I could hear the rain pelting down on our roof. The noise of the guns firing miles away made me jump every so often. I had not put a date on my musings, but it could have been any day. But today is special as it is my birthday and after a pleasant little tea party of bits and bobs, various comestibles and weak tea, I am sitting here on my cot, thinking. So, if you will allow me, I will turn the page ...

October 23rd, 1917.

Hello again, Dear Reader,
 Don't know why I started like that as I am not only the only reader, but the writer as well. No one else is going to see this, my journal or diary or whatever I should call this... my history perhaps? Just received this blank tome from parents for my birthday. Yes, today is my Birthday so, Happy Birthday to me, Happy Birthday to me, Happy Birthday to meeeeee! Seventeen today! Don't know how Dada did it, but the parcel arrived today right on cue for my big day. Already shared some gob stoppers with the girls, at my age gob stoppers! Don't know what Dada was thinking! Pleased anyway. We drank tea to celebrate. Tea! Not very strong tea at that! We had cakes and some dainty little sandwiches. Not sure what was in them though. But we were happy for a while! You find me in

Lapugnoy in France at the Casualty Clearing Station between shifts. I can write that without the censor blotting it out as he will never see this! In my spare time, today I have eaten some lump cake from home and lots of sweets. No point in saving any as the girls know I have them and will swoop on me when they return. I'm not greedy or selfish, but I want them for myself! I have really got a sweet tooth since being here, I don't know why. I have been listening to the guns firing all day. Well I don't listen to them; they are just there. Luckily now we are far enough away from the Front not to feel the ground shake with each explosion, but the noise is still there. All the time. Noise! I have sat on my cot picking louse eggs from the hems of my uniform. I had to be careful not to burn the seams with the lighted candle, but it was effective. You can see the results of your hunt as you shake the trousers over a newspaper. It gave me a strange satisfaction to see their little dead bodies litter the news. I am not sure if they are more relieved than me to escape the cold and the damp, but am glad they get no further than my hem. When I was first here I suffered terribly from bites, but thanks to the help of my fellow drivers I soon devised ways to stay louse free; well most of the time. It is a constant battle though. Sophie joked that it was a war within a war. We have to smile at something I suppose. Our poor fellows at the Front suffered so much more than we did, so I have to be thankful for small mercies... I am so tired I will end here. I've had a lovely birthday and I now feel sick from all the sweets I've eaten. Perfect!

I first met Élodie Proux by the side of a sunken road near Lebeuvrière in Northern France, a mile or so from the Dressing Station near the Front. Her face was battered and bruised. She was huddled under a blood-soaked nurse's cape holding a young Canadian soldier tightly. It was as if she was willing him to be alive, but he was long dead and we had no idea how long she had been there. Covered in his blood and mud, and soaked to the skin by the thunderous rain, we nearly missed her as the storm was so fierce. Around her was the detritus of war. A bomb must have landed plumb on top of the Dressing Station that was once there. Bodies lay around in the mud, the contents of tents were spread about the sludge, snow white bandages, vivid against the filth of the mud, parts of bodies, some inside pieces of uniform, others just lying there looking so out of place in the dirt and the mire as if they were asleep, untouched and unbloodied. It was as if hell itself had opened up onto the world and was displaying all that was evil. Élodie sat in silent horror in the mud as we eased the soldier's body from her hands. Her auburn hair was cut short and was plastered onto her skull. Her emerald green eyes were dull and lifeless. She was deep in shock, her nurse's uniform stained with the young lad's lifeblood, her face an unnatural white mask creased with the track lines of tears and mottled bruises. The Canadian's body was placed in the back of the ambulance along with the bodies of some more of the victims. Élodie was wrapped in a blanket and sat huddled against me in the front, shivering and sobbing until we reached the Clearing Station at Lapugnoy. The fragrant orange blossom scent she wore seemed incongruous as we slithered through the mud and the rain towards safety, well relative safety.

My roommate in the Barn, Sophie Quittenton, was on leave back in Boulogne-sur-Mer, so it seemed natural for Élodie to share with me for the time being until things were sorted out. She hadn't said a word since we had picked her up. I found some water from the tub outside, thankfully today not having to break the ice to pour it. I had slowly bathed her bruised face, getting rid of the muck and the tears. Her eyes were still dull and listless, she felt heavy and was so quiet, unnaturally quiet. I undid her cape and asked her to stand up. She did as she was told. She put her arms up into the air without me saying anything, just like I myself had when I was being undressed by Alice, my nanny at home all those years ago. I pulled off her bloodied tunic and washed all the bare skin I could see and reach. She was almost lifeless as she stood there, limp and unresponsive, but then Élodie shivered and I wrapped a blanket around her slender shoulders. She moved unbidden and kissed my cheek. I felt a strange surge throughout my body and shivered myself, and led her to Sophie's spare cot bed. I helped her to lie down and placed another rough grey blanket over her. She smiled. The first time she had shown any emotion other than shock and despair. She closed her eyes and was soon asleep. I had managed to get most of the blood and mud from Élodie's blue grey uniform, but it had taken several attempts and I felt hot and sweaty. I was very tired after my ten-hour shift and wanted to sleep. Her white apron though was useless, it was just too blood-stained. I had shuddered as I had rubbed and scrubbed it, eventually tossing it aside. There was no head dress, I wondered what had happened to that. This had made me perspire heavily, despite the cold and that meant that my head started to itch, not a good sign! With Sophie away I had not arranged for anyone to check my hair for lice for some days and having combed my hair over and over again I was starting to feel really dirty. How I longed for a hot bath, and some clean, dry clothes. Everything was soaked from the never-relenting storm. It always seemed to rain here which I hated. But at least I wasn't getting shot at every day, I suppose I should be grateful for small mercies.

  I woke the next morning and looked across at the sleeping French nurse. She seemed so at peace. I would have to get away on duty soon, it was almost six o'clock. Though still wet outside, I could see it may be a brighter day later. I had hung up the French nurse's uniform and checked my own socks again for fleas. Nothing there. I wrapped Alfie's rugby scarf around my chest and pulled on a thick cotton navy blue blouse. I had a pair of silk knickers on and then a big pair of bloomers, all in the interests of warmth. Well admittedly the silk was also in the interest of luxury; I did love the feel next to my skin. The bloomers though highly unattractive, were of necessity. Again, unbeknown to him Alfie had donated several pairs of his rugby socks to me and I pulled on a couple of pairs. I wasn't bothered about what I looked like. I just wanted to be warm and dry, though red and yellow hoops on one foot and green and white on the other were a tad unsightly! My dark blue uniform had hung up overnight and I pulled it on. It was still damp. I shuddered again. That was all I seemed to do, shiver or shudder. I suddenly felt so unhappy and sank my head into my hands and started to cry.

"Mamselle Poppee." She made me jump, I had never realised how many ees there were in my name. "Mamselle…" It was a small voice coming from her bed.

"You are all right?" I answered in French, shaking myself from my gloom, "I am well Élodie, how do you feel?" I got up and stepped over to her cot and brushed her hair from her eyes with my hand.

"So much better, *merci*. I was so frightened. I thought I was to die…"

"You are safe now. Your papers are under your pillow. Your clothes drying and clean. You can wear my spare uniform when you rise."

"I will get up now, there is work to do."

"Are you sure? You can still rest?" I asked, but she was already sitting up.

"Mamselle Poppee."

"Just Poppy will do Élodie."

"Poppy." She had removed all those extra ees

"Yes, it isn't my given name, but one all my friends gave me."

"We are friends?"

"B*ien sûr.* The best Élodie, as long as you are here."

"I will stay here then." She smiled and it was a radiant smile. Her whole face lit up, but it was her eyes that smiled the most. Large and sparkling emerald green, she was so beautiful. I handed her some socks and a scarf and intimated what to do. She giggled as I wrapped the scarf around her slender chest, but I assured her it would be worthwhile.

We stood by my ambulance in identical blue uniforms. Élodie was rather dwarfed by hers as I was somewhat taller than her. Élodie moved my beret slightly and pushed an escaped hair underneath its rim. I felt my skin tingle where she touched me and my tummy seemed to turn into honey. I could not explain the feelings that went through my body. Élodie smiled again.

"We are back to the Front?"

"Yes, some Belgian boys will need collecting. They attack later today so we pick up the results."

"We pick up the pieces you mean."

"I know Élodie, but we do our job. Get them back here as soon as possible and we help how we can."

Somehow, despite all the red tape that surrounded us, Élodie was allowed to stay. The German bombing had destroyed her unit just before we had found her trying to rescue the young soldier. We had heard the explosions from the Front and thought it strange that behind the line was getting so much flak and then saw the result of their onslaught. I had hoped to God that the Germans had not been targeting the site because it was a hospital and that the Red Cross would have been clear for all to see. Perhaps it had just been one of the many mistakes of war, but I also knew that everything did seem to happen for a reason. I cannot say what that reason was, but had I known then what I know now, I would have just been grateful. I suppose I shouldn't have been surprised that a Dressing Station had been targeted as they also often attacked our ambulances when they had the chance. I've gripped many a steering wheel, holding my breath when I heard an engine in the sky. To be frank I was surprised how poor their marksmanship seemed to be, both with the bombs they dropped that missed by yards and the spumes of bullets that flew either side of the old bus. I wasn't going to complain though! Anyway, there were already some French nurses billeted at Lapugnoy, along with some Russians and a few enterprising Americans, but they were living in tents towards the west of our base. Because she had stayed with me the first night it was deemed fair and square that she could remain in the Barn. A rare occasion of common sense prevailing during a time when madness and lack of humanity dominated.

November 1st, 1917.

Dear Dada,
I hope you and mother are well. I am as to be expected! Cold and wet a lot of the time but hey ho it is what it is. You'll never guess what I have been doing for some weeks now... so I will tell you...FIGHTING! Not in a bad sense, but I have been tutored in a Chinese martial art. I know not what it's called as the Chinese coolies don't speak such good English, but it's something like tie chee. Yes, it is exotic! Chinese coolies who help out digging and suchlike are based near us and I saw them out one morning doing this thing that I think they call tie chee. I don't know if it's spelled like that, just that it's pronounced like that. They let me join in and it was really relaxing, and a group of them split aside and started to fight using all the same movements and they let me join in that as well! So, for six weeks or so I have been in the ruins of a village that I cannot name, moving, and holding and grappling in a quite unladylike fashion. BUT I have to say darling father that I feel much safer for it. I can ward off any unwanted attentions. The Chinese can disarm a man with a stick or a gun with their bare hands, but I haven't done that yet, but I can trip someone, break a strangle hold and actually throw a man onto the floor. I know the Chinese are tiny, but I know what to do at least. I feel a lot more secure. More news later. Should you tell mother? Not sure!
What I do need is something for my hair to delouse it again. Some soap as well if you could please. I've had to cut it even shorter, so short, that you had better warn mother about that! If I came home on leave with it like it is, she would have a fit! I tried having it in a chignon as the French call it, but it was too much fuss and the nasty lice invaded all the time! Now it is shorter it doesn't get attacked as much, but if you could send some that would be tremendous. The smell might be obnoxious but at least I won't be scratching myself to death. Sophie has been away somewhere on leave and I hope to go to the same place myself. Some good news is that

besides Sophie, I have found a new friend called Élodie, who is a French nurse we picked up on the roadside. Suffice to say her unit is no more. I can't add to that, but she seems nice enough. Has anything been invented that keeps the cold and wet out of the human body? My feet freeze as do my hands. I could make an absolute fortune if I could patent something that kept all parts of the body dry. Pity I don't have a scientific inventing bone in my body. I could write about it though! The rain gets everywhere. I have Alfie's scarves to give me layers of warmth but they get damp and do smell hideously. I need a coat that the rain bounces off, is there such a thing? Perhaps made of wellington boot material? Finally, if you can spare it can I have something sweet in my next parcel. Not to presume, but I do look forward to my treats from you both and from Mrs George, so jam, toffee, chocolate, marzipan, bulls' eyes... I could go on but will stop there! Give mother all my love, well keep some for yourself of course. Say hello to Mrs George and reassure her that all is well.

Your loving daughter,

Ophelia

November 4th, 1917.

Dear Journal,

As we know I am just seventeen and driving an ambulance here. I managed to bluff my way across to France because I could drive, and, thanks to my darling brother Alfie, I also knew how to check the carburettor or find a fuel blockage. He would always mock me when I was small, badgering him to show me how, but I knew I had a purpose. I didn't know what kind of purpose and I certainly hadn't dreamt about being in a war zone, but that's how it turned out! Sometimes when the men are screaming in the back of the ambulance I wish I was home, but needs must. I think I wrote earlier in this journal that I hate the sound of screaming. It never gets any easier and their screams never get any softer.

Mother is very angry that I came to France, but Dada stopped her from bringing me home. In fact, he was able to have stopped me if he'd wanted too. Old army, Boer War, you know what it's like. If mother knew she would divorce him I'm sure! In fact, this is one of only two things they have ever argued about. Me coming to France and my name. Dada insists on calling me Ophelia. His mother's name and my favourite Shakespearean heroine. Mother will call me Pandora. This is her middle name. It can get confusing at times, especially as all my friends and Alfie call me Poppy! I came to France partly to be near my big brother Alfie, but I have never seen him. That's no surprise, I'm not sure at times what I was thinking. We are all like needles in haystacks. I feel his presence though and that is enough.

We live in what we call "The Barn" It's an old cattle shed I think, a central area with stalls along both sides, we occupy the stalls and have a central area where we can meet and eat and smoke. The stalls seem to have almost been designed to snugly fit three cots in them, though most just had just the two. We put up a blanket on a string across the entrance to preserve our privacy. I heard that the drivers before me spent a whole week cleaning out the stalls and fixing the roof. It seems they had some real battles with some of the men at the base to keep their new home as the soldiers thought that they deserved a real roof over their heads rather than the women, but the battle was won, with the ladies successful.

When Élodie moved in we fitted her cot between mine and Sophie's. There was then no room to walk around and we had to shift our lockers to the foot of the beds. It did seem to make it cosier though. Mind you, we now need a locker for Élodie, she has nothing to put in it yet so we must find her some essentials.

Outside the stalls is our communal area. It had a wood burner in the middle attached to the outside by a long tin can chimney that wobbled its way to a window and took out most of the fumes. I rather liked it when we burnt logs from what was left of the now petrified woods outside. Other times it was coal or clinker which didn't smell so nice, but I was able to collect it from the railhead where it had dropped from trains, so it was free of charge... Perhaps I should add a piece here in my journal about life on the camp. Part I. Food. What about it you may ask, and I am only too happy to let you know. Breakfast of strong tea and when I say strong tea I mean it. It would allow a spoon to stand up in it. I am also not sure what the chemical taste is, for sure it is not tea tasting, it is something else indeed. Still, there is plenty of it! Porridge. Well they call it porridge. Sometimes it has the consistency of whitewash and tastes like it and at others it is as thick as the mud I drive through most days. Taste? Well that is the question. I cannot deduce what taste there is. It bubbles in the urn it's served from and continues to bubble on the plate. It tastes of... white heat and sticks to the roof of your mouth and can burn your flesh. There is always bread and some type of jam. Though again what the fruit is I have no idea, so it is red jam or black jam and sometimes it is orange when some marmalade sneaks through the customs. Margarine is the problem, it is an absolute curse to cookery. So disgusting. Sophie has often said she will take some to use on her axle to help it get through her journeys. My face will tell her what I think of it. Bread? Bread. Well it's so full of something other than wheat that I think we could use it on a chalkboard to leave messages from each other.

     Having written this, I am now hungry. I think I will leave my cot and see if I have any cake left from my last parcel from home ...

Poppy Flowers at the Front

Chapter 2

"I wonder if the snow loves the trees and fields, that it kisses them so gently?"

We had just delivered a group of wounded men. Most, thank goodness, were just bullet wounds. No shrapnel or gas. Nothing that would mutilate the insides or outsides. It also meant that they were a little more stoical and there was not so much crying out in pain. We were lucky I suppose that we had a gnarled old corporal with us who was keeping them in line and hushing them when they moaned. When I opened the back of the ambulance cigarette smoke streamed out like a fog, and several of the more able men stumbled down to be led away by nurses who would sort them into lines for treatment. Several stretcher bearers hurried over and with great gentleness lifted the severely wounded and moved them away to the operating tents. I was just about to wash the inside of my ambulance when the first shell landed and amid screams of terror I raced over to the shelter, bumping into bodies flying about in panic as I made my way. None of this stiff upper lip anymore. It was sheer horror and panic. Élodie saw me and grabbed hold of me like a scared child. I could feel the tears of Élodie as I held her next to me. The bombs rained down outside our sandbagged shelter. I had little faith in its safety, especially if one landed too close. We were soaked and covered in mud and terrified. I tried to soothe Élodie, but her tears were relentless, and I could hear other nurses sobbing as they too huddled together. Every time a shell landed Élodie would jump with terror and grasp my hand tighter. I hoped they wouldn't land on the Barn and destroy our living quarters. It was almost like home now. I smiled at Élodie at the thought, but she was oblivious. We were all in a hopeless position, totally dependent on where the bombs might land. It suddenly went quiet inside the shelter, Élodie wiped her eyes with her skirt, smiling thinly at me. The silence began to be interrupted by sobs all around us and moans from outside the shelter. I put my head outside the doorway and saw a scene of utter devastation. Tents had been destroyed, detritus was all over the ground, swimming in puddles of mud where the duck boards had been shattered, or plastered against the tents that had survived, or the ranks of sandbags that seemed to have escaped unscathed.

"Wait till the All Clear!" A matron shouted, but I could see two bodies close to the shelter. One was dead, the body decimated, the other was crying in pain. A piece of bloodied khaki sobbing into the mud in agony. I ignored matron and ran out to him, keeping my body low. I had no idea if the bombing would resume. I heaved him up onto my shoulder and he screamed in pain. I had to ignore him, and part carried, part dragged him to the operating tent which was luckily untouched. Half-way there the whistle for all clear was sounded and soon all was organised bustling action. An orderly came to my aid and we took the young man to a table and laid him gently down. His moaning didn't stop. His eyes were closed, his tunic soaked with blood, mud, and rain. Not for the first time was I thankful that my uniform was navy blue. I made my way through the returning doctors towards my ambulance and my next orders. Matron took my arm. "Stupid, Loveday. But brave, do have a care."

"Yes matron," I mumbled. To my right three tents were ablaze, so much again for the red cross emblazoned on everything, I thought. I looked up into the early evening sky. Every so often a red flare would light up the clouds above the Front a few miles away. There was now no sound of guns or shooting. It seemed peaceful. The rain of course still fell. The world seemed almost at ease with itself, but only for a moment as my Commandant, Lady Greenwood, beckoned me over and instructed me to go to Zone Three, which meant towards the death fields of Ypres, back to the Front to collect more wounded.

"I need to wash out the old bus." I protested.

"Sorry, no time for that Loveday, double clean tonight!" She smiled, unusually so as she was the most stoic of individuals. I revved up the cold engine as the ambulance jerked into life. I waited until a nurse got into the back and was off down the newly damaged road. Sliding through old ruts and new ones, towards the flares and the mayhem.

Back at the Barn that night with a candle guttering by my cot, I lay exhausted, but sleep eluded me. Besides me Sophie snored quietly, so lady-like I thought. Elodie was tossing and turning in her narrow bed. She was fighting demons it seemed, muttering and whispering in her sleep. What was going on in those dreams? I closed my eyes and breathed deep. I wanted so much for sleep to come.

"Poppeee!..." Her scream split the night. I rolled over onto her bed. Despite the freezing cold, she was sweating, I could feel the dampness on her arm and her face as I touched her cheek. Sweat and tears.

"What is it Élodie?"

"Sorry, a *cauchemar*, a bad dream..."

"Again?"

"*Je suis désolé*, I cannot help ..."

"I know, I know." I tried to sooth her, "but you are safe, no one can hurt you
here."

"Just the bombs Poppy, the bombs, the fleas, the cold." At least she was smiling.

"I will keep you safe my darling, don't worry. What was the dream, the *cauchemar*?
You never speak of it," I said.

"I cannot Poppy, you would hate me, let me sleep." She turned away from me. "I will be fine now."

"Do you want a candle?"

"No, it will be dawn soon. Go back to sleep, désolé, sorry."

"No matter Élodie, don't worry about me." I left her as she tried to get back to sleep and sat on my cot and looked at the huddled form in the camp bed. Élodie shifted and twitched and muttered as she fell back to sleep.

I was sitting at the side of Corporal Lewin's bed.

He was a very formal soldier and would only call me Miss Loveday or Ma'am. The other soldiers I spoke to called me Poppy. It was strange how some formalities still remained, even with the world as it was. I was closing in on the end of Westerman's *The Sea-girt Fortress*. My volume had several pieces of paper with various names on them, stuck in different parts denoting where and when I had reached a particular page with a particular soldier. I held Corporal Lewin's paper in my hand as I reached the last few words. The island fortress was just about to fall, and I was trying to make this sound exciting! He lay in his bed staring ahead. He never said much, but he did seem to enjoy the reading. I had to be quick with some of them as they were to be either shipped back to England or were unlucky enough to return to the trenches. Lewin would soon be sent home. I had written to his wife to reassure her that she would be getting all of her husband back, which was not always the case. I was not sure about his mind, however. He had, like so many, seen things that could never be unseen and would take those sights home to his wife and family.

"Thank you, Miss Loveday."

"It's been a pleasure Corporal," I said.

"Do you know when I'm going home?"

"Quite soon I hear, you'll find out before I do, I'm sure."

"Well can I thank you now, Miss Loveday. You have made things so much easier. Though where I'll get a copy of the book if I go before you finish it, I don't know." He laughed for the first time since I'd met him, and this was a cheerful sound and made me happy. There weren't that many laughs here on the ward. At the Barn yes, but this was work and was a serious place, so it was a pleasant change. I checked where Matron was and bent down and kissed his forehead.

"It really has been a pleasure, Corporal Lewin." I said and moved onto the next bed and another soldier. I flicked through the pages to find out who was next and as I found my place I sat beside another bandaged young man.

"Got a kiss for me as well, Poppy?" The cheeky young

thing said, and I wondered what I had let myself in for.

November 7th, 1917.

Dearest Pandora,
  How are you my darling? We all miss you so much. Even cook asked me to send you her love, which I am happy to do. How is everything going? I hope you are safe. We read a lot about what is happening and of course your father has his contacts, so we know some of what life may be like.
  We are having to find new ways of eking food out as we are having some shortages. I will still send whatever we can to you, which I hope you will enjoy. Cook will be baking some special cakes she says, and we will post them to you as soon as possible.
  We have few horses now as the last of the really healthy ones, were taken by the Army. Maybe you will meet them? I jest of course! I doubt if they would survive very long over there.
  I do love you my darling Pandora, the house seems so empty without your laughter and your arguments. Yes, I even miss our disagreements. It is strange. I have found it hard to let go of you my darling and do look forward to you returning home on leave soon.
  The village is very quiet. The men have gradually disappeared and many of the young women have gone to the cities for work. I have no idea how some of the farms will cope when it comes to harvest time.
  Alfred does seem to write a mixed-up letter with no real order. I am finding it hard to concentrate at the moment, there is so much going on and we don't seem to be in control. What it is like for you must be even worse.
  Remember it would not be a bad thing to come home. All is forgiven. We love you so much.

Mother

Lapugnoy seemed at peace. There was no gun fire in the air, and I could actually hear birds singing. I knew I had to make the most of that, it wouldn't last long. I had managed a little lie-in. No one had disturbed me leaving our little room and I was grateful for that. Despite being so tired, it was very rare that we could stay asleep for long once the first of us was awake. People didn't really concern themselves about others so carried on without a care in the world, talking loudly, joking loudly, living life at a louder level of decibel that's for sure. I left the Barn and stretched my hands as high towards the sky as I could, feeling cracks of bones and ligaments snap. In the distance was the loud crump of cannon fire and in the sky I could see black clouds. At least it wasn't raining this morning. I eschewed breakfast and made my way towards the used ammunition dump, where I found Élodie sitting on a stack of empty shell casings. Where their payloads had landed heaven knows. The damage they'd done was replicated by the damage done to our own soldiers, by German bombs, our tents full of the wounded, evidence of their evil intent, all lined up in neat rows in a muddy field. The Barn stood aloof to the tents, the only brick building for miles. Though pock marked with shell fire, despite the huge red cross painted on the roof, it still stood and our rooms were secure enough. All too obvious to the world was that this war was going nowhere. Élodie looked up, she was sketching.

"What are you drawing?" I asked. She handed me the pad. In charcoal; she had pictured the inside of one of the tents. Rows of beds each with a head popping out from the blankets. The blackness of the charcoal against the white page gave a funereal quality to the drawing. I turned the page. A shell hole with a corpse hanging at the edge. Water at the bottom mirroring his pose as he tried his fruitless escape. Again, just black and white. Stark and real. The next page featured a series of drawings of soldiers. Smoking, digging, running, marching, all so life-like, it was as if I was looking at a photograph. Her talent was stunning, and I found myself tracing each figure with my fingers, I don't know why, as if to check that they were real or something.

"It's me!" I squealed as I turned the next page.

"You can tell?" Élodie asked shyly.

"Of course, Élodie. It's perfect."

"You may have it then." She smiled.

"And this of you?" I asked as I turned the page to a self-portrait that caught my eyes completely.

"If you wish, *Cherie*."

"I wish." I said, glancing around before kissing her cheek, "Of course I wish."

"Why so excited?" Élodie asked.

"I don't know. These are just so beautiful, even though they show such pain." I spread my arms out wide, "You are so talented. I didn't know you were so skilled."

"I love to draw and paint. I was at the university to study Art, but after a year, the war..."

"Stopped you?"

"Stopped so many things. I moved into nursing to help. But yes, I should be in Florence or Rome drawing. Instead I stop blood, trying to help wounded boys."

"Which is important."

"I know," Élodie whispered.

"You can start again, when this is over."

"I don't know. Life will have moved on. Time moves on, perhaps I missed my chance."

"Don't Élodie, you have a gift. You must use your gift."

"We shall see. For now, I have my book of memories." She held the book to her chest with both hands. "I see this in my mind's eye and also on the paper."

"I have it all here." I tapped my forehead, "I will never forget."

"We should never forget, *Cherie*," Élodie said softly and kissed my cheek.

Post from home had arrived. I unwrapped my parcel with slow pleasure. Another book, Percy Westerman's latest, *A Watch-dog of the North Sea*. I thought back to my father reading to us in his study, sat snuggling up to him on his big leather settee at home. All derring do. Boys Own stories. I would put myself in the male lead and escape for a while as I saved the nation. It was the same with the Sexton Blake books he had sent, when I read them I was always the one who burst through the door, it was me, Sexton Blake, gun blazing, ordering my female sidekick Tinker to do her best to defeat whatever stood in our way. I giggled to myself. I threw the packets of gaspers on my pillow. I would hand them out later to the girls who smoked. They just made my throat sore and gave me a cough. I couldn't see the attraction, but the minty Bulls Eyes, now that was nice! I popped one in my mouth sucking with relish and put Dada's letter to one side to read later. That would be another treat at the end of a long day. Under yet another knitted scarf, I now had seven, were some cut out Times Crossword puzzles. I glanced at them and noticed in pencil one clue had been answered in each. Silly Dada, I thought, and saw that the answer had no relation to the clue. MISSING, OPHELIA, MOTHER, TERRIBLY, HOME, COME, DARLING, YOU, SAFELY, FATHER... A puzzle within a puzzle, but rather easier than the actual crossword. I rearranged them on my cot; it didn't take long; it probably wasn't even right, but it made sense to me; he was such a soppy man. MISSING YOU TERRIBLY DARLING OPHELIA, COME HOME SAFELY, MOTHER, FATHER. That made me laugh out loud, but then my tears came, and I hugged the new scarf to my face, sobbing my eyes out. My mother's scent catching my eyes as the tears rolled down my cheeks.

    I just couldn't get warm anymore. It seemed endless. Wet and cold, cold, and wet, I'd stand by a brazier, the burner in our barn or a fire outside and rub my hands, but all that would happen was that I'd get smoke in my eyes. The cold just stayed with me deep in my bones with the damp and the itching. I had my woollen mittens on with a pair of leather gauntlets over them and still it was frozen. My hands seemed numb. I looked over the windscreen through screwed up eyes feeling the snow set on my eyelashes. There was so much snow the wipers could not clear it, so I had to face the elements with the windscreen down to have a clearer view. It was blowing a real blizzard and my chest was covered in snow. My eyes stung. I had mislaid my goggles, though I didn't really like to wear them even though my eyes stung under the wind and the snow. It didn't help being so tired. It had been a double shift with another pointless push at the Front, which meant that there were also more trips from dressing station to clearing station as severely wounded needed moving on quickly. It was like some horrible conveyor belt. A nightmare existence for all concerned. I was so tired and so cold. No matter how many of Alfie's scarves I wrapped around me it was always cold. I had to concentrate though, getting my eyes focussed through the snow on the road ahead. At least with the road being frozen the tyres were not sinking deep into mud, but still they slipped every so often throwing the ambulance to the side and causing cries from the wounded behind. Thankfully, I eventually got us to the railway sidings, and we could unload our passengers. An orderly and I put another stretcher on the frozen ground to await collection. We exchanged him for another stretcher. It held a severely wounded boy, as he didn't seem to be a man yet. And, he would never become a man.

"Is it time for tea, mum?" The young soldier asked me. His eyes bandaged; his sight destroyed.

"Nearly, darling. Are your hands clean?" I asked, then shuddered.

"Washed 'em special, mum," which was a lie as both had been blown off and the boy was dying. I stroked his head. He lay on the stretcher in my ambulance, white as a ghost.

"Will dad be home soon?"

"Not long darling, he's busy but he'll be chuffed to see you."

"I hope so, mum. I've missed him, I've missed you both." I felt a large lump in my throat and was finding it hard to breathe. The boy was drifting into sleep, a permanent sleep. The morphine was working. "I do love you, mum."

"I love you too." I kissed his forehead and he was gone.

My tears spilt onto his face like rain.

"Come along, Loveday, work to be done!" A Matron called into the back of my ambulance. I eased the boy's head from my lap and pulled the blanket over his head before getting unsteadily to my feet. The Matron put out a hand to help me out,

"Never ever gets any easier, Poppy, but never let it get easy."

"No, matron."

"Now off you go. Bring some more chaps back for us, there's a good girl."

I thought I had finally finished my shift and drove back to Lapugnoy and went through the revolting ritual of cleaning the ambulance out. I washed out the back with the water freezing as it hit the floor. This will be a death trap I thought, and almost smiled as I thought about how many were dead at the end of each journey. It was usually at least one, sometimes more. I poured the foul-smelling disinfectant onto the icy floor and it managed to turn it back to water and I pushed it all away out of the bus. An orderly came over and gave me the wonderful news that I was needed to go back out to a Dressing Station in a different sector from this morning. The generals liked to share out their death. I wanted to scream, I was so tired and had started to relax, thinking I would be able to sleep soon, but instead I swallowed hard and went back through what was now turning into rain and the mud to the front of my ambulance to find Élodie sitting grinning behind the wheel.

"My turn to drive, *Cherie*," She smiled, but then clambered across to the passenger seat, "But you have been crying?" She reached for my hand and squeezed it.

"Young lad died in my arms again." I started to cry once more. "It's too much, just too much."

"I know, Poppee, but we have to go on, we can help many others."

"But so many, so many. They come back with pieces missing. This young boy no hands, no eyes, so much pain. I cannot bear it."

"You have to, Poppee, you must, they rely on us, on you to get them to safety."

"But what life faces them after the war at home, legs gone, faces ruined. Blind, all manner of things. How can they return to normal?"

"None of us will find this normal again, *ma mie*. This is not your problem. You do this job, you do it well and then we have done our piece."

"And when the war is over?"

"It will never be over for some, but you can decide what to do..."

"When it's over? Will this ever be over?" I got out and cranked the engine. Thankfully it started on the third turn, I would have gone mad if there had been a problem now. I jumped back up onto my seat and slammed the door shut, then rammed the gear stick into place

"It has to end, Poppee. It will end."

"But who will win in the end? All they do is bomb and blast away, gaining nothing, losing lives. It's madness!"

"I know, but it will end. Nothing can last for ever. Tell me something, *très jolie*, something nice. Try to forget for a moment." The bulky ambulance started to skid on the muddy road, and I laughed.

"Well I am with you."

"And that is nice for us both. What about just you?"

"I found no lice this morning."

"That is better. But still not nice just for you. I don't want your fleas!"

"The rain looks to have stopped."

"Come, Poppee, there is more surely?"

"I got my leave, have you heard of yours?" I asked.

"Not yet..."

"I hope we can both go to Boulogne together. I need a rest."

"You need a bath more!"

"Why, do I smell?"

"No more than usual!" she snorted. "We are here."

Élodie pointed to a line of soldiers and stretchers. One by one the orderlies placed them in the back of the ambulance and Élodie went to join them. An officer with a bloodied head bandage took her place in the front seat.

"You're a sight for sore eyes, miss," he said smiling
"Just as you are. Bashed your head?"
"Just a glancing blow, be right as rain soon." He must have been twenty if a day.
"How does it feel?" I asked.
"Bad as when we played Caius before we came over. More blood than damage I'm sure."
"Caius? I hope to go to Queen Aethelflaed's one day, when all this is over."
"Good show, nice College, all those young ladies!" he grinned.
"Those your men in the back?"
"Some of them. Good bunch of lads."
"They all are..."
"What's your name, driver?"
"Poppy, to my friends."
"Can I call you Poppy then?" he smiled.
"Of course, captain?" I asked.
"Llewellyn."
"Welsh?"
"God's own country, Poppy." He said proudly.
"Though no accent?"
"You know what it's like, had to lose it to move on."
"I have some Welsh in me somewhere. My Dada is from Wales, my mother very English."
"Where are your people now?"
I started to offer my story, leaving out the landed-gentry status of my family. He knew Leicestershire and appeared to be listening intently until I realised he had gone to sleep. I smiled to myself and continued driving in silence. The rain started to come down heavier and the sky became blacker. Though mid-afternoon, it was soon as dark as night and the rain turned to hail. The headlights danced through the rain

and picked up every rain drop that fell to earth, highlighting them like diamonds. A fork of lightning arced across the sky, followed shortly by the rumble of thunder mirroring the sound of artillery that we had gotten so used to. Straining at the wheel, I turned the lumbering ambulance into the Clearing Station at Lapugnoy and parked alongside the main admin building, tents lined up either side of it. I touched the captain on the arm.

"Here we are sleepy head." But he didn't move. Naturally he had died on me, right next to me. I let my head fall onto the steering wheel and started to butt the centre with my forehead, sobbing my eyes out. There was no matron or Élodie to stop me crying. They would have failed anyway.

November 13th, 1917.

Dear Dada,
Hope all is well. Apologies for the muddy paper, but you can imagine how it is. Just taking a break before my next run. The rain never stops. If it does, it means it's snow. It's quite a lark! But getting clothes dry is so hard.
It is all so hard, in every sense. We see so much blood; it is heart breaking. Thank you so much for the tuck and your silly puzzles. Keep sending the gaspers, I don't partake but the other girls are always cadging. Alfie, I hope is well. He wrote last week and seems very busy but safe at the moment. Mother did mention cake in her letter. Where is it I ask?
Mother seems to have forgiven me. I wrote to her. I feel I am doing so much good here, my work is so worthwhile, and I suppose if it allows another man to go to the Front then all is right with the world. We all can help in our own way. It is horrible though, too horrible for words and do people at home want to know I ask?
More books would be wonderful. I read them to the wounded, so kill two birds with one stone, so to speak. Mind you, I almost know them off by heart as I have so many patients in their beds awaiting adventures and scheming

detectives! Confectionery of all sorts more than welcome. They keep me going at the wheel. Cake would be nice if you have the ingredients. I am hoping to have some leave soon and look forward to seeing you all. I hope you will be at home. I don't suppose Alfie has any leave, does he?

I've met some really sweet soldiers in my time here so far, what amazes me is that they are so personable and then go away to shoot the Germans to pieces. How does that affect the mind? One day all calm and relaxed and the next in mayhem. Perhaps they are never relaxed, we don't really see them unless they are wounded and then they have a certain calmness about them, especially if they are not long for this earth. Oh Dada, it is such a waste, but I'd best stop this or the censors pen will rip through to the other side. Do you keep my letters Dada? It would be interesting to know what does get blacked out. Do my letters have much censorial intervention you never say so?

It's strange there is so much going on but so little I can tell you about. I am quite safe though. Tell mother. I don't know if anything has been crossed out by the censor, I hope not. Tell mother I have her letter; it came as I was writing this to you. So, will love you and leave you my darling Dada. I love you both so very much my darling mother, my dearest Dada.
All my love.

Ophelia

Chapter 3

"O, wind, if winter comes, can Peace be far behind?"

I felt a warm surge at the thought of Élodie. This was all I seemed to feel now, a dry mouth when we spoke, a warm feeling when our hands brushed. I knew something was happening with Élodie and I didn't quite know what to do about it. To be honest I didn't really understand any of the feelings that were going through my body. I did understand guilt. Part of me realised it was different, part of me realised my feelings were wrong. Wrong for whom? I refused to accept it was wrong no matter what I was told at church, because part of me wanted to be with Élodie so much. I shivered to get myself back into the moment which was not that difficult. And so it went on never seeming to end. Never-ending blood today, mud tomorrow with the rain, but always the blood. I wasn't sure when Sophie would return from leave. I missed her, she had been so full of life and chatter. Always jollying me along when I felt down. A real product of the aristocracy. The pair of us together. Sophie was a few years older than me and lived near London. She had a younger sister, Sapphire who was living at home, and was in love with a soldier with whom she had kissed her goodbyes in 1915. Since then they had written to each other as regular as clockwork. How could you sustain a love affair under these conditions I wondered? Was it even possible? In her case it seemed it was as they were to be married when all this was over. If it ever would be, I often thought to myself. Sophie wanted this to happen sooner rather than later. I thought she ought to wait. Who knew what the war would bring and how we would feel when it did eventually end?

For a special treat we were to see a film from Hollywood. It was taking place in one of the large mess tents and the place was packed-out with soldiers and smelt appropriately. We were sat to the right in our own small roped-off Ladies Section. How demure. The sight of Sherlock Holmes in action might raise the testosterone level in the men and we would be unsafe from their advances. I just wanted to stay clear of the rank body odour smell, though they could not help it. I sniffed to see what I was like and Élodie gave me a queer look. She of course smelt of orange blossom as she always did. I had read about the smart William Gillette somewhere and was now to see him in real life, well at least on film. I had first read of Holmes as a child along with Sexton Blake and the rest of the sleuthing gangs and had my own view of what he should look like. Gillette was that man; he was Holmes with his sharp chin, hooded eyes and pipe. Though there was no speech it was clear he was a fine actor. There were so many reel changes though. The soldiers were easily bored and heckled during these gaps. Smoke filled the tent and the light from the projector was cutting through the smog and I kept feeling it at the back of my throat, but needs must. Élodie would squeeze my hand every so often and almost jumped out of her skin at one point, her hand almost crushing me before she started giggling at the silliness of it all. I wasn't sure which Holmes story this came from as it seemed a mixture of many. The Tommies cheered as the baddie was chased down. We only met Watson almost at the end of the film, which was odd, but such was the director's choice. Ernest Maupain played the evil Moriarty to perfection, all wide-eyed and extravagant gestures. I had seen him in "The Raven" before I came out to France. It made me laugh, though this was no comedy. What was missing was a musical accompaniment but we had no pianist here. That was a shame, music always adds to the theatre. Marjorie Kay played the love interest, but I couldn't remember if I had ever seen her in a film before. As the lights went up the roof was lifted by the Tommies who were obviously more than satisfied with the outcome, predictable as it was. I would have preferred something with Mary Pickford. I had seen a couple of her films recently and though predictably saccharine, they had more of a story than this gung-ho fare. I had loved watching *Poor Little Rich Girl,* that was a real pleasure and she was so pretty.

Élodie and I made our way back to the Barn. It was a bit of a relief to get out of the smoke-filled tent and I breathed deep as we came into fresh air. Clemmie was alongside us and Sophie in front. Sophie had of course loved the romance. Clemmie the action. Back at The Barn we chatted as Élodie made cocoa on the stove and Elsie toasted some bread. What a perfect night. Why was life so difficult? Would it be like this if it were portrayed in a film?

November 14th, 1917.

Dear Reader Diary Me Poppy
This is written directly to me, and for no one else. How can I explain? I see her and my tummy turns upside down and all I can feel is a sensation of loveliness. I cannot describe it, but my heart beats faster and I find it hard to breathe. My cheeks go red. I don't feel clumsy, but I feel something. A honey glow inside me, a shiver on the outside, it's so strange. Then we touch and I tingle everywhere, especially... I cannot write where. But I feel different, special, chosen. She seems to occupy all my thoughts. Her touch... how is this so? What does it all mean? I do know, but should I say it? If this is what I think it is ... Girls get sent home for this... Is that a disgrace or is it just wrong to punish them for their feelings? What are their feelings? Do they love each other? Should they love each other? Boys, men, mean nothing to me. I have never felt anything. We will have to talk. What does she think? I see her watching me and I feel as if a ray of sunshine is on me, warm, peaceful, excited... How can it be all those feelings? We need to talk, but how...

What if I am wrong? Are my feelings wrong? What can I do? What does she feel? Our French nurse has disappeared with a patient to Paris it seems. She was rushed off without notice and I realise again how much I miss her whenever we are apart. Must be a special patient to go to Paris, I sometimes have to drive one to the coast to one of our many hospitals, but never to Paris. I would like to go to Paris and see the sights. We hear of bombs being dropped on the city and my fear is that the things I want to see will be destroyed. How a city as beautiful as Paris can be attacked is beyond me, but you only have to look out towards the battle front to see that so many pretty villages have been erased from the earth and will probably never be rebuilt. But can you compare Notre Dame or the Eiffel Tower to a village hall or a village church? Well you can actually. They are all created for people, they are people's homes, places of worship, places of education. All should be sacred. None should be wiped away from our eyes. Those who sent the bombs were truly evil and I include those on our side as well.

    Well Diary, it's not for you to decide. I thought coming over here was the biggest thing in my life, but maybe there is more. That's the whistle for work so off I must go. Until the next time!

November 15th 1917

My sweetest Poppy,
    I am here in Paris missing you so much. I will give this letter to my new friend Private Appleby who drove me and the wounded officer here. I have been able to have two days leave as a treat for coming all this way. They didn't tell me till I was away from you. I feel as if part of me is missing without you. I cannot explain it. Still I am in a peaceful place. Well, at least it is at the moment. Paris still fears attack by the Germans. Paris is so empty though and so quiet. There is none of the bustle I remember, but it is no surprise. There are no men, but we know where they all are. Well there are some very old men! It is so quiet though and that is what I notice the most.
    I have been to a delightful soiree at Madame Barney's. It was exquisite. So many artists and writers. They danced and everything. Even though times are hard, here it was a true celebration. I met the artist Romaine Brookes and she gave me such good advice and Dolly Wilde. She is driving ambulances

and is a wild creature. She is beautiful in that strange way her uncle was and is fascinating in everything she does. I was able to do some sketching and I will share with you when I return. I walked by the Seine. There were more people fishing there than were walking in the streets. They are all trying to find food. I haven't seen too many children, where they are I don't know. We will both visit Madame Barney's soiree when we come to Paris next, though who knows when that will be. There is a knock at my door.

Sorry, I return to this letter after a night of bad behaviour. Too much drinking and carousing. Do not ask as I cannot tell! I have been a terrible person. My head aches and I can write no more. I will see you in a few days.
Tu est ma mie, Élodie

I had drawn the short straw. No one was left on camp, some were on leave, others en route to the Dressing Station and they needed help to bury the bodies. I shuddered but smartened myself up and got to the ambulance. It was only a short distance from the tent that acted as a morgue to the graveyard with its row upon row of wooden crosses. Heavens, I thought as I looked out from my ambulance at the sad sight. Of course, as I had put on my smart uniform it began to snow. The sky suddenly grey and gloomy. A cliché to say it matched the mood. Soldiers came to the ambulance to take out the shrouded bodies. No wood for coffins, it was all being used to line the trenches. They might as well have turned the front line into graves. So many bodies had disappeared there. It seemed so desolate here at Lapugnoy. A slate grey sky flecked with the snow and nothing else for miles where bombs and bullets had altered the landscape. It was strange to never see trees except for the strange blackened stumps and sculptures that they now resembled. I felt the snow tickle my face, shivered, jumped as a volley was fired over the coffins and next watched as the whole sorry spectacle was repeated. Eight times the snow-filled air was fractured by the sound of gunfire. Ahead to the

North we could hear the rumbling of cannon fire. It seemed an apt backdrop. Cannon fire, a priest intoning words that would benefit no one, especially the dead, together with the volley of rifle fire sent pointlessly into the sky. Eventually all the bodies were buried, and I trudged back to my old bus, slipping where the mud was beginning to freeze, but just staying on my feet as the wind ripped into my coat and started to burn my face. This was a horrible place. Dark and damp, freezing cold and heartless. A sergeant banged on the side of the ambulance to signal their work was over.

"Don't your boys want a lift back?" I asked. He laughed grimly.

"No thanks, Miss, we've got to fill in the graves now. We'll be some time."

"Shall I wait?"

"No Miss, we'll make our own way. The walk helps clear their minds ready for tomorrow."

I smiled, understanding and stepped down out of my cabin to turn the starter handle. Despite the cold, it gunned into life straightaway. I gave the sergeant a feeble wave and was off. The snow was creeping up my windscreen. At least my wipers were working this trip. I was glad I didn't have too far to go. The engine complained frequently on the way back. I thought perhaps I would ask a mechanic to take a look at it. I was fine with the regular simple things, but if it was too complicated a repair it was out of my league. Changing gear was becoming heavy and my arm and shoulder ached like billy-o. I would see how things went.

Later, the Chinese coolie who told me to call him Jimmy C, but who I called Chan out of respect for him, raised his hands again. I mirrored him as he swayed to the left, then the right. He put up his hands high and I responded and then as he moved towards me, I pushed his hands away.

"Correct Miss Poppee." He smiled. Then he pushed me on the chest, and I fell flat onto my bottom and into the snow. "But protect self always..." He laughed, and I grimaced as he helped me to my feet. All these hand movements to learn and then all the responses were mind boggling.

"But what if a fighter does not use moves?" I asked.

"You still use … he not know, what you know…" Chan said. It sort of made sense. Chan took up his stance again and repeated his movements and so did I. He suddenly lunged at me and I responded correctly, and he ended up on the floor. It was strange, I used so little energy, but he fell back hard. It was the same when he pushed me to the floor. It didn't feel any great effort, but I went down like a sack of spuds.

"Breathing Miss Poppee, control of body, control of mind." He often repeated that mantra and when I was on my own, I would go through the patterns of movements I had learnt. They all had beautiful names like 'Clouds' and 'Grasp the sparrow's tail,' for goodness sakes and it was always a question of repetition and memory. Each time I met Chan we would learn something new. I would watch as the other coolies stopped from self-defence and went all out into attack. They would leap high and use their feet as weapons, kicking and chopping as their opponents defended themselves. I looked forward to that, but Chan kept me going with the basics. Every time I saw him and his friends it was a bonus, as they or I could be moved on at any time, and no one would be able to tell the other as it could be that quick. I was also wary of the fact that we were often told not to mix with the work coolies, but how inhumane was that. They worked like dogs and we were supposed to ignore them? That made no sense, but Lady Greenwood had told me to mind myself once and I did keep an eye open for people who might criticise me. Luckily they were all busy at the Front, protecting freedom!

Rest and relaxation were soon over, and it was back to work. They were again an orderly short, so I helped stretcher a boy into the main tent. I smiled at Élodie, who was bandaging another boy's leg at the far end of the tent. She returned her beautiful smile and I felt my heart start to race. Matron was arguing with an officer who was shifting his feet with embarrassment. A soldier with a rifle was by his side, looking equally at unease.

"We will not have a gun in my ward!" I heard her say.

"Sister..."

"Matron Jones, if you please, captain. I will not. He can wait outside..."

"But the prisoner..."

"Is dying," she hissed. "He will not be running off."

"He can't die yet, Matron," the captain almost pleaded.

"Why, so you can shoot him later? Just get out. Take your guard with you. Loveday! Stop gawping, bring that fellow over here. Well captain? Why are you still here?" We took our patient to the empty bed and lifted him gently onto it. Matron stood there muttering. I had never seen her looking so cross, but also so sad and perplexed. Had our war sunk to a new low? Could it sink any lower?

"Can I help, Matron?" I asked.

"No, thank you, Loveday. Fellow shot himself in the face. They want to keep him alive so that he can face a firing squad."

I felt sick and looked over at the man. His face was swathed in bloody bandages. His feet were moving in agony as he tried to deal with his self-inflicted pain. Matron was just looking at him, it seemed so unusual for her to show any emotion. I left the tent and saw three ambulance drivers walking through the rain towards Lady Greenwood's office tent. They all had their equipment with them and none exhibited the fresh eager faces that new girls had, so they must be going home. It was strange how I only knew a small circle of drivers, those on my shift and those who shared the Barn. I gave a group of VADs a desultory wave, pulled my coat collar up and made my way to the canteen determined to meet someone new and make friends. To no avail. Unsurprisingly, it was my shift drivers alone in there. All loud and excitable. All had a large tin cup in their hands. They waved me over with catcalls and laughter. Overexcited as ever.

"Bovril or tea?" asked Florrie. "I'll get them." The canteen tent was busy, shifts beginning or ending, as ours was. We were all exhausted.

"Is there a difference?" I smiled.

"Well, there is to the creature that gives us Bovril," laughed Sophie who had returned with a blaze of gifts and laughter.

"What creature would that be?" I asked.

"Loveday, you are so ignorant!" laughed Elsie.

"Well?" I demanded.

"The Bov," Clemmie offered.

"No, the Bovrasaurus," Elsie assured us all.

"It's the Bovcat!" screamed Sophie.

"Make it tea then!" I laughed. Someone muttered and caused more laughter.

"How many people do you know outside this group?" I asked.

"Not too many, not enough time to make new chums," said Florrie.

"Three girls leaving by the looks and I don't know any of them."

"Three? Wonder why, it's so heavenly here!" scoffed Clemmie.

"I don't know why. The weather is so good and work conditions second to none." Sophie smiled.

"Second to none indeed!" I mocked.

"Should we try to be friendlier?" asked Sophie.

"And then get sent home for acting disgracefully? I don't think so!" snorted Clemmie.

"Everyone needs a friend, Clementine," I said,

"Shouldn't that be a rule that you make when you first come to a place like this?"

"Well, we all got thrown together and those you fall amongst with first you become pals with," Elsie said firmly.

"So, you didn't choose me as a pal, I was just thrown at you?" asked Florrie.

"No, Florrie, I mean, well I'm not sure what I mean. We all come from such different worlds and we would never have met if we hadn't been here. Different parts of the country for a start," Elsie started, but was digging herself into a hole.

"Different classes as well," said Clemmie.

"I think we have all been given a great chance," I said, "I mean, when would we have met otherwise. We are almost kept apart in what we would have called normal life. This has meant we really do see how the other half lives, and I don't mean that in a condescending or patronising way. We all know Sophie and I have been more than lucky in life, but we are doing our bit as well as anyone here. We don't get any favours here."

"That's for sure. It's the one time on earth that we are all equal. All as one. The perfect socialist existence," smiled Florrie.

"A revolutionary amongst us!" laughed Elsie.

"But it is true," I said, "we are all equal. I don't assume anything about anyone here. I just want to do my job as well as I can, and I expect everyone else to do the same. That we are all such lovely girls is an added bonus." They laughed.

"Bovrodile!" shouted Clemmie. They were almost hysterical, and I was not surprised. Everything was done to excess here, so the humour though not particularly funny was grabbed hold of at any opportunity. If you thought about it hard enough, it really wasn't funny, but my eyes were full of tears of laughter. I laughed and shaking my head, scanned the tent. I saw Élodie with a group of French nurses. There was also the exotic sight of the so-called Russian princess, who was reputed to have run away from the Romanov court and settled with us. It seemed a bit far-fetched to me, but we all had our different masks. I had lied to get over here, so what other secrets could there be. Just then Élodie looked up and our eyes caught. Hers sparkled and I felt a jolt in my chest, from where I had no idea. I smiled and Élodie returned it, her face lit up, then she turned away as someone spoke to her. I yawned and clapped my hand to my mouth, I excused myself and left for the Barn.

Élodie arrived somewhat later that evening and sat on the far edge of her cot and sighing, she pulled off her headdress. She wiped her forehead and now that she was close I could see that her eyes were red and watery. "Bad day?" I asked.

"Same as usual really, though that suicide, he died."

"That's awful, maybe for the best though what with his awful wounds and then
a pointless court martial."

"He was murdered Poppy." Her voice was icy quiet. I froze.

"He had been stabbed through the eye. A white feather on his chest. Someone is so evil..."

"How could that be, in a busy ward?"

"It would only take a second. No one has time to look around, to think."

"That's madness though, who would do such a thing?"

"Matron has no idea. The Provost office is not pursuing it, better dead I heard someone say. I couldn't believe it."

"But they must. If it's murder?"

"They have told us not to mention it, to forget it. Another casualty of war."

"His family?"

"His officer is writing, died of wounds apparently."

"But they can't, can they?"

"They have Poppy, all is covered, all is forgotten. One life more, who is to care? It is like a nightmare within a nightmare. I found him dead. The knife up to its hilt pinning him to the bed. I put up a screen and got matron. There were so many in the ward, but nobody appeared to see anything, or mention it. Matron fetched the guard. He fetched the Captain, then he the Colonel. He summoned Matron and me to her office and told us to forget what we had seen, that he did not want a big outcry, and this was not important as the man was to be shot anyway. I tried to ask but he silenced me. Matron could only give me that look of hers. She knows it is wrong. I was dismissed on direct orders of silence. Matron stayed, and I could hear her argue, but it was to no avail. All is to be how do you say, swept under the bed?"

I nearly smiled, but knew it was no longer appropriate,

"Carpet, Élodie, swept under the carpet. Did matron

say anything else when the colonel had gone?"

"Just to try to forget it. She was very angry, but for the colonel to order this, it must be important. I don't know why though, it does not make any sense. Surely the Army cannot be happy that murder has been committed?"

"Perhaps as they were going to kill him anyway. It ruins their chance to show an example of him. How disagreeable for them."

"So, it could be someone sympathetic to him? It would have been a quick death?"

"But the white feather, that shows someone who is vengeful."

"To throw the scent away?" I smiled, her use of English was not always perfect, but this made her cross. "It is no joke Poppy, someone evil is about."

"I know, it's your English, not what you are saying. Forgive me." She suddenly hugged me and I could feel her sobbing.

"It is wrong Poppy, the poor boy. Bad enough he shot himself, but then this."

"I know my darling, it is wrong. We shall find out who it was."

"But how?"

"I'm not sure yet. Do you have a name, a regiment?"

"I have some details and there was the guard sent to watch over him. They were of the same regiment. But he died alone, afraid so far from his home. He died in what should have been the safest of places. Everything about it is wrong. He deserves so much better."

"Is the guard still about? He might know more. Wipe your eyes Élodie, let's find out."

Typically, though, the whistle went to summon me to drive my ambulance. I kissed Élodie on the nose and ran off to my charger. It didn't want to start, but after several efforts on the heavy hand crank it coughed into life. A nurse in the back, destination in my head, it was down the unforgiving road towards the field station at the Front. Ahead the sky was filled with black plumes as shells exploded in the air. I could hear the noise above my engine and knew this was not going to be good. The sky was getting darker and darker as I neared the Front, and the explosions louder and louder. I was in a convoy of about six, a couple in front veered off to another sector. I think I heard them before I saw them, but I can't be sure. They just appeared from nowhere, two German planes that swooped over us like birds of prey. Except birds of prey are silent and don't spit death at you from their guns. The explosions rocked the ambulance. How they could bomb us, I wondered, since we had red crosses on our roofs. They knew what we were. Mud erupted into the air in front of me as a missile hit the road. Should I stop or carry on, I wondered, what was a better target for them. But why were they doing this?

"Are we safe?" The nurse behind me shouted. I almost laughed.

"Not really, I'll try to be. Just hang on!" And I could imagine her gripping the seat behind me, eyes closed and tears streaming down her face because that was me, save for my eyes which were wide open and seeing everything in front of me. Another explosion erupted in front of me and the ambulance ahead veered and slid, but carried on. Next bullets came. I could see them pock-marking the side of the roads. Broken branches were falling into the road as the rounds tore them from the dead trees. Still we managed to keep going and the colleague ahead was still making good progress. More noise was followed by the sound of gunfire. It was strange I hadn't heard the shots fired at us, but when our RFC boys started firing at the Germans it was as clear as day. I did pull over then, to check my passenger was all right, but also to see the dogfight above. I got out of the cabin just as a German plane exploded into a ball of flame to my right and tumbled out of the sky. I was pleased, though I knew I shouldn't be, but he had tried to kill us.

Were we so innocent? I thought so. We would have helped if a German came into our wards as we often did. We were not the enemy. But to the German pilot, everyone was the enemy. No longer were we seeing the game played as on the playing fields, but as a dirty nasty occupation. A game no longer. After parking up at our destination, I opened the back of the ambulance and my nurse almost fell on to me, sobbing her eyes out. She clung to me as if she was drowning and I held her close. I don't know why I was being so stoical, part of me wanted to dissolve into tears too. It was no fun to be shot at, none at all. A couple of French fighters swooped down, the big cockerel emblazoned on the side of their planes. We could make out the moustache sported by one of the pilots and the grin on the machine gunner as he started to open up on the remaining German. They had him trapped between them now and almost teased him into defeat, swooping up and then hovering over the top like hawks whilst the British pilots confronted them face on. There was gun fire and then another explosion as the German erupted into another blazing ball of flame. The pilot had had no chance of escape and burned with his plane. The French pilots flew away, seeming to waggle their wings at the British who came down really low and waved to us at the side of the road. My nurse had calmed down now and waved back. I just thought, how can he show off like this, he had just killed someone, a son or husband, another human being, a brother perhaps and he was treating it like a game. What had we turned our young men into I wondered?

    Her night shift over, Élodie found the canteen almost empty. The tea in the urn was warm and tasted of disinfectant. She wished she had some coffee. She missed that more than anything. The English and their tea! She smiled to herself. No concessions made here to us who didn't actually like tea, it was just stewed muck most of the time. The coffee when it did come wasn't there long enough to stew. That told everything! She looked across the canteen tent and saw the soldier who had stood on guard until the moment that Matron kicked him out. He stood politely as she asked if she may sit with him. His boyish face split into a grin.

    "Of course, miss, I mean, nurse."

"Are you back to your unit now?"

"Why, what have you heard?"

"Well, the prisoner died, didn't he?"

"Well yes, but I hear another is coming in."

"Another attempted suicide?"

"S I W I hear, there's so much of it."

"Do you blame them?" Élodie asked.

"S'not right Miss, we have to do our bit. Poor bugger … sorry Miss, poor bloke who shot his face off went too far. Most just put a bullet into their foot or leg, or hold their hands up for snipers to shoot. He made a right mess of it."

"He must have been at his wit's end?"

"We all are miss, but we have to get on."

"Was he in your regiment?"

"Yes, Fourth Rutland. Jamie Briggs. God knows what the officer will tell his parents."

"The truth, do you think?"

"Who knows. It's all gone quiet, I've been told not to talk about it."

"Did he have friends?"

"Not really. Didn't really know him. If he had some mates, he might not have done it. Who knows?"

"What's your name, Private?"

"Peter Saunders."

"How long have you been here?"

"Two years, six months. Though I'm not counting." He smiled. There was no real humour in his eyes. He was pale faced and exhausted as all the men seemed to be. Tired with the war, tired with life.

"Did Jamie have enemies?"

"Sorry miss. I was told not to speak." He looked uncertain for a moment, adding, "He was a nice lad though. Too nice for the army, but you know how it is. All sorts sign up or are sent over. He had to make do."

"In what way?"

"He was your artistic type, if you get my meaning." Élodie did, which made it all the worse for poor Jamie

Briggs. Élodie finished her tea and bade the soldier farewell. She was tired, but her head was spinning. She needed to get away and walked across to the rubble that was on the edge of their camp. She looked back at the tented village, with its hospital and soldiers' quarters, the cook house and then their barn. They were lucky to live there. Smoke curled out of the makeshift chimney and she imagined the warmth of their tiny space where they tried to laugh and joke and forget about the miserable war. She stepped over fallen brickwork and sat at the front of the ruined church. L'eglise Saint-Pierre. She could see the dull morning sky above her. The roof had been destroyed some time ago. In front of her was a makeshift altar with a wooden cross balancing against the wall. She fingered her rosary and bowed her head. All she could think of was the Canadian soldier. How had that happened, she asked herself. She shivered as she remembered the crump of the bombs as they had landed all around them. How they had destroyed their dressing station and had destroyed her friends. They were helping people. For God's sake, there were two Germans under their care, and they had all been killed. Then there was the Canadian boy, and there was Poppy. She smiled at the memory, but then felt tears sting at the corner of her eyes. Part of her wanted so much to forget about what had happened, but it wouldn't leave her mind's eye.

November 24th, 1917.

Dear Diary,

The Barn, my home for the past few months, was just as it says a barn. A former barn. We slept in what was once a stable. It was quite cosy, but still cold. There was a row of seven down one side. In the middle of the Barn they had split it up with all different types of boards to create more sleeping areas and then on the other side there was a communal area with a sink attached to a water tank outside and a large stove and a pipe that twisted its way out of a window where the smoke could escape. Behind the Barn were rows and rows of tents which we serviced with wounded soldiers. In front was the parking area for our ambulances. We each had our own or shared one with a colleague. Mine stood not exactly sparkling, but clean enough and doused in disinfectant nearest to the Barn. I didn't want to move far! I had put a waterproof sheet over the engine and was confident as ever that it would start in the morning or if called to arms during the night. Thankfully that didn't happen too often, but we had to be ready. I am in our small, snug communal area, drinking tea. The gossip from the other girls went over my head. They were mostly moaning, but in a good-humoured way. All had stories, be it the soldiers who tried it on with them, or the soldiers who didn't. That used to insult them more it seemed. I had no interest as you know. Matron was often the butt of the nurse's gripes though my contact with them was mostly positive, but there again I was only in and out of the surgical tent rather than having to do a ten-hour shift. I could imagine some had rather barbed tongues working under the pressure they had to live with.

    I am not sure how many trips we did today. From Casualty Clearing to the Train or Dressing Station to Clearing, the ambulance can do the trips without me it seems, which is ironic as I shouldn't even be here. My terms of service clearly stated that I had to be between the ages of twenty-one and forty-five. Why those arbitrary numbers? It encouraged people to cheat, me included. I am still not sure how I carried this off. What was the reasoning? How old do you have to be to expect to see death every day? Do you become obsolete when you are forty-five? Madness.

    Also, in the terms was the idea that no VAD should question any work we were given. Question? I have a hundred questions and am not allowed to express them. Is this the new world our soldiers are fighting for? We should be allowed to ask anything. Why we are fighting, would be the first question I would ask. Why indeed?

    Perhaps the most amusing thing I read before I signed was the thought that we must not expect a joy ride. Indeed? We are at war and we come to the Front and expect an easy life? Who are they fooling? They countered that by saying there *would be moments of slackness as they called it. To be honest I've not noticed any slackness at all in my time here in France. Every day there was something to do, if not ferrying patients we helped with the burials, or we helped move patients around, and on top of all that was keeping my beloved ambulance clean. That was a tour de force. Many of the girls give their old bus a name. I hadn't, it seemed to trivialise the position we are in, but each to their own.*

I do pride myself in keeping it clean. The paintwork I can do little about. There are the odd chips where flying bullets have caught it. Frightening I have to say, but so far I have been unscathed.

I know the underneath of my bus well. I spend time under there when we are being strafed or bombed. Such fun. I also tinker under there, keeping things tight and oiled or greased. Not with our porridge but with thick black glutinous lumps of grease that then cannot be removed from my hands for days! Under the bonnet is also a friend. I keep that as clean as I can. The belt is always tight, the spark plugs clean.

It was the innards that was always so depressing unless it was clean and empty. When full of louse-ridden bleeding broken men it was a place of horror. The moaning and screaming like being in Hell itself. To clean up after that was also horrible. I cannot even think to write what was sometimes left in there for me to clean and disinfect. I shudder as I sweep and wash it out. It takes an age and is often finished at night, so I need lamps to guide me. I hate to miss anything. I want a clean ambulance, it is my one contribution to this mess that I can control.

Chapter 4

"The frost makes a flower; the dew makes a star."

"Any gaspers, Poppy?" Clemmie asked and I reached into my overalls pocket to find those sent by my mother.

"Excellent, Poppy, thanks." They were shared around and soon the air was full of smoke. That with the taste of the tea was most off-putting, but beggars can't be choosers. The stove was firing off plenty of heat and I felt quite content. We could hear the rain pounding on our tin roof and I felt sorry for those who had to work in the tents and then live in the tents. We were often damp but they must be even worse. Some would come into the Barn trying to persuade people to swap beds, but it didn't work. It had been a piece of luck that Élodie had been able to come in, but we had to squeeze an extra cot into our stable to make room. I was still amazed that the usual red tape hadn't intervened, but I was so glad that it hadn't.

"You on leave soon Elsie?" asked Florrie.

"Yes, me and Clemmie are going to Boulogne-sur-Mer."

"We can't wait. Is it far from the station?" asked Clemmie.

"Not really. You not cadging a lift in an ambulance?"

"Maybe, depends if anyone is going that way. Otherwise it's the train."

"You meeting anyone there?"

"Maybe I am, maybe I'm not. But I have my chaperone and I'll be hers."

"Sounds promising, bring some biscuits back, will you?" I asked.

"Poppy, you and your sweet tooth," Florrie laughed.

"I know, but I must. It keeps me going." I knew I was whining a little as the other girls started giggling.

"Bring some coffee, Elsie." It was Élodie, she rested her hand on my shoulder and tingles flowed up my spine.

"I'll give you some money, but I must have coffee."

"What is wrong with tea?"

"Pah, it is awful. We French need our coffee. I've not had any since … since I don't know when."

"Don't send her into a maudlin, Florrie, change the subject quickly."

"What's maudlin?" asked Élodie.

"I'll tell you later as long as you don't become it." I smiled and Élodie looked even more puzzled. Florrie stood up and took my cup and went to wash up. She rang her hands complaining about her chilblains and the cold water. Élodie jumped into her chair.

"What a day we've had. It never, ever seems to end."

"I think we made ten trips to the Field Station today," I said.

"You must have. We have no more room. I think they may be looking to put some more tents up," Élodie said.

"God," I sighed, "Just what is the point?"

"We had another S I W today. He's under guard again. Shot in the shoulder, though how he managed that I have no idea."

"I suppose if you want to go home badly enough, you find a way," said Florrie.

"Bloody cowards!" Elsie snapped.

"Have a heart Elsie. It is awful up there. You know it is. You can't blame anyone."

"But he lets all his mates down..."

"The government has let his mates down," I said.

"Poppy, treasonous talk!" laughed Florrie.

"Poppy is right. Our rulers do the damage. The boys pick up the pieces. Still, we must not fall out with each other. Poppy, can you wash my hair for me?" Élodie diplomatically added.

"Can I have the last of the hot water, ladies?" I asked.

"Just fill it up again, Poppy. Does anyone want a cuppa before?"

To caress Élodie's auburn hair as I washed it was a

real treat. The tingles it sent through my body made me want her even more. I was able to take my time, feel her closeness and not seem out of place. She sat on a low stool with a towel around her shoulders.

"What is this maudlin, Poppee?"

"Sadness really, a state of sadness. I don't ever want you to be sad."

"I am not sad. I am content."

"With this, Élodie?"

"With my life. I feel I am doing worthwhile work. I do my bit for my country, your country. I do my bit for myself. I cannot stop what is going on around us, but I can help..."

"But it is like trying to stop a flood."

"We have each other; we have our love. What could make me happier?"

"There is that Élodie. Now let me comb your hair. Then will you do mine."

"We have no more hot water," Élodie complained.

"I am used to the cold water. I have toughened up since we left England."

"What is this England of which you speak?" Élodie laughed.

"You idiot. I cannot wait for you to come and stay."

"Will I be welcome?" Élodie asked.

"As a friend. I am not sure about ..."

"I joke Poppee, I know it is difficult."

"So, this new patient?" I wondered.

"Yes, shot in the shoulder but done it himself they say. Must have very long arms!" Élodie laughed. Her kohl-rimmed eyes sparkled as they looked up from her stool. "Is my hair safe?"

"Yes, nothing there. I'll get some water as you dry it a little." The sink was empty, so I put my head under the tap and wet my hair thoroughly, filled a bowl full of water and slopped it over to where Élodie was sitting. She got up and put the damp towel around my shoulders. Her hands were soon massaging soap into my hair. None of your beautiful scented shampoo, but some harsh smelling carbolic type that brought tears to my eyes. At least it would kill anything it touched on my head. I was surprised my hands hadn't rotted over the past months.

"I spoke to him. He was evasive. Wouldn't admit it. Said he knew Jamie Briggs the suicide and that he was sad that he had died."

"Did you tell him the truth?"

"No, I just said he'd died of his wounds. For some reason, he seemed relieved. Sad and relieved a strange mixture."

"And the new man?"

"Another S I W, but then his wound was badly infected. It seemed quite an old one, not fresh, but you can't always tell."

"Must be hell out there if two men from the same platoon try to kill themselves."

"We know it is hell. We know that for sure." Élodie closed the book and the eyes of the listener were also closed. Either she'd bored him into sleep or ... who knows. She looked down the tent, then at Poppy's book. Six men had heard Percy Westermann tonight as she had offered to let Poppy have an early night, and to be honest, she was getting a little bored with reading the same text over and over again. But what else could she do? Carry six different novels about with her? This for the best part made sense. She looked across the centre of the tent and saw the suicidal patient, Ralph Giles. He looked at her.

"Come to gloat?" he asked spitefully.

"Gloat? What does that mean?" Élodie was puzzled.

"It ... no don't bother. What do you want?"

"To see how you are, to see if there is anything I can do to help." He looked at her.

"You don't care that I tried to get a ticket home?"

"Did you though? It seems a strange place to get a wound." His face reddened.

"I was drunk," Giles explained.

"But still, harder to hit there. Unless someone did it for you?"

"What do you mean?" he blustered.

"Oh, come on Mr Giles You didn't shoot yourself. That's an old wound."

"No ... I... This was my own work." He turned his head away.

"Why do you want to get home?" Élodie asked gently

"I had to, I hate this war, I hate what I'm doing ... we..."

"We?"

"My friend. We were going to..." He hesitated, turning back to face her. "Could I have some water please?" Élodie helped him drink. He moaned as she helped his head back to the pillow.

"The guard here ... he implied..."

"I can guess what he said. Silly bastard. Sorry. It's ridiculous," Giles said.

"You knew Jamie Briggs?"

"He's my, was my best friend. We came over together. We both come from Lowestoft, went to school together, then signed up."

"But why if you don't..."

"It was fun, we got swept along. We became part of something. We didn't feel excluded. Here's me saying it was fun, just like a game. It soon became all too real. It was not a game for long, though those at home seemed to think it was. I could never understand them. They didn't want us to die, but didn't give us any option about not signing up. The women were the worst with their white feathers. I think we left at the right time. Boys younger than me were getting targeted by feathers and notes and by comments from women to their faces. Fourteen years-old lads being told that they should be over here, fighting. It's a madness, a bloody madness."

Élodie understood, it had been like a contagious madness. Boys, brothers, fathers signing up, whole streets, most of a factory or a village. All signing up to fight in what they thought would be just a game and over by Christmas. What fools they had all been. "But it didn't help?" she asked.

"At least we were together, but Saunders started making comments, insinuations, all very quietly, but made sure that we knew that he, you know..." Giles voice was so low, that Élodie had to strain to hear it.

"I can guess. Did you fight him?"

"No, we decided that the best way was out of it all."

"To kill yourselves?"

"We couldn't see any other way. If he reported us, we'd be shot, any day at the Front we could be shot. One or the other, or both. I couldn't have lived with myself if I was on my own, so the best thing was for us both..." He started to cry. Tears flooded down his face. Élodie took his hand and squeezed it.

"We were desperate. I was so frightened, of exposure, of getting shot in the trenches, or caught up in an air raid. Every day I woke up frightened. I couldn't bear it. Jamie was the same. He became a shadow of the man I knew, we both did. We decided we were going to do it together, but we only had one pistol. We thought that it would be easier than with a rifle. Jamie had it. I don't know what happened, I suddenly thought how stupid it was, what a waste, that I wanted to live and to be with Jamie. I tried to stop him. We struggled and the gun went off and hit me in the shoulder. He grabbed at the pistol and we were still trying to get control of it when it went off again. It was the worst thing I had ever seen in all my life. Worse than any of the wounds from battles." He sobbed again, his shoulders shaking uncontrollably.

"Half his face was gone. I couldn't understand how one bullet could have done that. Then I looked across and saw Saunders. It was him. He had fired at us and hit Jamie. He was smiling. He lifted up his rifle again and was looking at me straight in the eye. I just got to my feet and ran down the trenches." Giles had tears in his eyes.

"Why didn't you report him?"

"And say what?"

"But they will shoot you and he'll get away with it. He's even here now." Élodie was astonished.

"I can't risk the shame."

"But the shame of desertion and wounding yourself. Isn't that worse?"

"Not in my eyes, not in my family's eyes. They knew about me hating war. The other would break their hearts."

"But he murdered ..."

"How can I explain it. How could I twist it so that they didn't find out the truth? This way..."

"But Briggs, he was murdered, stabbed. It must have been Saunders!"

"What good will it do?" Giles was adamant.

"Justice!" Élodie hissed.

"What justice is there in this world anymore? Thousands shot and killed or maimed every day for what? To move inches forward or inches backward, or just to stay still. What does one or two more deaths mean?"

"But he killed your friend, your love ..."

He looked at her and smiled softly. "He may have killed Jamie, but he could never kill our love. I can take that with me to the grave and die happy."

"Please Ralph ..."

"No, it'll just take its course." Élodie squeezed his hand.

"As you wish, Ralph." She paused and swallowed hard. "Do you need anything else?"

"No thank you, but it was good to talk to you. I think I can rest easier now." Élodie stood up, smoothed her uniform and picked up Poppy's book.

"Good night then, Ralph. Try to get some rest." She made her way out of the ward. Private Saunders stood there with his rifle in his hands, staring at her.

"You seemed so pleasant over tea, Private." Élodie said quietly. "But I know what you are, and I will bring you down, make no mistake." He just continued to stare at her as she walked out into the fresh night air. All Élodie wanted to do was to feel Poppy's arms about her and she knew that all would be well.

I hadn't seen Élodie since this morning. She hadn't finished her shift I supposed. For some strange reason I felt longing for her inside my tummy. She now helped me get through each day, through just her presence, nothing more. She had become another reason to stay here in Lapugnoy, a reason to wake up in the morning. At times such as these, I needed her more than ever. I had to go and assist with burials again. I hated this duty. The white shrouds so neatly tagged and stacked up in the tent showing off the effects of modern warfare in an all too unpalatable way. It was something we all had to do, but you could never get used to it. I met up with the chosen few outside the tent that acted as a store for the bodies. It was like hell on earth. They would only be there for a day at the most, but the smell was horrendous. Indeed, the smell of the living could be quite awful at times as gangrene affected their limbs and rotted away their lives. Most of those with stretchers wore masks. No one was particularly cheerful. The orderlies who did this regularly seemed to have run out of their macabre jokes, and it was just going to be a case of getting on with matters at hand. It was cold which helped I suppose, but not too pleasant. We went inside the tent and there must have been about twenty shrouded corpses. Stacked neatly on shelving. The smell was overpowering and oozed through my mask. I helped my partner load a body onto our stretcher and we made our way to the rear of the camp to the graveyard, where the required number of graves had been dug. Beyond the fresh pits were row upon row of simple wooden crosses on top of the interred. There must have been hundreds. At least they were at peace now.

Most had names on, some had 'Known but to God' and sometimes we had carried pieces back from the Front and had no idea of who or what they had been. It was really distressing. We laid our stretcher down by the grave side and two more orderlies lifted the shrouded figure off and lay them by the side. I picked up the stretcher and returned to the tent. As I entered the tent, I could smell a slight scent of orange blossom which at least made me feel better as it reminded me of Élodie.

We removed another soldier and repeated the process. As we returned for the fourth time, the scent was so much stronger. I suddenly felt a shiver go through me. Why should Élodie's scent be here. Had she placed a corpse in the tent? That would not have been her job, the wards had orderlies for that. I asked my colleague if he could smell it, in case I was imagining it.

"Yes, it's odd. Over there?" he suggested. We went towards the rear of the tent and it was stronger, coming from the rack of bodies. The smell of death was overpowering, but the orange blossom could almost be tasted, it was so strong. I looked at the shrouds. Most were blood stained, or off colour where gangrene fluid had seeped into the material, but there was one that was almost spotless. I went towards it and the orange blossom scent got stronger. Fear surged through my body. This could not be happening. This couldn't be Élodie. I scrabbled at the shroud to reveal auburn hair and a mass of bandages wound around a head. We pulled the body onto the floor. I felt tears streaming down my face and found myself muttering, "Please God, no don't let this be happening."

We pulled off the shroud and before us was a body wrapped up tightly like a mummy. It was deathly still. I felt my heart racing and sick in my mouth. This could not be happening. I pulled the bandage from the face. It was Élodie. She was deathly pale. A gag stuffed into her mouth. I pulled it free as my partner unwrapped more bandages. I put my face to her lips just as she gasped and rattled and almost exploded into life as the bandages were released and freed her to breath normally. Slowly her eyes opened, she smiled and I hugged her to my chest.

"Élodie, thank God. What happened?" She closed her eyes and was once again unconscious. There was chaos around as soldiers ran in, followed by Matron.

"What on earth is going on, Loveday?"

"It's Nurse Proux. I have no idea," was all I could say. Soldiers lifted her onto a stretcher, but thank God, she was taken a different route, away from all the other inhabitants of the tent and into a ward. Matron by her side. Before she left, she cruelly told me to finish my shift on the ambulance. She had no idea, but there again why should she?

November 26th, 1917.

Dearest Diary

What an awful day. I thought I had lost her. When I saw her there all pale and still, I honestly thought she was dead. Thoughts flashed through my mind. How would I live without her? What would I do if she was dead? In that instance I knew my love was complete. I could not love anyone as I loved her, my dearest girl, my beautiful Élodie. What had we come to? A man puts her in with the dead. Did he intend her to die? God knows.

They found Ralph Giles. He was dead. Another stabbed whilst he slept. Would he be at peace? It was monstrous. What was happening to people? War was making people go mad and behave outside the norm. Or more frightening, was this the norm? My stomach is ice. I must think of something else. Write something else...

Who would have thought that after all that chasing Alfie around in the tractor I would have ended up here? I just did it to irritate him and it did! It made me laugh. Then I would sit in his lap as he held the wheel and off we would whizz. When he let me take control it was such fun. When the engine conked out, he would show me how and why. Blimey, I remember Nanny going mad when we both came home to the Hall covered in oil and grease. She used to really hurt us as she scrubbed us clean but all we could do was giggle. Happy days indeed. He was the perfect big brother. He is still the perfect big brother and I miss him so much. I miss everyone so much. Sometimes my chest gets so tight and I can hardly breathe as I think that perhaps I will never see them all again. I have no idea what Dada is up to. He seems to flit over here for some reason or another and only Alfie ever knows. Is our Alfie involved I wonder? Mine not to reason why. I do know that mother is less than happy and that makes me sad. I just want her to be proud of me. she sits at home moping. Well, that may be unfair. She organises committees and sales and raises money and helps everyone. She just wants me to be with her, but this is what I want to do, to do my little bit.

"He couldn't find it in himself to kill you."

"But he killed two men."

"You are too beautiful to kill, but what did you say to him to make him do this?"

"I must have been the straw that broke the camel's back. I accused him of the murder. I don't know why. I just felt he knew something. He spat out your name as well. He told me that we were all going to be taught a lesson."

"But he didn't kill you, that was odd."

"So, he just left me with the rotting corpses."

"Élodie, he's dead now, the provost shot him as he made a run for it."

"Will the truth ever be told about Jamie and Ralph?"

"A certain truth will be told. Matron persuaded the Major. She told him that Saunders murdered the two men after shooting Jamie Briggs at the Front earlier. That he had obviously had a mania, that the two dead men were not at fault."

"He accepted that?"

"Yes, or Matron was going to complain about him allowing a murderer into her ward."

"I love Matron Jones," said Élodie.

"I need more Narcisse Noir. It's all emptied onto my uniform."

"I'm so glad it did, I smelt it in the morgue tent. Don't know what would have happened if it hadn't."

"Fate my darling. But now you will get me some for Christmas."

"Of course, but where would I be able to find some. Here of all places?"

"Well let's not think about that. My head is still sore, I reek of Narcisse Noir, but I'm alive."

"And I'm so happy that you are!" I said.

"We need a holiday, Poppee. Perhaps we should ask if we could go to the Front and work in the no-man's land."

"It might be safer. I'm getting fed up with you or me being a target."

"Well, you should take the bull's eye off your back!" Élodie laughed.

"It's not funny, Élodie. We seem to meet the most improbable situations without even trying to. Problems seem to heap themselves upon us."

"Maybe it is all a case of being in the wrong spot at the right time."

"Wrong time, Élodie. Wrong spot is right. Dada said these were dangerous times, but these seem unnatural times as well."

"It is unnatural, but it is no surprise. We have all that evil only a few miles from us, Poppy. All those men killing each other, all the bombs and the gas. A whole world seemingly geared to destroy one side or the other. Or maybe both. An industry of evil has sprung up, geared to destroy and to find different ways to do so. Is it any surprise that the evil seeps into the souls of people? This Private Saunders, and others. They are infected by evil and it must show itself elsewhere. On both sides of the trenches."

"I suppose you're right. Evil will prosper when men allow it to. They certainly aren't trying to stop it, are they?"

"Some have too much to lose. What have they invested into this war and what profits are they taking out? This will be a problem for years to come, long after the war has ended."
"I know, all the wounded and maimed. What are they offered? What world will our boys have when they return home? Which side will win, we could all be speaking German in five years' time? We don't know what will happen and when it is over, because it has to end."

"God willing."

"When it's finished, will we still see arms being produced at the same rate to protect from conflict again? An ever-building race to make the weapon that will promise to overcome the enemy's next weapon. It will become never ending, Élodie."

"We must not worry about that now, *ma Cherie*. Let us worry about what we can control."

"And what may that be?" I asked.

"Your ambulance!" Élodie laughed.

"Your hands in the operating theatre."

November 27th

Poppy old Bean,

Uncensored letter for you so don't leave it lying about. Tom Farrer's dropped this off for you as he's on his way to have a spot of leave. If you see him give him my socks back! I do know you've been stealing them you beast. What if I had a game to play in? Best be in good condition after this has all ended as I do like them!

Moving forward at a pace. Germans appear to be folding where we are. Still a long way from you but who knows, we might suddenly join up in the middle somewhere. I can't be too obvious with my news as there is always a danger others will see this, but we have got through the bloodiest of battles unscathed and I hope my luck holds out till it's all over. I've done some office work behind the lines and also a bit of hush hush stuff put my way by the old man. We never did find out what he did in the past and I guess we never will find out what he knows. I will say that he is my hero. He is a clever and resourceful chap for his age! I jest of course, we are only as old as we feel and papa must feel like he is twenty-one. Goodness knows what affect this all has on poor mater. She must be at her wits end worrying about us all. So be gentle with her when you get back to Blighty. When I saw her last, Mother seemed as happy as she can be with you over here. I'm sure once it's all over she'll understand, but she does love you.

Rumour had it that Pops was over here recently, but I didn't see him. Wink wink! Not sure what the old warrior is up to. No good I'm sure! I can't remember when I last had leave.

Lucky old Tom!

It's been horrible here as you know. Too many lads getting it in the neck. Sad to say it's best some don't make it out, the injuries they are getting, but you see that every day. I can't help but sit here and sniffle away at times. I have to write to wives and mothers, or sisters, to tell them what's happened, and it really does break my heart. Some days it's over twenty letters to people I've never met about young lads I've never met. It takes its toll. I try to find out a bit about each lad, but it begins to get too impersonal and I don't think I'd like to receive a letter like that, so I do try hard.

Mother sent me some cake, hope you got it too. She does insist in sending gaspers. Don't know why. What do you do with them?

Did some work with father a few weeks ago? Can't say what but very exciting. BUT do not get jealous. You are doing as much as me in the scheme of things so don't be rash and try and win the war on your own. I know what you are like! Hope the vans don't play up too much but with all the teaching I gave you it must be a doddle keeping them on the road. Now you can see why I was so bossy!

I had best stop now as getting cramp. I don't want to sound soppy Poppy, but I miss you and I love you. Do take care of yourself and I hope to see you in one piece soon. Try not to worry too much.
Yours as usual!

Alfred

Chapter 5

"Before us fog, behind us fog, and beneath us a sunken country."

November 28th, 1917.

Hello dear diary, or is that Dear diary hello? Who knows? Who cares?

    My hands are so cold. They are almost always blue and hurt a lot of the time. Gloves don't seem to give me any warmth and I'm afraid chilblains will cripple me if I am not careful. The cold wind seems to be eating into them as I grip the steering wheel. Can wind enter the body? It would be interesting to know. Suffice to say. It is cold! I just cannot get warm at the moment. I cocoon myself in scarves and socks and big bloomers and then my uniform and heavy coat and that's just to get into my bed! The weather is horrendous. The driving even worse. My eyes are so sore, my cheeks rubbed raw by the wind. Oh, I do moan, but here I can say what I feel like. I don't want to moan to the others as they all know how horrible it is. At least I have Élodie. She makes everything worthwhile. She is my life. She is so funny and so cheerful. I don't know how she does it, working in those tents, patching up bodies and then coming to the Barn usually all cheerful, though tired. I don't really know too much about her. Well, to be honest I know nothing except that we had found her by the roadside. She hasn't said anything about her past. She is a mystery, but she is a very pleasant mystery. One day we shall sit down and talk about her life. She knows all about mine. We have to share.

    We are out in a bit of land destroyed by shelling. Nothing but blackened tree stumps and rubble. As you can see, I am writing and Élodie is drawing. She is so talented. Perhaps she will return to study art at university when this war ends. Who knows?

Élodie sat on her favourite shell casing. She looked again at her sketch book then back at me. I put down my diary. "What is it?"

"Your face against the sun is like an angel's."

"Élodie, you are such a romantic. Show me your drawing." She held up her sketch pad and indeed there I was. An angel with wings and a halo. The sun blazing down over my shoulder. All portrayed in pencil, but giving the idea of colour with all its different shades and nuances. She was a wonderful artist. It was so clearly my face, she was so clever. "Beautiful," I gasped and got up to sit with her on another shell casing. "Show me your Paris sketches." She flipped back pages in her sketch pad. I was stunned at the beauty of them. Places I recognised from my visits and from some old photographs. They were so real, so immediate. I felt as if I was there. She had to be able to do this and have much success once this war was over. If ever it was over.

I saw a familiar face and waved at Chan and he bowed low. Out of respect I bowed back. He walked towards me and bowed again, a big grin on his face. "How are you Chan?"

"Well, Miss Poppeee, and yourself?"

"I am tired, but happy to see you." His smile became wider.

"Then if happy, perhaps we should try new move?"

"I would be happy to."

"Then what rules you remember from last time we spoke?" I thought back, it had been some time.

"Use the mind, not brute force, to stay in your centre."

"That one is easy, the next?" As he spoke, he sank into his stance and brought his hands up in front of his face.

"Calm the mind, relax the body and maintain an awareness of the body." I sank down and this reminded me. "Initiate all the turning from the hips and waist."

"Very good, Miss Poppee." His left hand flicked out towards my face and I was just too slow to parry, and his fingertips brushed my cheek.

"The legs initiate the forward and backward movement," I said and tried my own little attack.

"In calmness there is movement, and in movement there is sinking," said Chan and this time his feet moved, and I found myself on the floor with a thud. He helped me up and we bowed again.

"Your feet move very quickly, Chan. Hard to prepare for."

"Sink your hips, Miss Poppee. Then you are alert. Hands up. Get mind focused on action. Try to anticipate." As he spoke, I struck out with my left leg and caught him beautifully and it was his turn to hit the floor. "Good, Miss Poppee!" His smile never left his face. "To begin stand in Single Whip." I obeyed and he explained as he showed me. "This called Snake Creeps Down, Golden Cock, Leg Kick." Whatever that meant. I had no idea. "Breathe in, Miss Poppee. As you inhale, use your back leg to push all your weight to the front, freeing back leg. Sink onto the front foot, and slowly place back foot into a longer stance." He showed me, this seemed simple enough and I tried it a few times. "Keeping leg on right side of line." He used a finger to draw a line in the earth under our feet. "As you exhale, open your hips as the back foot opens this much." He showed me a perhaps ninety degrees arc. "You are opening to the back corner. As the torso turns, the right arm stays in the single whip position, left hand coming to inside of right elbow."

I followed his movements, concentrating hard. His explanation plus demonstration meant it was more straightforward than the description he had given at the start. But as I may have mentioned before, all these exercises had a name or were bits of other exercises joined up. It was difficult to remember, but what else had a girl to think about on the Western Front? "As you inhale, sink onto the right leg pushing the knee directly over the right foot. Then must sink low as comfortable, keeping torso upright make sure no lean, then sink onto the back leg."

We did this a few times until I had perfected it then went back to the start and joined everything together. "Left leg sweeps forward as if showing off the left foot. As you exhale, begin to transfer the weight to your front foot as it turns. Feel as right arm is pulling the right leg forward and up. Bring all your weight onto the left leg, as the right leg comes up parallel to floor, then you are into Golden Cock stands on Left Leg. If your balance good, bring the thigh parallel to the ground. Then kick right!" His foot seemed to explode out of nowhere and finished an inch from my face. I jerked back. "No flinch, Miss Poppee. Must trust. Now you do."

I followed instructions. He put my various limbs into the correct positions, and it seemed like no time at all that I had come to grips with what he had shown so far. Sweat was pouring from my face. I blinked away the saltiness that was stinging my eyes. I would have to have a cold shower tonight. But still we weren't finished. "As you breathe in, slowly kick right leg forward toe pointed. Right arm extends forward, left arm pulls back as you kick. As you breathe out, leg and arms come back to position, all weight on back leg." So, there we had Snake Creeps Down, Golden Cock, whatever. Chan bowed and ran off towards his camp. I tried a few more times and was very pleased with what I had discovered today.

I walked back towards Élodie and we returned to camp. Shame about the cold shower though!

"We have an Oberstleutnant Kunz who has to be escorted back to the German lines, a repatriation in time for Christmas." I looked at Élodie then back at Captain Porter. "They have insisted on a normal ambulance driver with the armed escort, so we would like you to drive, Miss Loveday, and take Nurse Proux to assist."

"Very well, Sir." It seemed a strange order, but needs must. I must have shown my feelings on my face.

"This is a request, ladies, not an order," Captain Porter said.

"No, it's all right, Sir," I smiled.

"He is in a poorly condition, but needs to get back in one piece."

"We'll do our best, Sir, but why is he going back?"

"Not for you to know, young lady," he paused, "suffice

to say you will be returning to
us with a repatriated British officer. Leave at, oh seven hundred hours. An officer will accompany you. Good luck!" Outside his office, I looked at my watch, six-thirty.

"Well I never." I whistled for some reason.

"The prisoner exchange?" Élodie suggested.

"I know, but why do they need us, seems odd."

"Orders, *ma Cherie,* you know how they say."

I always amazed myself as to how I kept the ambulance on the road. I recalled the tractor on the estate that I had been allowed to chug along in, getting under the feet of our gardeners as well as Alfie as I learnt to drive. This was not too dissimilar; they were both cumbersome and heavy under the steering wheel. I wished I was in Alfie's little motor car that swept along the roads like a rocket. I loved to drive that, but only when Alfie was in a good mood. He allowed me to have full rein in the paddock and I would drive it alone at the wheel, Queen of all I could survey. On the twisty winding roads near Loveday House it was a different kettle of fish, he would always have a hand ready to put on the wheel to steady her down. All I wanted though was freedom. I didn't get much of that in the lumbering ambulance. It always had to go the same few ways, from Base Hospital to Dressing Station, or Clearing Station, or railhead and back again. Always the same, ruts and mud. I felt I could drive the route blindfolded, but was never tempted to try. I was also amazed that they called the muddy tracks we chugged along roads. Bombs and the wet weather had churned up cobblestones and they had deteriorated so much, no matter how often the sappers and Chinese workers came in to repair them. My shoulders were screaming at me, but I had hardly travelled any distance. Élodie called through the hatch, "Is all well, Poppee?"

I didn't dare take my eyes off the road so shouted even louder in response, "Bon!"

I heard Élodie call, "The guard, he is asleep. The patient restless. He almost hit the roof then!"

"*Desole,* Élodie!" I almost laughed at the vision Élodie

had described and gripped the wheel tighter as I bounced the ambulance along the rutted track. We had left Lebeuvrière behind and were continuing East, towards the Front. I looked ahead and saw black clouds bursting in the sky and realised how close I must be to the Front. I hadn't passed any soldiers so was hopeful there would be no assault this morning. No one going and no one marching back. Must all be at it on the Front.

"Can you stop, Poppy?" called Élodie.

"What's happened?" I shouted back.

"Just stop, *Cherie* and come around."

I pulled into the side of the road and jumped down from my seat. I ran around to the back and tugged the doors open to be met by a luger pointed at me, Élodie face down on the floor and the soldier slumped in the corner with blood trickling down his face. Kunz was looking at me over his luger. His face now free of bandages, with a steely glint in his eye.

"Feeling better, Herr Kunz?" I asked.

"Very well, my dear."

"Is he dead?" I nodded towards the guard.

"No, he is just stunned, though so inefficient to sleep whilst on the job." He stepped over Élodie.

"Remain on the floor nurse as I now have your driver in my sights. I must take my leave of you."

"But we were taking you home," Élodie said from the floor.

"Home? An interesting thought."

"But what of the British officer?"

"No need to worry about him, ladies, he is not your concern."

"But..." I started.

"Just get into the ambulance and lie next to your colleague." Élodie looked at me, face set as stone.

"I cannot let you," I said. The gun belched fire. I jumped having no idea where the bullet had gone.

"I do not miss often my dear, and I will not miss next time. Step into the ambulance if you would."

"Please do as he says, Poppy," said Élodie. I scrambled

up and lay down beside Élodie. I felt her hand reach for mine and I squeezed it tightly.

"Now stay here for a short while and I will be on my way." He closed one of the doors.

"But your wounds!" Élodie exclaimed.

"I have no wounds," he scoffed.

"But the blood?"

"There is too much blood, so I didn't need to spill my own."

"Where are you going?" Élodie asked.

"No need for you to know. Farewell ladies." He slammed the door shut. I tried to get up straight away, but Élodie held fast to my hand.

"Leave him go Poppy. We help this man and get back to our lines. This is very strange."

Later, we sat inside Captain Porter's office. Having declined his offer of a gasper, he lit one for himself and looked at us sitting there like two schoolgirls in the headmistress' office. He slowly drew on his cigarette and looked almost unconcerned at our news. "And he ran off which way?"

"We were inside the ambulance, but I don't think it was towards our lines." I said.

"Towards the Germans?"

"We cannot be sure," Élodie said.

"He shot at Poppy, we kept our heads down."

"You did the right thing, ladies. Did he say anything unusual?"

"Not to worry about the British officer we were going for." I looked at Élodie.

"Does that mean he has been released?" Élodie asked.

"I cannot say, except we did find the original Kunz in the mortuary tent earlier today."

"So, he was an imposter!" I started.

"It would seem so." He stood up. "Thanks for your efforts. Do not mention this to anyone please."

"No Sir." I said meekly, though not knowing why I felt

like this. Secrets and lies, that's what these men were all about, playing their little games. We didn't even know if this Kunz was on our side. I wouldn't put it past them all. It was still early, and we sat in the canteen tent waiting to go on shifts. We can hear the cannon fire from the Front. We would have to depart soon. Every so often the ground would rumble like it must when an earthquake happened as an extra-large piece of munitions exploded. Élodie jumped every so often and I put a reassuring hand on hers.

"Quite safe here, Élodie," I whispered.

"I know, for the time being anyway." She smiled, but her face was pale and worn.

"You look tired," I said rather obviously as we all were.

"Just the excitement of this morning, Poppy."

"What a lark that was!" I smiled back at her. "I wonder what it was all about."

"That's for clever clogs Porter to know," Élodie said.

"Clever clogs? Where have you got that from?"

"I listen," she giggled

"I know when to pick up …what do you call them?" She paused.

"Colloquialisms, Élodie."

"Well, I didn't know that. I was going to say sayings," she laughed, "I have learnt yet another word for my growing vocabulary."

"You speak English, *très bien*," I laughed.

"*Comme tu le faites français,*" She laughed back. I squeezed her hand again, then released it as a surge went through my body. I pre-empted the whistle that called me to work, as it sounded as I stood. "I must go. I will see you tonight."

"*Voyage sûr mon amour,*" Élodie whispered.

It was early evening and I was sitting alone in our small room picking at the seams of my uniform, checking for lice. I was a bit cold to be honest, dressed just in my underwear. A candle-light was close by in case I had to roast any little buggers I found in my kit. Such a pleasant activity!

"Can I come in?" It was Élodie.

"Of course." I felt the now familiar surge in my stomach as I heard her voice. I turned and saw the short auburn hair being shaken out of her nurse's cap and her cloak being thrown towards her cot. Élodie smiled, her eyes sparkling.

"How are you Poppee?"

"Well, we finished early."

"That is good, less boys to bring home, less work for me …could you …" I tugged her uniform over her head for her and Élodie stood there in stockings and underwear.

"That is so much better. I would like to run in the fields like this!" she smiled.

"I used to do that when I was small. No clothes, running naked in the rain!" I blushed at the thought.

"I would like to see that," Élodie whispered, and I looked at her, suddenly realising what my feelings had meant. "You are so beautiful I…" Élodie started.

"I cannot stop thinking about you," I found myself saying. I smiled a bit feebly, "we are all we have here."

"No not like that. I want to touch you." I felt the familiar surge in my stomach. But then it was as if a dam had burst. "I see you across the base and want to hold you tight to me," Élodie continued.

"Élodie…" I didn't know quite what to say. She looked at me, her face reddening, her breathing heavy.

"I cannot explain my feelings, Poppy. I see you and my heart beats faster and I cannot breathe."

I wasn't sure how to react. This is exactly what I had felt and had not been able to explain to myself or perhaps I could. I was attracted to Élodie. In a way I had not been attracted to anyone before. My feelings surprised me. I had liked many people in my time. I loved my parents, I loved Alfie. I had never loved another man. I had never had feelings for anyone despite my mother pushing me, but for Élodie… I suddenly realised what I was feeling. It was an attraction, for a woman. Could this be right? I had been brought up to believe a woman should fall in love with a man, but for me this sudden feeling that had been stirring itself inside me for a while now had come to the fore. I was attracted to a woman. I was attracted to Élodie. My thoughts were interrupted.

"I touch your hand and my body feels as if electricity is going through it. I tingle and dissolve. I feel weak, yet so happy."

"I do as well, Élodie," I admitted, and her face lit up.

"I think I am in love with you," Élodie continued. "We are so close together here, so near to death. No, it's not that I'm not afraid of death. I'm drawn to you, not to a man, I've never been ..."

"I understand."

"Do you? To me, wanting you seems natural, it seems so right. I don't truly understand this."

"I do though, Élodie, it is just because we are so near to death that makes us think differently. I'm drawn to you as well. I think I love you."

"Is it love?"

"Can that be what it is?"

"I am sure. I do not want to be with a man. I want to be with you."

"You make me feel different ..." I managed. "I'm not sure what…"

Élodie took my hand, I felt myself going red and again felt the familiarity of my heart beating faster. The insides of my stomach once again churning, melting, turning into that honey feeling. My mouth was dry.

"This is *très difficile* ..." started Élodie.

"You can say what you like to me." I said.

"It's how I feel," Élodie replied. I smiled and took her hands in mine.

"You've been through a lot these past few weeks."

"No, it's not that, or perhaps it is, I'm not sure."

"How can we know until it happens to us?" I asked.

"I never lay with a man, ever."

"Neither have I," I realised I was whispering.

"I have never wanted to. I have no interest." Élodie

took my hands from hers and kissed them gently.

"Don't Élodie..." But I didn't mean it, I was confused. I could only see one reason for my feelings, and she sat before me. I felt the warmth in my tummy starting to make its way through my body.

"I think I loved you from the first time I saw you," Élodie said, kissing my wrist, sending shivers down the length of my body.

"You make me feel so warm inside, Élodie, I've never had ..." I didn't know what else to say. Élodie looked into my eyes. Her cheeks glowing, her green eyes sparkling.

"May I kiss your lips?"

"I ..."

But Élodie's lips were on mine. Like butterflies dancing she was so gentle and I felt so aroused, I had never felt like this before. My insides seemed to be dissolving as I sat there. It felt wonderful, but I pushed her away and gasped for air.

"Élodie!" Her orange blossom scent was intoxicating me as I breathed her breath. I then pulled her close and my lips found hers. This time it was not so gentle, it was fierce and passionate. I suddenly understood everything. I understood the surges that I had felt jolt through my body when we had brushed together. The tingling when Élodie had kissed my cheek in greeting. The warm gooey feelings when we had held hands to negotiate the muddy paths. I understood it all. Why had this taken so long to unravel, why had I been so blind. I pushed Élodie away again, gasping for air, my heart thumping, fit to explode from my chest. "Why did I never realise this?"

Élodie buried her face in my shoulder and whispered, "Love is strange and we have a strange love. I know it is not seen as right. My church does not allow it, but how can you fight love?"

"I don't know, I don't ..." I felt overwhelmed. I had such emotions going on in my body. My stomach felt as if it was melting every time I saw Élodie, I had had no idea why until now, I realised I had love for her in a very different way. I knew that I was a sensual creature, I loved to feel the sun in my face, the wind in my hair. I loved to feel the touch of Élodie's fingers on my skin. Now I knew why.

December 3rd, 1917.

My dearest diary

    Now I understand. Now I can see what all those strange feelings were. I am in love. But I am in love with the wrong person, with a girl, Élodie. How can this be so and how can it be right? Strange, I know it must be right, but girls are getting sent home because others see it as wrong. Well I suppose everyone sees it as wrong. What will Dada and mother say. How can I tell them and Alfie? Well Alfie will be all right. He loves me and everything about me and he will love Élodie as well. Dada would as well. Mother? I am not sure she has changed so much since her suffragette days. Will she still believe women can behave as they wish when it is her own daughter? Why did this happen to me. Why can't... Why should I worry, I am in love, let me enjoy that for now? Secrets will be kept until the time is right. Would it hurt mother to let her know? So many questions, so many problems, all I have done is fall in love. In love with such a sweet girl, my dearest girl I kiss your name and want to kiss your mouth.

    Such sweet feelings, but now as I look outside, I see that the rain has fallen like the proverbial stair rods and steam seemed to be rising from the mud at Lapugnoy. I think if there was a hell, this is what it would be like, a primeval swamp now scorching under the afternoon sun. Nurses in the hospital tents wiped their brows with their forearms, almost melting in their heavy cumbersome uniforms. No concessions were made to the weather. Inside the tents, it was sweltering, the sides of the tents that had just been sheltering them from the storm were now lifted to get some air into the patient's lungs. I was grateful that I didn't have to work in there, that I could get out in the ambulance and open a window to get a bit of a blow. I never got up enough speed to be really cool in the rare bouts of hot weather that we had, but I could unbutton my overalls if I was careful enough to watch out for the eagle-eyed matrons.

It was such a change from the wet and freezing weather we had endured and I knew that it wouldn't be long before the rain returned. I glimpse Élodie walking briskly to the tent. Walk, don't ever run was the order, no matter what calamity was about them. I'll stop writing now, I must speak with her ...

Élodie was exhausted and only halfway through her shift. All she could hear was the moaning of soldiers and the orders of the pressed doctors. Matron Thomas was stalking about ordering hair back or complaining about a mark on an apron. It was usually blood, what they were supposed to do about blood Élodie never knew, it was always blood. Sophie smiled across at her. Élodie returned Sophie's smile, she was friendly, and they had gotten on immediately. She was full of her trip to Boulogne-sur-Mer, their hotel, the food, the hot baths. She made us jealous. She told how she had met her fiancée, Edward, there and had to find a chaperone to sit at their table. I had laughed.

"Three's company, Sophie."

Élodie looked quizzical.

"It was fine. She knew when to leave us alone. There were couples at every table plus one. They must get fed up!" She laughed.

"How do they find these chaperones, are there that many spare ladies of a certain age about?" I wondered.

"Mine was from the hospital. You ask around, promise to pay for their grub and they come along to be bored for a few hours. Luckily mine was on duty early most mornings so we were able to sneak away and ..."

"Sophie!" I gasped theatrically, "I'm shocked."

"What is going on?" asked Élodie.

"I'm sorry darling," Sophie said grinning,

"I'm so full of love that I forgot my place. Let's talk of other things."

"No Sophie, tell me about the bath!" I laughed.

Sophie, long blonde hair, and the complexion of an English rose broke into a grin. "It was just soooo divine darling. All warm and so full of suds. I thought the floor had disappeared and I would ride down them like the bath was on a layer of snow. It was memorable!"

"Sounds super!" I agreed.

"It was. Still it will have to last me now for weeks. Soon back to the nit-picking routine here."

December 4th, 1917.

Dear Me it's December 4th, 1917.
That's not self-admonishment, but an introduction to writing to myself. Seems silly.
I'm looking into a mirror. I'm not vain, I hasten to add, but you will know this as I get to know myself. Does that make sense? Well, no matter. Admittedly it's in the half light. Sophie and Élodie are fast asleep. There is a bit of movement outside our room, but whoever it is, she is trying to be quiet. Outside I can hear the rain fall and it is splattering on our roof. No leaks so far, but it is chilly.
Back to me. I can see my eyes. Blue, but with no sparkle. My eyes used to sparkle. I'm not sure if they only sparkle when I'm happy, though that's odd as I do feel quite happy, at the moment, for reasons I will explain later if I can. Well dull eyes and black rims around them. Not kohl, there's been no make up for a while. No, this is tiredness. My skin is really dry. I need more cream, must ask mother for some. The wind and the rain and now the snow really whip into us and I can almost feel it marking me some days. The goggles we have are worse than useless and I have sore eyes as well. Maybe that's why there is no sparkle, it's been worn away. I laugh. I have to laugh otherwise ... but I am happy. My hair, goodness my hair! It used to be so long and luxurious, then I cut it and it has to be said it is rather clumpy, I didn't do a very good job! It's clear of lice as far as I know, but you have to be on guard. As long as it's short it seems to keep them away, but in my clothes, it seems a different matter. I am constantly onto the hems with my candle. The little devils end up crisps when I've

finished. Sophie had a nasty attack the other day and she is rather close to us in our cots, so we have to guard against the swine hopping across.

Well, now I have to reveal it all. I have feelings for someone. I shouldn't I know, but I do. This may not be the time or the place to fall in love, but I think I have and I know many would see it as wrong.

I cannot tell Dada or mother, or even Alfie. Maybe I will tell Alfie, if only we could meet up. I do miss the big lump. Knowing he could only be a few miles away is really hard. Knowing that he may be so close and may be killed is even worse. Still, me, my feelings. The touch, even a brush against my skin sends shivers down my spine and a warm honey feeling inside. As if they were melting. I have never felt like this before. It really is I have a warm melting point which does not make sense. My insides turn to goo, between my legs it seems to explode and all I want is to be skin to skin holding them close. Only I will read this, why do I tell myself what I know? Do I need to reinforce my love with words? If only I could reinforce them with actions. Though I am also at a loss as to what to do... Life and love they are both such a puzzle.

The road was almost sunken underground. Either side of us were banks of earth, past them were the broken trees of war. Nothing had been left unspoilt. Houses, farms, complete villages, and hamlets all had been smashed to smithereens. High explosives had taken their toll and above the parapets above the road the view was a wasteland. Ahead were our front lines and the dressing station. Behind was the clearing station and the railway, as well as our homes. We were in the middle. Sometimes planes flew overhead squawking gunfire and fighting each other. My nurse sitter was in the back asleep I presumed, as long as she didn't keep hitting the roof as we bounced along. It would take about half an hour to get to our destination and she had looked so exhausted I had told her to crawl into the back. The ambulance was clean as this was the first trip of the day. The sun was trying to get through the clouds ahead and it seemed another pleasant enough day. Ahead there were some small crumps and the clouds seemed quite low. The sun was being filtered through them and looked quite beautiful. I looked ahead and saw the cloud moving slowly towards me and realised that it had filled up the gap between the two banks either side of the road. I could see above the cloud and the sun was brighter there. I suddenly realised that it was not cloud and banged on the partition between me and the nurse.

"Gas!" I shouted, "Wake up! Gas!" I pulled my mask over my face and straight away my sight line was gone. I stopped the ambulance and got out waving at the wagon behind who saw my mask and understood. I pulled my beret over my ears and wrapped my scarf around my neck, then banged on the back door and yanked it open. The nurse thankfully had her mask on, and I pulled the door shut and pointed to lie down. We would just have to wait for the gas to clear and leave us in peace. I pulled the nurse's coat up over her neck, hiding any bits of flesh I could see. Depending on what kind of gas this was, it could damage any skin showing. The gas attack was like fog in London. It insinuated its way everywhere. Our masks worked thank goodness, but we could see it enter the ambulance and slowly make its way to the ceiling. We were both fully covered, and I hoped to God my colleagues were as well. Trouble was that we would be bringing those who had been too slow or unlucky back to base today. I don't know how long we waited in the ambulance, but eventually there was a bang on the side and a voice shouted,

"All clear!"

I ran around to the front of the bus and jumped behind the wheel. I knew I had best be as quick as possible now. The sun was still shining brightly, and the wind was lightly blowing dust up from the fractured cobbles of the road. It really was a pleasant morning. The dressing station was mayhem. But it was an orderly mayhem, if that is possible. I could see everyone had a role and everyone was doing a job as I helped unload our patients with the orderlies on duty. We were not quite overwhelmed, but close to it. There were rows of stretchers of coughing, retching soldiers who had been too slow. Others stood leaning on colleagues, coughing and spewing up pink foam, trying to control their breathing or lack of it. Others had bandaged eyes where the gas had eaten into them. It was like Hell itself without the flames.

We quickly had a full ambulance. I had two sitting in the cabin with me gasping and wheezing. Coughing and choking on their own body fluids. I wanted to be sick but had to be strong. I got back to the Clearing Station in under half an hour and the men toppled out or were stretchered away. I found the hose and was diluting the mess that was on the floor before brushing it away. Disinfectant followed. I wiped off the front seat of the ambulance and was on my way again, to be met by even worse cases as the gas had had more time to work its way into their lungs. If ever you could meet walking death, this was it. Some didn't know it, but they didn't have long to live. It would be a hard and nasty death. I think I cried all the way back to the Casualty Clearing Station and for most of the rest of the day. Crying for all these boys who were in the wrong place at the wrong time, who had forgotten their masks thinking it would never happen to them. This war had happened, why had they assumed that there was nothing worse that could happen?

It took a long time to get to sleep that night. I didn't see Élodie at all as she was overrun with the consequences of my work.

Élodie wiped her forehead with her sleeve, so tired she could barely stand. She tucked the young soldier's arm under the blanket and stroked his cheek. He smiled with gratitude.

"Will miss you Nurse, when they send me away."

"At least you will be going home with everything intact," Élodie smiled down on him.

"A blessing I suppose, but all me mates ..."

"Can carry on quite happily without you. No one wins a war on their own, no matter how important they think they are."

"I don't think I'm important Miss. In fact, I don't think I count for very much at all. But I had to come over. I had to be here. What would they have thought if I'd stayed at home, whilst all me mates died?"

"I know Private. I know. You boys all think it is so important not to let each other down, but who is letting you down?"

"Whatya mean, nurse?"

"Well you are here, fighting and your friends dying and your officers they lead you into all the mess you face risking everything and them dying, then there are the, what do you call them, the brass, far away, sending you this way and that. Never sure if what they are doing is successful or helpful, just a case of doing something."

"And all we do is die ..."

"Yes, you die, but not this time. So, you are a lucky boy."

"I hear some Frenchies have turned mutineers nurse. Will you mutiny?" He grinned, then winced from the pain of his wound.

"No, I will stay at my post, Private. I am doing some good after all."

"We aren't, are we?"

"One day we will discover if you are, but it will take some time. Now get some rest. You need to be strong for your journey tomorrow, it is not easy on those ambulance trains."

I sat on my cot. Sophie was asleep on hers on the other side of our little world. In the middle Élodie's empty cot waited for her return. We had been so busy today; the ambulance had not stopped, and we had finally finished well after dusk. The gunfire from the Front had ceased except for the odd flare and rattle of machine gun fire. They couldn't rest out there. Someone was constantly having to make a point, though I was never quite sure what the point was. The flares were bright in the distance and filled the sky with light. It would have been quite magical if it wasn't accompanied by gunfire. I heard our curtain rustle and a white faced Élodie came in. She looked at

Sophie's sleeping body, then crawled onto her cot and pulled me towards her. We kissed and I felt a warmth flow into my tummy.

"My love for you," Élodie whispered. "It's unbearable."

"I cannot control that my love."

"No, I don't want you to, I want it to be uncontrollable, well at least when we are alone."

"If only we could be in control enough to arrange that," Élodie sighed.

"When the war is over, and we live in the small cottage by the sea."

"Two sisters who hold hands a lot."

"Who never leave their home except for groceries."

"Two old maids who will die with the love of their life by their side."

"And nobody will know," I laughed.

"Well, a few, but we will know. We have our love and we will know." Élodie yawned.

"And show, I need to show you my love."

"And I will show mine. And we come back to the problem of never being alone." And she turned and was asleep almost at once. She hadn't even got undressed; she still had her boots on. I smiled to myself as I untied her laces and gently eased them off. I pulled her blankets over her and blew out her guttering candle. How I loved her, how I loved her. When could I truly show her my love?

December 6th, 1917.
Dearest Diary of my deepest thoughts and dreams

Sitting here in the dim light so close to my dearest girl is an agony, a torture that I cannot bear at times. My candle is letting black smoke sneak up towards the ceiling and I am freezing despite all my layers of clothing. My hands hurt and my shoulders ache. I am a wreck. Though tired I will write something. Why am I telling me that I am doing this anyway? I am so confused. I see all the young fellows about camp and hear all the comments they mutter to each other. Sometimes they want us to hear them and other times they are talking just to each other, but just too loudly. But what do I feel? Florrie and Clemmie and even my beautiful friend Sophie all go red and giggle. I feel nothing. They will comment on someone's appearance. Something we would never have done before the War. Well I might have, but I was only fourteen at its outbreak so said many silly things. But here?

The men are sometimes quite open about what they want from the nurses and VADs and we have to keep away from them. We could be sent home in disgrace, losing any rights we once had, whilst they might be put up on a charge as well, so it's best to keep them all at arm's length. I would rather keep them further away. There is no attraction. Sophie has her gorgeous fiancée, but is still flattered by their words. How times have changed for us all. I am different. I am one of so few. Am I unnatural? Élodie would say not, but is she unnatural? What is unnatural? Her church says one thing and perhaps that is why she goes so rarely these days. I like to sit in the ruins of L'eglise Saint-Pierre and I know that Élodie goes there sometimes, but she never sees a priest. Has she lost her faith? Is that now my fault because of our love? So many things to worry about.

Then outside today there was the snow and the hail. All building up towards Christmas. That is one good thing coming soon as well as our hoped for leave. What a treat that will be ...

Chapter 6

"You are ice and fire, the touch of you burns my hands like snow..."

Élodie stood naked behind the makeshift screen as I tipped the pitcher of water over her head. She squealed like a child. I tried to hush her, "People will come to see what the noise is about!" Élodie danced as if on hot coals, hugging her body,

"But it's so cold."

"Just wash yourself whilst I fetch some more." I left the ad hoc shower area to go to the taps and waited for the container to fill.

"Carbolic soap, I hate it!" shouted Élodie.

"Kills everything dead."

"The smell will be the dying of me."

"Grow up, Élodie!" I called back at her, but she made me giggle.

"Look at my skin."

I returned laughing, bucket at the ready. We had been here for months and still had no proper showers.

"Your skin is beautiful. Your whole body is beautiful."

"Don't Poppy..."

"A few baths in goat's milk will sort you out."

"Goat's milk, pfft. *Tu est fou!*"

"It will all be over soon, then we'll be back to normal."

Élodie stood there vigorously rubbing the foul-smelling soap into her body, under her arms and between her legs. She was not embarrassed in the slightest about her body. I always wanted to hide in the communal showers, didn't want anyone to see me. British reserve of course.

"Pfft! What is normal anymore, Poppee. Things will never again be the same. I know France will never ... all the dead boys..." She started on her hair and I doused her by surprise. Her scream was again piercing, and I burst out laughing as Sophie ran out from our quarters.

"What the Devil? Oh, it must be Élodie Proux! Shush or matron will be over!" She laughed and returned inside the barn.

"Élodie! Be quiet!"

"You are an assassin, Poppee Loveday!"

"I..."

"You kill me with your cruelty." I couldn't stop laughing as I made my way back to the water tanks once more.

"You are an idiot, Élodie Proux!"

"But I am your idiot."

"So, true my darling. Let me check your hair."

"But it's so cold!" complained Élodie.

"Best out here than in your bed." I combed through Élodie's short hair for lice, but found none. "One more rinse, Élodie, then it's bed for you."

"Am I being punished for my noise?" Élodie smiled angelically.

"Only with the water!" And I doused her again.

Our leave had come at last, but we had to finish a job in return for a lift to Boulogne. We had six officers to deliver to a clinic there for further treatment. They were all full of it, none of them wanting to show the others that they were scared or wanted to go home. It was all stiff upper lip and wanting to be back at the Front as soon as possible. How on earth would their men cope without them? A lot better than you think, I mused to myself, grinding out another gear as we skidded along the road. This was so much better as we got further away from the Front. It hadn't been attacked from the air for a while and was in good order. The one problem was the stream of soldiers marching against us, making their way towards the Front. It never seemed to end. All hunched over carrying great sacks of equipment and weapons. Not really talking to each other, not looking up from their boots, just marching stolidly on. It was getting dark as we neared Boulogne-sur-Mer. I didn't want to run over a line of troops and was pleased when we reached the clinic and deposited our men. I was to leave the ambulance there for collection and we strolled down into the town to find our hotel.

The hot water streamed steaming from the taps. Suds piled high, almost spilling over the edge. We stood naked in the bathroom. Holding each other close, jumping from one foot to the other like over excited children waiting for Christmas to come. I stepped away and pointed to my legs and the ingrained dirt that circled my ankles despite all my efforts to keep clean. Élodie laughed then suddenly pushed me to one side and leapt into the bath sending water and foam splashing all over the floor. I squealed, then laughed almost hysterically,

"How could you Élodie?"

"We are at war Poppee."

"We are on the same side."

"I could not wait."

"Neither can I." I turned off the taps and climbed in, facing Élodie.

"I never dreamt you could be so selfish, Élodie."

"Shellfish, what is this shellfish?"

"Selfish not shellfish, and you know very well, Élodie." Élodie took my left ankle in her hand and started to scrub away the dirt.

"How am I a shellfish my Lady Loveday? I worship you. I wash your feet." Élodie was almost hidden by the suds, water lapped at the side of the bath, threatening everyone in the rooms below if they had not already been drenched by Élodie leaping into the bath. I felt so aroused under the touch of Élodie and shivered despite the heat of the bath,

"Will the dirt ever disappear? Out damn spot!" I recited.

"Macbeth!" squealed Élodie.

"Yes!" I laughed.

"The great Willyeem Shakespeare."

"You know it?"

"Of course, Poppy, our education system is to be feared around the world. We put up with Shakespeare, whilst we really love Moliere and Racine."

"Who?" I smiled.

"It is you English who are Philistines. You and your Donne and your Blake. Why not Baudelaire or Proust?"

"Indeed, Élodie. Now you have rubbed my leg raw, can you do the other one?"

"Oh, *désolé* Poppee. But at least it is now clean despite the blood!" she laughed. Legs finished I stood and sat between Élodie's legs, who wrapped her arms around me as I leant back into her body. We luxuriated together in the warmth.

"When I was growing up we always had a time limit on bathing, our nanny said our skin would shrivel and die."

"Shrivel?" Élodie asked.

"Wrinkle up, you know, we were always pulled out ready or not and wrapped up in a giant towel."

"How nice for you."

"It was nice. We were wrapped up like a cocoon in a thick warm towel then rubbed silly until we were dry. It was divine." As I spoke, I gently rubbed at the dirt on Élodie's legs, slowly but surely erasing weeks of mud.

"It sounds like it. I am jealous Poppee. And with your maid, you were spoilt Poppee?"

"I always hated it really, the idea of someone serving you. I never liked it, but thinking back now it was really nice. Especially with my long hair."

"Your hair was long?" Élodie's eyes widened.

"We all had long hair; you know that. Then we came here. I used to sit on it, my nanny was useful then, it took an age to dry. Now with my bob it's just minutes."

"Your hair is nice, Poppee. I don't think I would like it long."

"I know, it took a bit of getting used to, but just think if we were looking for lice in such lustrous locks?"

"Locks, Poppee?"

"Hair, such long hair my love." Élodie nuzzled into my neck,

"I think I could stay here forever, Poppy."

"Yes, we can wallow together."

After the nightmares of the Front this was almost

heavenly. The froth from the soap made it look as if they were lying together in clouds. I scooped some up and blew it away. I felt Élodie stroking my body and started to dissolve just like the froth.

"I don't want to go back," I whispered.

"Shush Poppy, don't think about tomorrow, think about now."

"It's so horrible, it's just …"

"Hush *ma Cherie*, let's forget just for a little while." Her hands continued to caress me and despite all, my mind was soon elsewhere. She was so gentle and her fingers reached inside me and started to explore and tease and I gasped. My whole body seemed to be shaking as she found the perfect place.

"To bed, Élodie, let's go to bed." Élodie stood and helped me to my feet, I felt shaky and weak kneed. She had emptied me of strength. I made my way towards the large bed and Élodie wrapped a towel around me and rubbed vigorously drying me off. I repeated the effort for her then dropped the towel and pressed my hands upon her breasts as she leaned into me. Her mouth found mine, her tongue found mine. Our bodies collapsed onto the bed and we were locked together, flesh on flesh. Élodie felt her way inside me again and I inside her. She convulsed and moaned and I almost stopped as I thought I had hurt her, but she pushed my hand back inside and moaned with pleasure into my ear before her lips were on my body finding places of pleasure I had never known existed. This was what I had been waiting all my life for. Élodie was what I had needed all these years. I was so in love and my body was flushed and swollen with the pleasure of it all.

Dressed in clean uniforms, sharing Élodie's Narcisse Noir perfume, we went downstairs to find our seats. We sat opposite each other at a small table in the dining room feeling as clean as new pins, which I had to explain to Élodie. We were close enough for our knees to touch under the table and made do with that, though we would brush each other's hands or arms every so often as we discussed the menu. It was like

Christmas, not a great choice, but so different from the food we were used to at Lapugnoy. Every table was filled. At least we had no need for a chaperone as at many there were three seated, two women and a man. One woman looking awkward and out of place as the other two lovers only had eyes for each other. Other tables were occupied by three or four men in khaki. All looking spick and span. It was a wonder there was enough hot water in the hotel.

We looked at the menu. Heads close together. Élodie whispered into my ear what she wanted, but it all revolved around when we returned to our room. I shushed her feeling my cheeks redden with her suggestions, she knew how easily it was to embarrass me.

The sea rolled in across the shingle making strange sucking and swishing sounds. Élodie giggled as she mimicked the noise. I danced on the stones and made my way into the water, my skirt hoisted up to me knees. I realised how unladylike I must look, but as it was near midnight, I had no real worries about my stock in society. The moon was high though and we could see down the empty beach. The smell of brine and the noise of the waves left us in no doubt as to where we were. Élodie took my hand, her other grabbing her skirt to keep it dry. It was ridiculous, we were only about two hours from our camp and another three from the battlefields, but this seemed like a different world. True during daylight we saw hundreds of soldiers, but most would have returned to their camp down in Etaples for the evening. Here was just a strange peace and quiet. A world apart from where we were used to, a different world now I had my dearest girl by my side. Talking of a world apart, it was also strange that the Americans had come to France this way, but as yet they were one of the few nationalities we hadn't seen. Canadian, South African, Chinese and Russians yes, but no Americans. Maybe they shunned our beautiful beach for their own delights wherever they may be. The sea was up to my thighs, I wanted to swim, but knew I ought not to without undressing and on this beach though deserted at the moment it could fill up at any time, so

I put my wishes to one side. Élodie stumbled and I pulled her towards me to keep her balanced and our lips touched, and I dissolved into her for the briefest of moments. Swimming was then forgotten. I just wanted to get back to our hotel and our bedroom.

We had three wonderful days and nights. Much of our time was spent in our room. Not all of it to sleep. When we did go outside, we strolled hand in hand through a town that bustled with trade as if there wasn't anything happening less than fifty miles away. We smiled knowingly at each other as we passed the young couples, one party in khaki, the other in a bright coloured dress, followed discreetly by an older woman keeping her eye on their morals. At least we had our freedom, we just seemed like two friends promenading together. Who knew what we attended to in the safety of our bedroom? I felt so happy and could almost measure the weight of my work being lifted from my shoulders as the hours passed. Élodie was losing the greyness in her face and her green eyes were sparkling as she too was refreshed and reinvigorated. The only downside being that soon we would have to return to the mayhem of Lapugnoy and not know when our next leave would be.

"Concentrate young lady!" I snapped to myself. I was tired and my eyes ached. We were back. Nothing had changed except that we were cleaner. It had started to snow again. The long journey to the Advanced Station seemed to take forever and then the bumpy road back seemed to take even longer. My bus bounced along the lanes and I pitied the poor boys in the back. Ahead I could see a dogfight unfolding in the sky. This didn't happen very often, usually we had the sky to ourselves. When the Germans did attack from the air that made it all the more frightening, but if our boys or the Canadians or French reigned supreme in the skies we would be safe. A plane suddenly blew out thick black smoke and started to spiral towards the trenches. I couldn't see who had won, but as the winner dipped his wings, he made his way to the West, so I assumed he was one of ours. What did it matter though? One more dead boy falling from the sky. More dead boys in the ambulance to be sure and many more to come. My beautiful leave was well and truly over.

December 10th, 1917.

Dear me Diary I should say!
Had a long talk with Lady Greenwood. She is talking to all the girls. She is trying to look to when the war may be over to boost morale. She spoke about our hopes and prayers for the future, about our families. She said she'd known mother in her challenging days as she called them when they both protested for suffrage. She made me laugh with some of her stories and I felt at ease in her presence. I'd best not repeat what she said my mother got up to, but it saddened me that she has lost her fire. She used to be full of it when she came back after a demonstration to the London house. Anyway, I suppose we all learn to live with our new responsibilities. It was just like talking to an old friend. She asked about Élodie and her painting and showed me a drawing Élodie had done of her. Of course, it was beautiful. I thought how talented my dearest girl was and what should she do with her talent.
When we talked about my future, Lady Greenwood agreed that I should get a degree and mentioned her old college in Oxford and promised to write to them putting my name forward. Yes, she said, it is still about who you know and how to use your contacts and as she gave them enough in charitable donations, the least they could do would be to look favourably on any suggestions she made. She said if the blasted war ever ended that she would be going back to be Headmistress in her school in Norfolk. Nemesis Hall, she called it. Goodness knows why. She said there would be summer school teaching work there if I was ever interested and that perhaps I should consider teaching! We had tea and cake! It was lovely. She said how her school was and would be a beacon of excellence for all the girls who went there. She wanted them to be rulers of the world. She certainly has a lot of fire! It's nearly the end of 1917 now and I wonder what

we have in store. Snow of course after a few dry days and so my fingers are now really cold. Everyone is asleep. Sophie is snoring and I can hear one of the girls talking in her sleep. Not sure who it is. We need to celebrate the New Year. The Christmas Tree is looking sad. It is sad. I had another good cry today. Seems the only way to get through the day. Do the driving, clean out the bus, have a good cry, head for the mess tent and hope to goodness the good cook is on duty. She was today!

We lay in our cots, side by side at last. Wrapped up against the cold. My nose was just above the blankets as I looked across at Élodie. She was crying.

"What is it my love, we were so happy." I floundered.

"I have to tell you something, Poppee," she whispered.

"You can tell me anything my darling."

"Promise you will not hate me?"

"I will never hate you." I reached over and put my hand on her shoulder and squeezed.

"It is about when you discovered me."

"By the road-side?"

"Yes," she swallowed hard.

"The soldier you tried to save?"

"I didn't save him, Poppee, I killed him."

"What?" My head jerked up and I sat up.

"I killed him, he tried to rape me. The bruises on my face were from him."

"But how?"

"He had seemed so nice. He had a slight wound. I was helping him to our theatre when bombs started to fall," Élodie whispered.

"I remember."

"The tent, the doctors and my friends, the nurses were all killed. We were sheltering in a hole. Hiding. Then his hand went to my skirt and was grabbing at it. There was so much cloth he could not get under. It would have been funny but ..." She paused tears filling her eyes. "I slapped his hand away and he punched me so hard. No one had ever hit me before; it was a shock. I told him not to be foolish, but he carried on. He was like a wild thing, hitting and slapping me, trying to rip my skirt. He was laughing like a mad man. I pushed him away."

"My poor Élodie." I reached over and pulled her close.

"It was as if the bombing had triggered something inside him. He exploded just as the bombs had. It was horrible. He kept trying to get through my skirt, he made my nose bleed. Ripped my head dress off. I managed to push him away and get out of the shell hole. I ran to the road where you found me, but he grabbed my leg and we fell. He got out his bayonet and waved it at me. I remember telling him not to be stupid. We got into another fight; his hands were everywhere. It was horrible, he put the knife to my throat, and I thought, kill me, that would be better than rape, so I grabbed the knife." Sobs wracked through her body. "I dream of this, every night. This is my nightmare when I wake you. I grabbed at the knife. He pushed me to the floor and was at my skirt again. I remember kicking him and then he just went limp and there was blood everywhere, somehow he had managed …"

"But you were cradling him."

"You came just as this happened, I had pulled out the bayonet and thrown it as far as I could but could not get from underneath him. I was exhausted. I was trying to push him away when you came but can imagine what you saw." Élodie's voice was almost ghostlike.

"But it wasn't your fault."

"I still killed him."

"Do you think he would have shown you any mercy if he had had his way with you?"

"He was a boy."

"Man enough to rape, not a real man though."

"My nightmares, all I see is his blood." Élodie started to cry again.

"Why did you not say?"

"How could I, to say to *ma mie* that I murdered."

"It was self-defence if anything, Élodie. No one can

blame you." I almost pleaded.

"I blame myself ..."

"Élodie, he was evil. You were right. You are in the right."

"I need to confess my guilt."

"No Élodie, you mustn't."

"To a priest, I need to ask forgiveness to see what I should do." Her tears took over and she lay sobbing in her cot.

I didn't know what to do or say, save for, "Élodie! You don't need forgiveness." I felt very cold. The blankets of my cot could not stop me shivering, but it wasn't the temperature, it was what Élodie had told me. My blood had turned to ice. I could not blame her for her actions. I could not judge her. If I was fighting for my body, for my life, what would I have done. Rolled over passively and let him have his way. I think not. I would have done the same but thank god I had never been put into that position. I reached out and found her tiny cold hand and squeezed it gently. I sensed a change in her breathing as sleep at last overtook her crying and carefully eased her hand under the blanket. I looked into her sleeping face. I turned and looked up to the ceiling. What an absurdity life had brought us. What could be done? There was no evil in that beauty.

"You have heard?" Sophie said quietly.

"No what is it, war about to end?" I laughed.

The seriousness of her reply put an end to levity. "Fraser and Monroe are being sent back in disgrace."

"Disgrace, what do you mean?" Then it dawned on me. "But what harm ..."

"Undermines us all, according to Commandant. The rot will set in."

"But that's insane. They do their job so well. What difference does it make who they love?"

"I know darling, but what can we do. It's in the rules and regs."

"I'll speak to her." I declared.

"But what can you change, you may be sent home yourself for insubordination."

As she spoke those words, I winced at the thought of being found out for what I was and being sent home. In disgrace, what disgrace, to love someone? It shouldn't matter. I felt so angry. I had to speak out. I could not let this go without a fight. I stomped through the mud and the rain. So bloody typical to get filthy before I could even start work. I banged on her door and was welcomed inside and offered a seat, as if she had been expecting me. Lady Greenwood had left her private school in Norfolk to serve here. She had turned the school over to be a hospital and now ran this station like clockwork. We didn't see much of her, but she had my respect. Until now. I couldn't believe this would happen. She was to put me straight.

"My hands are tied, Loveday."

"But Ma'am, you have discretion."

"Until the higher ups find out and I'm afraid someone has spoken to them. It's out of my hands." She was adamant.

"Someone told tales?"

"I cannot say, but the word came from above."

"But..."

"They were good girls, Loveday, too good to lose really, but there is nothing more I can do. If they are your friends."

"I don't know them ma'am."

"Then why?"

"The principle. Here we are fighting an enemy who would destroy all we believe in. The freedom we believe in. Who has the right to say what they want is wrong? To fall in love with the wrong person, shouldn't they have the freedom to do that?"

"If only it were that simple Poppy. Those in positions much higher than me see this as a way of destroying the fabric of society."

"But..."

"I know, I know. It is a nonsense, but until laws are changed and minds are changed, we are fighting for only a certain type of freedom. A certain amount of freedom. None of us can be truly free. It's impossible."

"But ma'am, we must have a purpose, a belief. We can't accept what certain people say as the truth. Is it the truth that God only wanted men and women to lie together? Why would so many people fight against God's will if it was the case?" Lady Greenwood smiled.

"Now you bring God into it, along with the politicians, and before that we have the army and the nursing corps. We can't fight everyone, Loveday. You will have to pick your battles one at a time. For the moment, I can only say I am really sorry. I tried my hardest for them both, as I valued them as people. As women. Sometimes one has to accept a fight is lost. This one before it began, I'm afraid."

I looked at her and saw they were the sincere words of a woman who cared and cared deeply about this. But they were the words of truth. Sometimes one couldn't win. It was like our battles at the Front. No one could win it seemed until that one thing that gave the advantage. The one thing that gave momentum to a cause. Would we ever see that on this issue, or would I die before I could achieve that freedom? It made my heart heavy.

"Get yourself on duty, Poppy," she smiled, "you are doing so much good, along with the other girls. Think of that."

"And our spy, Lady Greenwood?"

"I have no idea at all who she is. It may even be a spurned soldier. Just take care." I nodded and stood, smoothed my coat down and stepped out into the storm, chilled to the bone. As I walked back to the Barn, I thought how I had been unattracted to anyone all my life until Élodie. Neither men nor women had meant anything to me. I had spent over a year here in France surrounded by women and never once was there a spark of temptation with anyone. Then Élodie came along. Why had I not realised this was what I was. It was strange. Then these girls who were being sent home, when did they realise they had desires for each other. Had they always known or had something happened to make them feel this way? It puzzled me and I was aware of the feeling that we still had to hide it, our attraction to each other was anathema to so many, to society at large and now especially to the army, to the church, even to God, and this made little sense to me. I shivered again. What was to become of my love? What indeed?

It was back to the old formula. I had on two big pairs of navy blue bloomers. I looked ridiculous as added to them was a pair of Alfie's rugby socks. I had my hands in the air and Sophie was holding onto Alfie's long school scarf and I twirled round to allow it to wend its way over my bust band, my other piece of silky comfort. I was now twice my normal size and sat on my cot to pull on another pair of socks. Sophie threw me my blouse and buttoned up her own before putting on her tie. We started to look more normal as I squeezed into my trousers. At least I would be warmish today. We both grabbed our gas masks and mackintoshes as we left the Barn and strolled through the early morning haze to the canteen.

"I hope it's porridge!" Sophie laughed.

"Me too!" I grabbed her arm and we carried on giggling. It was quiet at the moment, but we had heard rumours of another assault so were not surprised when we heard the guns open up from behind. I could imagine the hail of metal flying through the air before exploding on some poor German boys a few miles ahead. It just added to the waste and the pointlessness of it all. We sat at a table and sucked our spoons clean of the porridge. It filled a spot as did the bread and margarine. How I longed for some butter and some of the jam our cook at home, Mrs George, used to make. Here I was never quite sure of what was in the jam. Sometimes it tasted metallic, other times too sour. It was just the luck of the draw. Tea, of course, was wet and sweet. Not always hot, though this morning it was. We were lucky as it wasn't as stewed as normal. How our cooks could get so much wrong was beyond me. I was just going to start a discussion on jam when I saw a weary looking Élodie enter the tent. She was pale and drawn and her white apron filthy from her night's exertions. She hadn't been seen all day yesterday so must have worked through day and night. She smiled as she saw us and came towards our table. Sophie jumped up to get her a drink.

"Thank you, Lady Quittenton," Élodie smiled.

"So formal, Élodie!" Sophie laughed, "You look dreadful!"

Élodie laughed thinly. "I feel dreadful. I just need this so-called tea, then I have to change and go back."

"So-called?" I smiled.

"Yes, you know it isn't really tea, but some medieval concoction made to suppress our men's sex drive."

"Élodie!" Sophie squealed.

"Yes," I added "and to make them more aggressive on the battlefield. A weird mixture indeed!"

"Ladies!" Sophie said, "You cannot be serious!"

"We only have to look at how you drive to know it works!" I said. Élodie almost spat out the last of the elixir as she laughed, then stood up.

"No rest?" I asked.

"No, over five hundred boys yesterday and last night. More expected after this push."

"It's due soon, listen to the guns." The sound was indescribable. One long roar, each shell fired merging into the next, a continuous raining down of explosives and death.

"We had some Russians in last night," Élodie said quietly.

"And of course, lots of Canadian boys," said Sophie. I felt Élodie shiver.

"All of them a long way from home," I said.

"I don't think they know where home is anymore. Some spoke a little French, others a little English. They have no idea what's going on. Or why they are still fighting," said Élodie sadly.

"Well I'm not sure why we are still fighting. It's just endless. One yard forward, two yards back. That's if we are lucky."

"Another push today and how many will be killed?"

"It's always more when we try to advance. Perhaps we should just stay put." I said.

"We have stayed put. I wonder what a map of our gains

and losses look like!" Sophie said.

"A line that has barely changed," I said.

"Well let's have no defeatist talk, ladies!" Sophie laughed.

"I held a brain in my hands last night," Élodie said out of nowhere.

"My God, that's awful!" I said.

"He had all this bloody bandage on his head, and I was holding him steady. Matron removed the lot and his skull had gone and I was just left holding this pink and bloody brain. It was incredible. All this time and I've never seen one in one piece. Poor boy died of course. I didn't know what to do with it. Matron was a bit stunned as well." She smiled with the grim stoical humour that war had brought to us all.

"Bloody hell, Élodie! What did you do with it?" Sophie squealed.

"Put it in a basin. Hurried to the next bed. Matron was a bit slower than usual. Not surprised. Then what do you think happened?"

"Same again?" I ventured.

"No, silly. A shell went straight through the tent. Missed Matron by centimetres. If she had been moving at her normal speed, she would have been by my side."

"What, just missed you as well?"

"We watched it fly. It was so strange. The canvas must have slowed it up, or maybe we imagined it. We heard the whistle and felt its wind that's for sure."

"What a night for you!" Sophie said, impressed. I realised that Élodie was asleep, just sitting there at the table, sleep had consumed her as she sat there talking. The whistle outside calling us to our ambulances jolted her awake. She smiled sleepily at me as I bade farewell for the day.

"Try to get a little rest if you can, sweetheart." I whispered.

"*Fais attention,* Poppy," she replied.

I boosted my ambulance bonnet open and checked the plugs and fan belt. All tight and clean. I topped up my radiator and went around the wheels checking for faults. It had been too dark to do this last night. All seemed ship shape. I winked at Sophie who was sliding towards me on the ground from under her engine.

"Oil leak!" she grimaced.

"Anywhere obvious?" I asked.

"I think so. Lend us a spanner." I took some over and she fiddled away for a few minutes, before appearing again, now covered in mud and oil.

"What a bloody start to the day!" Sophie moaned.

"Bloody indeed!" I laughed. "Fixed it?"

"Hope so, don't want it to explode *en route,* do I?"

"Chance would be a fine thing!" I laughed. "You take care now."

"I will, see you later!"

My shoulders ached. My head ached. My back ached. I ached all over. The ambulance bounced up and down on the heavily rutted road, every bounce sent a stab of pain through my body. I hated to think what it was doing to the wounded men in the back. I was struggling to keep the old bus stable, but at times it seemed to have a life of its own in the mud as it slid along ruts and travelled how it wished. It was near dusk and I had been driving almost nonstop since dawn. My eyes stung with fatigue. There had been yet another pointless offensive earlier in the day and we had been picking up the detritus ever since. This offensive that was planned to break through had of course failed. They always seemed to founder. I didn't think they had moved forward an inch in all the time I had been there, stalled, stymied, stalemate. All the S's I thought and thought of a word the soldiers might use also beginning with S. They were more to the point than me, but then I smiled to myself, it was *shit* indeed. I heard stifled moans from the back of the ambulance, where there were just four men on stretchers, the fewest I had transported all day. Obviously, they were running out of boys to damage and send back. The ambulance caught another pothole, I winced as I thought of the pain the men in the back would feel. I tried to drive as fast as possible to give them a chance of treatment and survival, but I knew that each jerk of the wagon could open up a wound again or damage already broken bodies. It put my own aches and pains into perspective.

I hated all this. I hated the generals for sending the boys on fruitless missions, I hated the guns that spewed death. I detested the bombs and their indiscriminate decimation. I instinctively ducked as a bi plane swooped low over the road. Yes, I hated the planes that spat death. I shook my head and screwed up my tired eyes. I had to snap out of this. Hatred is too strong a word, too strong an emotion. I couldn't be all consumed with hate, it would leave me with no feelings for anything else and I knew I had someone I wanted to give everything to back at the Hospital. The ambulance in front of me turned off to the right and I followed. As it parked by the tents the back door opened and out jumped a small figure who sent my heart racing. Élodie. Survived another day. I looked across at the smiling face of my dearest girl. Her emerald eyes were shining again. Her red lips looking so kissable, her cheeks flushed after the excitement of the day. Here she was, alive and beautiful and I wanted her so much. She seemed to burn into my eyes. She smiled. The unseasonable sunshine glittered on her face, her eyes sparkling.

"It's so warm today," I said.

"Unnaturally so, it'll snow tomorrow I think!" Élodie laughed.

"I hope not, but then it is Christmas soon!" Élodie took my hand and squeezed. The normal tingles went through my body.

"Let us go for a walk to shake away the feelings of the day and perhaps we can find a secret place, who knows." Her eyes seemed to sparkle even more, what was she up to? We made our way south of Lapugnoy, through barren, broken land. Villages that once had names like Marles Lesmines and Calonne-Ricouart no longer existed. Any vegetation or buildings there had been were black-smoked and broken. Nothing seemed to be in one piece. Beyond the ruined village was a field of pockmarked mud. Shell holes seemed to overlap shell holes and we stumbled as we made our way forward. Then the mud turned into grass and we could see bigger shell holes surrounded by hillocks of grass or mud, but there seemed more mud. We had left Lapugnoy a few miles behind us and there were no soldiers or inhabitants about. There was nothing here so why should there be? We rounded a quite large crater and I could see the grass was high, it towered over us, unnaturally so. Élodie took my hand and we moved into the long grass. She sat down and flattened the grass next to her.

"Here *Cherie,* here is our secret place."

She started to pull off her clothes and as I knelt beside her, I did the same. Down to my bust band and knickers, I caressed her smooth skin. She reached behind me and undid my band. I stepped out of my knickers, then knelt again and felt the warmth of her body as I held her close. Skin to skin after such a long time. My body shuddered as I felt her fingers on me, her lips everywhere, like dancing butterflies. Wherever they touched, it seemed to burn and my body arched as her fingers entered me. I could not help but to cry out and my moan was lost in the air, I returned the favour and felt Élodie's body tremble and heard a soft sound in her throat. Her secret place. Our bodies also had many of their own secret places and I found most of them that afternoon. At last sated and drained we lay there. Élodie was drawing circles on my stomach and was whispering in French into my ear. I just lay there exhausted after our love making and wondering why Élodie had never brought me here before. I felt so free, lying here naked. My body warm and content in the sunshine. I stared up into the pale blue sky, no clouds, no planes, but sadly no birds. Where had they all flown to, or were they all dead? Why should I think that when I am so content? I turned again to meld into her warm body and soon I dissolved again. I adored her and wanted this day to last forever, this moment to last for hours. Aching and exultant. I loved her so much.

I could not imagine a life without her. She was everything to me. Little did it matter that almost everyone in our society would frown upon this relationship. I knew it was right and as I glanced across at Élodie, her eyes closed and her dreamy smile, I knew it didn't matter in the least who we were and what we were. I had her and she had me. It was perfect. I rolled over and this time it was my hand that started moving slowly and the strange little sound from Élodie's throat started to get louder.

December 19th, 1917.

Dearest Dada,

I am writing quite late at night and with the light of a candle so do excuse! Had a perfectly horrid day, sorry if that's not what you want to hear, and I can't tell you why, but I wish you were here to give me a hug. Everything gets locked inside my head and can't escape. I don't get bad dreams but my friend Élodie *does. It isn't very nice. I don't want to upset you, but you will know the awful things we see. I can't look away like those at home do. Still back and forth we go, it is never ending.*

Is mother well? Tell her I am writing to her soon, it will be a prettier tale for her. Alfie? Any news? He hardly ever writes. I finished the Percy W you sent. I need another one or perhaps one from Sexton if he has one out. Once I read them, they do the rounds, but I make sure I get them back! They are always so glorious; war isn't a dirty business for Percy Westerman, is it? He seems to have loads of fun beating the Hun!

Need humbugs! French sweeties are nice, but hard to come by. Send me tons for Christmas, and I do mean tons!

And Dada when I write tons, I mean tons. I could use them as my bed or to surround my bath. Just send me plenty. I promise I will share. Honestly!"

Can you get mother to send me some face cream if she can? I know things are short, but I fancy the idea of hers now that I am getting old! Well, actually it's the wind and the snow and the rain howling into my ambulance cab. It is aging my flesh as we speak. I don't want to return home a wizened old crone and give mother something else to moan about!

Still raining as I write. Can't remember the last dry day we had any sun. Can't remember when I didn't have to wear damp clothes. Oh well. Write soon.

Merry Christmas if I don't get time to write before then. I probably will, but you never know how busy we will get. I love you and miss you so much. I don't think I will get any Christmas leave, mores the pity. I could do with whatever Mrs George's version of Christmas Pudding will be this year. She is a magician. Do tell her so I get brownie points for my return! Your loving daughter,

Ophelia

Élodie looked up as someone ran into the tent. No one was allowed to run. Élodie waited for Matron to bark at her, but instead she watched as she caught hold of the nurse and slowing her down, spoke quietly to her.

"His eyes are covered in bandages. He has his eyesight Doctor says, but do be aware, he looks worse than he is."

"I will, thanks," the nurse said breathlessly. She looked around as if searching and Matron took her to a bed. The nurse stood there for a moment staring down at the body in the bed, head swathed in bandage, his arms outside the bedclothes. She sat by his side and reached for his hand, but her scream pierced the silence of the ward. Wounded bodies jerked upright in their beds staring over at the source of the scream. They were well used to the sound of men in pain, but this was so different, a female howling in despair, her hopes somehow destroyed. She pulled her hand away sharply, as if a jolt of electricity had passed through it.

"That's not my Jim!" she hissed.

"But Nurse Sloan," Matron started.

"That's not my Jim, not my husband."

"But his papers."

"I do know my own man. My Jim had hands like meat plates. Look at those dainty things. That isn't him."

"Let's not make a fuss, Sloan," Matron tried again.

"Make a fuss? I've waited three years to see my husband and you try to fob me off with this man. He isn't my Jim. Let me see his face, let me..." She started to pull at the bandages. The patient groaned in pain.

"Nurse Sloan!" Matron took hold of the nurse's hands to stop her. Élodie had never heard Matron raise her voice before, but the patient started to cry out loudly. Nurse Sloan was near hysteria now. Matron looked at Élodie, she could only shrug and didn't know what to do. Nurse Sloan started to cry.

"What a to-do," Matron said. An understatement Élodie thought for sure. It appeared they thought this was her husband, but she thought not. How strange. "Let's get you a nice cup of tea," Matron suggested.

"It isn't damn tea I need, it's my husband Jim and this isn't him. I swear it."

"Let me, Matron," Élodie interceded and Matron swished away in dignified defeat.

"Let's go outside, Sloan," Élodie said softly and took her arm. They went to the exit and out into the fresh air. The sun was shining thinly through the clouds and it was cold. Nurse Sloan shivered.

"Someone's run over my grave."

"When did you last see your husband?"

"1915. He never came home for leave. Stuck in the trenches all this time. I left the hospital in Portsmouth to come here. You know to be closer somehow. He didn't visit. Didn't get hurt. Scot-free until he gets shot in October. That's what they told me. He was never one for writing. It seemed like fate that they brought him here, but..." She dabbed her eyes with her handkerchief, but did not stem the tears.

"And his hands?"

"Like bloody frying pans, like I said. He were the Blacksmith, he needed big hands and he was so muscular. He couldn't have shrunk into that shape, it just doesn't happen."

"I think not, Nurse Sloan."

"Those are woman's hands, not my Jim's. It can't' be him. We grew up together. I know everything about him. Ask anyone from my village back home."

"It may be a mix up over paper-work. We may have him somewhere else," Élodie suggested.

"Do you think?" There was hope in her voice.

"Look, I'll have a check. Where are you sleeping?"

"Tent Seventeen, over by air raid shelter B."

"I'll have a look into it and come around to see you when my shift ends. That should give me enough time. Where in England are you from?" Élodie thought she'd try to distract her, knowing it was hopeless really.

"Near Hereford. We grew up in the same village, the same street. Our parents knew each other from their time at school. It was so romantic really. Now this ..."

"I'm sure we'll sort it out. Now don't you worry. I'll make you a cup of tea and then you can get some rest."

"You are very kind, dear. It's been such a shock. All this time apart and then I thought I'd see him. Then this ..." She didn't have to say anymore. Élodie made some tea and saw that she was comfortable in her cot. She smiled.

"You get off to sleep, Nurse Sloan, try and have a rest. It's been a shock for you, I know. You'll see it's just a mix up. It's no surprise really, is it? What with everything in the air like it is."

"Perhaps, we'll see, but they seemed so sure."

Élodie couldn't think of anything else to say. She walked back into the ward to finish her shift. Her shift ended, all she wanted was to sleep, but she had made a promise and started her search. It didn't take too long, six tents were occupied, about three hundred men and there was a name for every bed. Élodie called out for a Jim Sloan at each ward and none answered or showed up on the bed lists. She returned to his tent and he still lay there. Unconscious now, unavailable to comment. Élodie finally made it to the registry and checked the lists for time of admittance and time of leaving. No one had left since Jim Sloan had been signed in this morning. He had come from the Front with three others. Élodie took their names and went back to find them. None of them really knew him, they had only been in France for a few days and they were all from different regiments. All she had to go on was the size of his hands. Could his wife be mistaken, or had she forgotten over all this time? More than three years had passed since they had been together. Would he have shrunk? That was ridiculous. Élodie couldn't believe that she was asking herself that question, but it seemed the only probable cause for his wife's distress. Well she would have to tell Nurse Sloan what she had found, or not found, and see what she wanted to do.

 I waved as I saw Élodie moving between tents and ran over to her. "What are you doing over here, sweetheart?"

 "Just on an errand, come with me and then we can go for a walk."

 "But you look exhausted, what's the hurry?" Élodie explained to me quickly, then asked, "Where's tent seventeen?" We looked around and I pointed. We made our way on the duckboards to our goal. I had never wanted to feel like this, but shamefully I was not shocked at the sight of a dead body anymore.

 Nurse Sloan lay on her cot. Still as a statue and as pale as a ghost. Her lips blue. By her side a glass. The faint smell of almonds gave it away and as Élodie stood next to me, a great sigh hissed from her lips and she turned her face away from the body. Just then a young girl appeared at the tent entrance. She just stood there, open mouthed. At least she hadn't screamed. "Call the Provost Duty Officer," Élodie instructed the nurse who had been shocked into a statue.

 "Go now!" I said sharply when she dithered and she pulled up her skirt and ran out of the tent, to be replaced minutes later by a red faced, breathless man of about forty who looked at the body, then at Élodie, and finally at me, his mouth open all the time as if trying to say something, but failing to remember what it was.

 "I met Mrs Sloan in one of the patient's tents," Élodie said. "We had a message for her."

 "I was accompanying Nurse Proux for moral support, it seems so strange," I said.

"Yes, Miss."

"Lady Pandora Loveday," I said, hoping the gravitas of my title might help us. He almost curtsied.

"This has never..."

"Poisoned, Captain?"

"Defreitas."

"Yes, Captain Defreitas. She has been poisoned. Cyanide I think, you can still smell it."

"Indeed, Lady Loveday. Almonds. Should we wait for the investigators here?"

"Perhaps not, you have an office?" I didn't really understand how I was able to react like this. Was I so immune to death that all feelings had been set aside, that I could just act in such a cold detached way? I had no idea. I didn't want to interrogate that thought too deeply. I wanted to care about every death, but didn't know if I had the strength to do so. And what help would caring be anyway. It did the dead no good. It might help their relatives to know that someone over here cared about their loved ones, but what good did that really do? I had to metaphorically shrug my shoulders and leave this burden behind. Life would be too difficult to live if I carried it all on my actual shoulders. Élodie left first and we followed her towards his office, it wasn't far, and he ushered us in. He motioned to two chairs and we sat demurely as he almost collapsed into the chair behind his document strewn desk.

"Would you like some tea?" he ventured.

"A coffee, if I may, *Capitaine* Defreitas," Élodie asked.

"For me as well if you please," I said, and he left the tent.

"So calm, Poppy." Élodie smiled.

"What is going on? Has she killed herself because it's not her husband?"

"I doubt it, that's so extreme, but who knows anymore what is going on in people's heads? Anyway, where would she get cyanide from? It's not kept anywhere that I know of."

"It makes no sense. The Provost ..."

"Will decide. You tell them what you know."

"What do I know? Her husband will have to be told."

"If it is her husband." Unusually another officer, Captain Porter, asked to see Élodie. She went to his tent and he showed her a chair.

"Smoke, Nurse Proux?"

"No thank you."

"Do you mind if I..." He didn't wait for her to answer, but as she nodded he lit up and breathed deeply.

"Tell me what you told the provost."

Élodie repeated what had happened. When she finished, the captain drew deeply on the last of his cigarette.

"And at no stage did you see his face?"

"No, he had eye damage apparently, though I'm not sure what. His bandage showed no blood which I suppose was unusual, unless it had been changed that moment."

"So, she only held his hand?"

"Yes, do you suppose she imagined it?"

"No idea, but it is damned strange. When he regained consciousness, we wheeled him over to his wife's body and he confirmed it was her."

"But that's just his word," Élodie said puzzled.

"Indeed. She was adamant?"

"Adamant?" Élodie queried.

"Sure, convinced?" Porter explained.

"Yes, but as I said, she was quite hysterical. Hands like plates she said. People don't make that up, do they?"

"No, they don't. Something is unusual here. We need to wait for someone from his old regiment to come through to identify him."

"But he will be sent home soon, is their time?"

"Plenty. Did you know Sloan?" A strange question she thought.

"No, neither of them. The nurse seems to have escaped my attention, but we are a big camp, aren't we?"

"Indeed, we are. But he couldn't have helped his wife kill herself?"

"If she did kill herself. It seems damn strange that she

would take her own life, but stranger things have happened."

"Unless she thought her husband was dead?"

"But still…" He lit another cigarette. "It's so damned strange. Well thank you Nurse Proux. You can get off now." Élodie hurried back to the patient's tent in the middle of camp.

"Sloan's long gone." The staff nurse explained, "Taken to the railhead. Got his ticket home."

"*Merde!*" Élodie spat under her breath. She bumped into me as she left the tent.

"He's at the railhead at Saint-Venant!"

"Already? Right let's go there!" I said.

"How?"

I ran over to some Signals boys. "Can I borrow your bike?"

"Can you ride this?" one said.

"Twenty gaspers?"

"Thirty?"

"Fine, give me the key. Hop in, Élodie!"

"My fags!"

"When I get back. Don't wait up." With Élodie hanging on for dear life, I kicked the bike into action; it nearly broke my leg as it kicked. Élodie looked rather small and frightened in the sidecar. I winked at her, released the clutch gently and off we went. If I thought controlling the ambulance was difficult, this was a completely different story. The bike seemed to have a life of its own, it was like riding a wild horse and the imbalance caused by the sidecar seemed to drag me the opposite way I wanted to go. It seemed the safest route was between our ambulance ruts until we could get onto some cobblestone road and once we did that, I felt more secure and opened up the throttle aiming for the Saint-Venant Railhead. We hadn't had rain for a day or so, the roads were not a quagmire, which was a relief, but still we bumped and skidded our way toward the railhead. Most of the time we seemed to be travelling sideways and my arms ached at the effort of keeping us on the straight and narrow. Élodie looked up at me with a white-faced smile.

"Slower home I hope, Poppy!" she breathed as I helped her out of the sidecar. We ran around to the train. It was still there, lines of stretchers on the platform and moans and groans filling the air. I spotted a matron I knew and asked her. I knew it was pretty hopeless.

"You'll have to look, Poppy. Paperwork got shot up this morning in a raid."

"Just when you wanted a bit of order."

"Can't be helped, but look at carriages fifteen and sixteen, I think they're for your Sector."

"You going to go home with them?" I asked as I started to move away.

"Yes, I've a week's leave."

"Enjoy!" I shouted as I began to hurry towards the end of the train. I turned to look for Élodie and could see her nowhere. Searching herself, I supposed.

At first, Élodie couldn't understand why a soldier was walking away from the train and towards some of the bombed-out ruins of Lozingheim. In itself, it wasn't that unusual, but on his arm, he had the band of a wounded soldier, he should be on the hospital train or with the recovering soldiers in their tent. She turned around to look for Poppy, but she was talking to a matron some distance away. She looked again at the soldier and he was ducking behind a half-fallen wall. She decided to follow. There wasn't time to tell Poppy, she would lose him if she did. When she had managed to scramble to the wall, she couldn't see him anywhere, but she heard falling bricks and a cry. She kept low and moved towards the sound. She looked around the corner of a ruined house and there he was, sitting in a heap of rubble rubbing his leg and talking to an officer who had his back to her. He pulled off his armband and handed it to the officer and listened intently to what must have been instructions, there was no way that Élodie could hear what was going on and she couldn't get any closer without being seen. She didn't know if this was Sloan, but it was strange, so she had to think quickly. The officer strode off. Was he telling the patient to return to his regiment, or to go to the train? He was coming back towards her. Élodie quickly tried to melt into the bricks when she heard a noise behind her. Just as she turned, she saw a face that she knew, but she also felt a stinging pain on her jaw, and all was black.

    I could find no sign of Jim Sloan. I only had his name, and no one seemed to know of him, though some had heard the story about his wife, and there were mutters of 'poor bastard' and 'poor sap' as I passed the racks and rows of stretchers. I got plenty of ribbing from the wounded, but no one had seen him. He was like a ghost. I heard a whistle blow; my time in the carriages was up. I jumped from the train and looked up and down, but saw no sign of Élodie. I hoped she wasn't stuck on the train. Steam gushed out and it was off on its way to good old Blighty. I smiled to myself, at least for these the war was probably over, but at what cost to them. Too late if Élodie was stuck, she'd have to get off in Calais. I strolled over to a small van that was serving hot drinks and ordered a tea. It was being run by a couple of VADs, but they'd seen nothing. Too busy flirting with our boys, I assumed, but who could blame them? The vile liquid they'd produced almost made me spit it out, was this tea? It tasted of chemicals, but it was warm on this rather cloudy day. At least no snow or rain. I asked a French *poilu* if he'd seen Élodie, but he didn't recognise my description. I didn't add that she had the most beautiful eyes in the kingdom; I thought that was too much information. I sat on a bench and awaited her return, grimacing each time I sipped the tea until I could stand it no more and threw the dregs from my cup.

    After about an hour, I realised this was fruitless. My tummy felt full of butterflies, I was scared I had to admit it. Élodie had disappeared into nowhere as had Sloan. I looked over towards the rubble of the destroyed village. That seemed my only hope. Another train was pulling into the station, all screeching brakes and blasts of steam. I heard ambulances pulling up outside, it would be organised chaos here soon. What a way to spend my day off! Where was Élodie? Had she come off the train and not seen me and gone back to

Lapugnoy? Was she indeed stuck on the train and on her way to the coast? I hadn't been frightened before, just a bit frustrated at her missing, but suddenly I wondered if something awful had happened. Had she been hurt, had she ... I saw one of our Provost men strolling down the platform and hurried over and described Élodie and my situation. Not that we were chasing a missing patient, but that she was lost. His answer surprised me.

"Well ma'am I did see a young nurse a while ago walking towards the old village. Thought she might be skiving, but then I saw an officer and you know I put two and two together. Thought I'd give them a bit of time."

"Where was this?" I asked, suddenly very, very scared. He turned and pointed. I started to make my way over.

"Don't forget curfew in an hour," he called after me. I waved acknowledgement, then thought. I turned back.

"Would you be able to get a message to Captain Porter at Lapugnoy?"

"Indeed ma'am."

"Could you tell him Lady Loveday was looking for Sloan and that Mamselle Proux has disappeared? Tell him what you told me. Thank you."

"Not at all ma'am. Consider it done, but do you need help now?" I shrugged, thanked him again and strode out towards the bombed village. It was amazing. Presumably, the Germans had been trying to take out the station, but had somehow missed and razed the village. The village was thus just collateral damage I supposed. Some damage! No houses had been left standing whilst the station seemed untouched. There were some shell craters along the rail line, but all rails must have been repaired, if they had succeeded at all in damaging them. What a fine mess.

Élodie's feet were wet; her clothes were sodden and she was lying in a pool or a puddle. Water she hoped. Her head was swimming; she kept seeing flickering lights in the darkness, tiny lights flashing on and off and moving rapidly across her eyeline. She felt something push into her stomach, another pushed at her feet. She flinched as she realised, rats, dozens of rats. She screamed into the gag that filled her mouth and heard only a muffled choke as the rats scuttled over her feet. She watched as the tiny lights reflecting like diamonds lined up and this time stop blinking. Just eyes that were staring at her, waiting for her to be still. She felt sweat on her forehead even though she was freezing cold and wet. Her hands were tied tightly behind her back. Whatever bound them was cutting into her skin and she couldn't move them. Her feet too were bound, and she could just about twist them, but she had no hope of escape. She waited in silent agony just as the rats waited. She blinked sweat away from her eyes and saw how the eyes of the rats were moving closer towards. She felt a sob rising in her chest, but it couldn't escape. Her nose was running, her tears were falling, and she worried that she would not be able to breathe. Shuffling and struggling she forced herself up into a seating position and bent her knees up towards her chest feeling a little more protected. She stared ahead daring the rats to move. Daring them to try. The eyes just stayed where they were staring at her. Her tears fell harder, she tried to breathe. Her chest ached with the effort. She had no idea where she was. No idea who had hit her. No idea who had dumped her in this rat infested, watery hole. Suddenly light poured into the room and she watched the rats scatter and disappear. Trouble was that a larger rat replaced them. It was a soldier. She recognised him. Certainly, he was the man that she had seen talking to the officer. She might have guessed, the bastard, the so-called Sloan. She shivered as he walked over towards her.

"Don't scream or I'll cut you." He removed the gag and she spat out the stinking rag from inside her mouth and started to cough. She felt sick and felt bile rise in her throat.

"What do you want?" Élodie gasped.

"Nothing, I don't need nothing."

"You're Sloan." Élodie guessed.

"Sloan? No chance of being him now, thanks to you."

"Spoilt things for you? Your boss unhappy?" Élodie sneered.

"I don't have a boss." But by his sudden shifty look, she knew he was lying.

"You aren't clever enough to work on your own. Anyway, I saw you talking. Who was that?" He snarled and swore.

"The plan was fine, it's worked before and will work again."

"But not for you though."

"They can find another match, no point as me going in as Sloan. There are plenty of others."

"But it holds you back? Why betray your country?"

"It isn't my country. I have no truck with you English. You destroy my country."

"English?" Élodie almost laughed, "You from Ireland? You betray us for that?"

"It is a righteous cause. I would do this a thousand times."

Élodie this time did laugh at him, "But you need to do it better."

"His hands, who would have thought his bloody hands. Then his bastard wife. How unlucky could we be? This has worked a hundred times or more."

"Your boss," Élodie repeated, "does he know you have me?"

"Perhaps."

"Does he know what I know?"

He kicked her hard in her thigh. She winced but didn't cry out. "What do you know?"

"Why would I tell you?" Élodie sneered. "All I know is that we've ruined your chances."

"We? Who else is there?" He kicked her again savagely and then grabbed her hair, yanking her head up towards him. He leant down until his face was in hers. His breath stank of wine and tobacco. "You will tell me."

She fought back the tears, but they filled her eyes. "No, I will tell your boss, Porter."

Poppy Flowers at the

Poppy Flowers at the Front

Chapter 7

"If there were no thunder, men would have little fear of lightning... "

"How?"

He shoved her away back into the water, shivers ran down her spine. She expected another kick, but he just turned away and started to pack up his rucksack. She looked around her as the rats returned. She closed her eyes to try to stop the tears from flowing, but with no success. She felt so alone, and she was frightened. She blinked open her eyes as a hundred tiny eyes watched her, waiting, but he ignored her, that to Élodie seemed even worse.

It had just been a guess, she could have said any name, but Porter's had stuck in her mind for some reason and now she could see why. But with him in his position he would have taken great care to cover his tracks. Was there any possibility that she would be able to outwit him, she wondered?

Looking for my Élodie I made my way over the rubble of Lozinghem and then stood listening. I could just about hear the noise from the station to the West, but that was it. Then the rain started. I looked around for a bit of roof to stand under and hurried across and shivered. There was nothing now, just the sound of the rain, splattering on the ground and then I realised that I could hear my heart pumping and the blood coursing through my carotid artery. A thump, thump, that seemed to be getting louder as my chest started to feel tighter and tighter. I was so frightened. I didn't know what to do or where to go. Where was my Élodie, I ran through different scenes in my head and this made me sick with worry. Who was the officer? Had she met him? Was she hurt? Why would she meet an officer? She loved me. Had... This was pointless. I looked out from under the low hanging roof into what must have been the old village square. All around had been battered, but I recognised the site of a café with chairs scattered everywhere and tables upturned and smashed. There were also the remains of a bandstand. It was shattered, but I could just about recognise it. The area was pock marked with small craters. The remaining walls scarred by bullet holes. How many had died here? Where were the inhabitants now? Where could they have gone? There were so many ruined villages like this one. As if to answer me, a small face popped up by a smashed window.

"Food, Mamselle?" The small boy made me jump. I looked down on him in his rags and dirt. Where had he sprung up from? I thought everyone had been evacuated years ago. Had he been here since the beginning? I hoped to God not, what kind of a life would that have been?

"Where are you from?" I asked pointlessly, having slipped straight into French.

"This is my home," he pointed at a burnt-out shell, then put his hand out to the side. He was tall, but so thin. He could be fourteen or ten, I had no idea. But he smiled and it was a beautiful smile.

"This is my sister." Another dirty child appeared. I couldn't work out her age either, maybe five or six, dirty blonde hair, but sparkling blue eyes that stood out from a pale mud smeared face. She met her brother's hand with her own. She smiled as a greeting and my heart melted. I patted my overalls, trying to find something for them.

"I haven't much," I handed them of all things a gobstopper each, holding up its movement towards their mouths with careful instructions to suck not to bite. I then found a small piece of chocolate and handed it to them, ashamed that it was so small and covered in fluff from my pocket. The gobstoppers came out of their mouths and the chocolate went in. They looked up at me with wide eyes, obviously wondering what else there was for them. I had no more, but I had made some new friends.

"Where are your parents?"

"*Ils sont morts*," the girl said quietly. Her brother took her hand, but she snuggled into his body looking for protection from unseen enemies.

"*Desolé...*" There was nothing else to say. Their faces were dirty, their eyes pleading for help. Tear tracks began to mark the small girl's face through the dirt. My heart was breaking for these two, how many more displaced orphans must there be in this town? I half expected to see small faces pop up all around me, but none showed. I swallowed hard.

"I'm just looking for a friend. When I find her we can get some food from the station."

"They don't like us there, throw rocks at us," said the boy.

"No..." I started, but knew it was probably true. "You'll be safe with me." He looked doubtfully at me.

"My sister is Jacinth, I am Raoul."

"My name is Poppy Loveday."

"*Les Coquelicot*. Like the flower?" Raoul said.

"Yes, just like the flower."

The small girl whispered in her brother's ear. He looked at me. "Jacinth says she will call you Loveday if that is all right?"

"Of course," I said.

Jacinth spoke to her brother again.

"*Les Coquelicot* reminds her of blood."

"There's no reason to explain," I smiled.

"What does your friend look like?" I quickly described her. Again, Jacinth whispered to her brother.

"A nurse?" Raoul asked her. The small girl nodded her head. My heart leapt. What did they know? Jacinth whispered to her brother again then looked at me as he repeated her words. My hand went to my mouth as she reached for my other hand and held it tight.

"A soldier hit your friend and took her underground, but the soldier is a bad man. He pointed a gun at us once, so we ran away."

"Where is this underground?" Jacinth pointed. "Will you take me?" The two small children looked at each other. Jacinth whispered again to her brother.

"Jacinth says of course we will, but you must be very

careful, the soldier is bad." I wondered if I should go back for the Provost first, but time was key. How long had Élodie been underground as the children put it? Who had hit her? Why? So many questions that couldn't be answered until I found my dearest girl. Then Jacinth gasped and put her hand to her mouth. Raoul pointed and we could see a soldier moving amongst the ruins. We watched the soldier as he pulled up a door and disappeared. We carefully made our way across. The door had been left open. I ventured towards it and then I shooed the two children to a safe distance and smiled to reassure them as they ducked their heads below a crumbling wall nearby. They waved as they did so. I almost laughed. I crept towards the entrance. I could hear a man shouting and then the sound of a slap. I looked into a black hole and could see nothing. I carefully lowered myself down inside, praying that I didn't find myself climbing on top of Élodie's captor. I reached the bottom of the ladder and looked about. I shivered as I saw scores of twinkling eyes in the darkness. I knew what they were. I heard another slap and my head jerked round and as my eyes began to adjust to the darkness, I saw the man towering over a bundle of something, but when he kicked the bundle, it didn't move. Then I heard Élodie snarl and I realised what the bundle was.

"You are so pathetic. Do you think you frighten me? Where is this so-called leader of yours. Do you slap me to make yourself seem important?"

"He'll be here soon Lady Muck. Then you'll find out real pain. I've been easy on you, just wait."

Another man coming. I had to sort this one out first, then decide what to do. I looked across the floor, I could still hardly see in the dark, but I did spy a large piece of wood. Perfect. I crept over to it and picked it up then moved towards where Élodie lay. Just as I closed in, I saw in her eyes that she had seen me. She spoke again.

"Tell me Mr Bully, do the ladies like you, or do you get what you deserve?" Silly Élodie, but clever Élodie. The man swore at her and kicked hard again, and I heard a burst of air explode from her just as I brought my plank down hard on his head. He crumpled and fell. I hit him again as hard as I could as he lay slumped in the watery rubble. I sank to my knees beside Élodie.

"Élodie, are you all right?" I kissed her bruised face and hugged her tightly. She winced and I let go quickly.

"A little bruised. Untie my hands I cannot feel them anymore." I scrambled with the knots and when finished grabbed the rope and tied the man's hands.

"Who is this man?"

"Sloan or the person pretending to be Sloan, though what he's doing here I have no idea." She was rubbing her wrists hard and shaking her fingers, searching for some feeling. She bent to untie her ankles and moaned softly as the blood rushed to her feet. She bounced her legs up and down in the puddle. Trying to rid herself of pins and needles. I tied the man's feet, then gagged him with a piece of cloth from the floor. He whimpered but showed no other signs of coming around. From the ground above, I heard Raoul shouting at his sister. She called something back then I heard a man swearing, then telling them to clear off. First in English then in French. In her squeaky little voice, I heard Jacinth shout at him, this time I heard the cocking of a pistol and another string of swear words. What a brave little pair; they had warned me. I scrambled and found our prisoner's gun and gave it to Élodie. I picked up my sturdy piece of wood and went to the ladder and waited in the shadows for what seemed an age but it was probably just a few seconds. Eventually a pair of legs descended and was followed by the rest of a body. I'll teach you to threaten children with a gun, I thought, and I swung the wood, catching him flush on the back of his head. He fell like a stone from the ladder into a heap and I kicked him hard for good measure. He was out for the count. A small serious looking face appeared in the doorway above.

"Ça va, Poppy?"

"*Bien merci*, Raoul," I answered and put my right thumb up. The face split into a huge grin and disappeared.

"Rope Élodie?" I said. She limped over with some and I bound our second prisoner

"This is one of the Provosts," I said to Élodie, recognising him.

"I sent him for Porter, so we'll get none of that help. I wonder where he's been. He wasn't watching me."

"Warning someone?" asked Élodie.

"So, we have Sloan, I saw someone with a wounded armband around here and that bully was the one. It must be him."

"I sent this Provost back to see Captain Porter. You don't think?"

"I think so, Poppy. It's the Irish in them both. Let's get out of here back to the children. I'm cold and hungry and I know they are as well."

"Of course, my sweet, can you manage?" It was a struggle to get her up the ladder. Even with the limited help from the two orphans it took what seemed like hours. When we got out the moon was high. The two children were shivering, as was Élodie. What a fine mess this was. I threw the door to the dungeon closed and put my arm around Élodie's waist and we started on our way back to the station. As Élodie found it easier to walk, we quickened our pace. Jacinth and Raoul scampered along beside us. We reached the railway station. It was dimly lit against air raids, but bustled with traffic, ambulances and cars, soldiers and patients. One line leading towards the Front, another towards the train and home if they were lucky. Élodie stumbled and I had to grab hard to make sure she didn't hit the ground.

"So dizzy, Poppy," she explained. I lowered her gently onto a bench at the railhead. Raoul and Jacinth sat either side of her, almost propping her up, but there was not a lot they could have done had she slipped. They were both so skinny and malnourished. I turned and looked up to see four soldiers moving towards us. One pointed at me.

"Nicked me bloody bike!" I heard him shout. Two were Provost men; I hoped these were on the right side of the law this time. But this was what we needed, I shushed the soldier and explained what had happened. I handed them the two pistols, pleased to get them out of my keeping.

"There's a Provost man in there. Don't be fooled by him whatever he says and do not untie him; he was going to kill Élodie. He was supposed to get help from Lapugnoy."

"Right you are miss!" one said. Both the provost men looked aghast and ran towards the dungeon. I just hoped they'd find it and the two traitors.

"Lots to do here first, feed the children, get Élodie to see a doctor, work again tomorrow." Élodie groaned.

"I'll come over with your fags tomorrow," I said to the sapper.

"There's no ..."

"We made a deal. Give some to your sergeant as a peace offering. Name me if you wish, I think justice will be seen to be done," I laughed.

As long as our captors were still tied up, two little rats joining their friends in a cage. The provosts could start that process when they returned. I looked down at the two young orphans. "Right, Poppy will find you two some food and you, young lady, a doctor. Stay here." I started for the platform to find a doctor. Ambulances were continuously arriving in the gloom at the railhead and I could hear a train spouting off steam. I turned to wave at my girl and found Jacinth trailing by my feet. She was such a tiny thing, my heart leapt into my throat and I lifted her into my arms.

"Come along my sweetheart, let's get you sorted out."

Jacinth clung to my neck as I spoke to a pipe smoking doctor. He tapped out his pipe and went off to see Élodie. At the catering van, there was a small line of soldiers. This time there were French nuns running it so perhaps the tea would be drinkable, and they would be able to do something about our orphans. Well at least they took the children and they waved as a nun led them away each with a large baguette in their hands. I felt a bit of a lump in my throat, but having recorded where they would be staying, I promised to write and to stay in touch. I needed to get mother to send money or something more practical to the orphanage. Another project for her! I then swallowed and took the traditionally foul tea to Élodie. As I did, I saw the provosts returning with the two traitors, because this was what they were, stumbling over the rubble.

"We'll need a report, ladies. Will you be back in Lapugnoy tomorrow?" a Provost asked.

"We both have shifts soon, if Élodie is well enough. Could you arrange for a lift?"

"Will do miss, we need to find Captain Porter. Any idea?"

"Is he the traitor then?" I asked.

"Well Mr Sloan here has implicated him."

"Porter may be at the German lines? They both have their cover blown. They are finished. Sloan may help. Porter is Irish so you know."

"Indeed, Miss, we'll report it. We'll get a car over here as soon as we can. Will you be all right?" I looked at Élodie who was drooping. She was exhausted.

"Yes, we'll be fine, thank you." I sat next to Élodie and she put her head on my shoulder and was asleep. A nurse from the platform, who we had seen about camp, but had never spoken to, rested a blanket over us. Élodie moaned something in her sleep and I looked down on my dearest girl, then looked up into the starless sky.

Later that evening, we sat demurely across from Captain De Freitas sipping rather nice coffee. He was a charming host, but was straight down to business.

"We assume you found Sloan after he met Porter."

"I think so Captain de Freitas, but you'll have to ask him," I replied.

"Well Sloan seems to be singing like the proverbial canary at the moment. He thinks it will save his skin."

"But the murder of Sloan's wife?"

"He seems to have forgotten that. Feels that he will get some kind of quarter for coughing up what he knew ..."

"He will hang, won't he?" I asked.

"Be sure of that Lady Loveday. He did a dreadful thing. Raised that poor woman's hopes. The real Jim Sloan has been dead two years it seems."

"What an awful thing to do to another human being," Élodie said.

"Evil," de Freitas said. "How low some of us have become these past few years. We could never have dreamt that this situation would have raised its ugly head. All rules seem to have changed."

"Were there ever rules in war Captain?" I asked.

"Perhaps not, Lady Loveday, but we used to hope."

"So, he took on an identity and was then to go to England, to do what?" Élodie asked.

She looked hollowed out. Her face was bruised, and she had a split lip. Goodness knows what the soldiers she was treating thought of her. I was so tired but couldn't imagine how tired she was. I had been offered a few days off, but we were down a few drivers thanks to something going around the camp. Lucky that us in the barn had dodged the lurgy at the moment, I thought.

"If all these chaps went home with superficial wounds or ones that that didn't really exist, they would have been redeployed. Some back to the Front, others on office duty."

"So, there would be a series of spies in our camp?"

"Yes, and we have no idea who they could be. German some of them perhaps, certainly some of our Fenian friends, but they will have hidden it well."

"If we could just catch Porter."

"I doubt if he would talk and I don't assume Sloan would know much that can truly help us. I suppose they could have trained together, but they wouldn't know what false names had been given."

"At least it can be stopped from here now."

"But what damage has already been done?" De Freitas choked.

"Ah yes, Captain, but what damage has been stopped?" Élodie said.

"Yes Captain, be a glass half full chap at least!" I said.

"Would this have anything to do with Kunz?" asked Élodie out of nowhere.

"Did Porter arrange that fiasco when Kunz escaped?"

"I have no idea, but don't worry your heads about that. I think I have all I need. You'd best retire. You need some sleep."

We thanked De Freitas and plodded back towards the barn. It was another moon-filled night, which came with the threat of bombers. I was so tired though that I thought I'd sleep through any raid. I closed my eyes and felt myself falling asleep where I stood.

"Come on, Élodie, let's get to bed." The barn was silent save for a few gentle snores. We pushed back our curtain. Sophie was sound asleep. Leaving all clothes and coats on we crawled over our luggage boxes and into our cots and were soon fast asleep.

Morning ablutions over, I looked over towards the noise of the barrage. Well to be honest, the way it echoed meant it could be coming from anywhere, but I was well used to driving towards it. I scanned over the village of tents and saw the long lines of soldiers at mess tents. Maybe their last meal before going up to the Front. As I looked at the rows of men, a face caught my eye. It was the biggest surprise when I realised it was Dada. I was even more surprised when he hugged me in public. Some good things come from War after all! Dada appeared in full uniform. He looked tired and his skin had a greyish pallor.

"Where have you been?" I asked hugging him tightly. "Why are you here?" He smiled and kissed me on the cheek.

"Need to know only this my dear, but it has been tiring. I was made to bring your Christmas gifts in person by your mother."

"But I have nothing for you Dada," I protested.

"Just seeing you is gift enough!" he laughed.

"Dada, you ninny, let's go to the canteen and get something hot." I said.

"Does it taste of anything other than hot?" he laughed.

"Wet," I said. He took my arm and waved as Élodie approached. She was limping slightly and her face was bruised. What would her patients think? She looked worse than some of them! What would Dada think? Mind you, he was too much of a gentleman to ask!

She kissed each of my father's cheeks and we all promenaded over the duckboards, towards the canteen tent. I was dying to know why he was here, but he seemed only happy to discuss the weather, and how we were feeling. We sat at the far end of the tent away from the groups of nurses on breaks and ambulance drivers having dinner. Sophie waved manically and ran over to greet Dada who gave her a big hug. He had never been this demonstrative before in public, how things had changed. Élodie set some mugs before us. "Do you want anything to eat, Lord Loveday?" she asked.

"In a while my dear, I'll just sample this." He sniffed at the mug and looked at Élodie questioningly.

"Tea my lord!" she laughed.

He got straight to the point. "We have had unusual happenings at this post. First Kunz and your little mishap and then this Sloan and Porter affair. It's quite unusual to say the least."

"Is this an area thick with spies?" I asked smiling.

"Most areas along the line have their concerns, but this is too many in too short a time. Given that there was the Provost and his mate, that's five at least."

"You think there are more?"

"I think we may have cleaned up this area thanks to you both, but I also worry about you pair."

"We're well, Dada," I said.

"But you have been involved in both affairs. I just came to make sure there was no more risk."

"No one will hurt us now, Lord Loveday," Élodie said.

"Just be aware."

"You came all this way to tell us that?" I asked.

"I was in the area. I've missed you darling; I thought

I'd use an official visit." He looked over to the tent entrance and beckoned De Freitas across.

"De Freitas here will keep an eye on you."

"We don't need babysitting, Father!" I huffed.

"Nothing like that I assure you, Lady Loveday. We'll just be aware." De Freitas repeated the words of my Dada. He saluted and left, passed by a driver who stood at attention next to our table.

"At ease, James. Grab yourself some grub, and wait by the car."

"Sir!" he saluted and left.

"Now, Élodie, what do you recommend?"

"Paris, Sir!" she laughed.

"Well, the rissoles are edible as long as they are the ones with meat in them," I said.

"Are there potatoes?"

"Of every sort, mashed and roast and boiled."

"Vegetables?"

"Mixed and usually very runny!" I smiled.

"Pudding?"

"Spotted dick and custard!" Élodie said.

"My word, so why aren't you girls bursting at the seams?"

"We often have to work through shifts without a break," Élodie explained.

"I miss meals because I am still on the road. Or they run out of grub."

"Or we are just too tired to eat," Élodie added. "Depending on what shift of cooks, sometimes if the wrong lot are on it can just be disgusting." Dada frowned.

"You will eat with me, now won't you? What would I have to say to your mother if she thought you were going without?"

"There's worse off than us Dada, you know that. Anyway, today's cook is a goodun, so let's queue."

It was odd whenever there was food, good or bad, there was usually plenty. They did run out late into the evening and hot food was replaced by bread, jam, and hot sweet tea. We would take the bread back to the Barn and toast it, especially if there was butter going rather than margarine. Who would have thought that butter was a treat? Toast and honey sent from home was a favourite, but now it was rissoles.

"Have you seen Alfie?" I asked.

"I have, he's very well. He apologises for not writing, but he is a busy boy."

"Where is he? Can you say?"

"Sorry, my darling, I can't, but he is as safe as he can be."

"It amazes me we haven't seen him. We had three fellows from his old school through here last week, all in different regiments, all hurt at the same time."

"So many are wounded, I suppose it's no surprise."

"When did you last see mother?"

"Seems an age ago now."

"She'll be going mad."

"I know, all on her own with those committee women. They actually do drive her to despair. Your mother wants to do something, but they all want to show they are doing something. Trouble is, it ends up with them preening and parading their children's wound stripes, whilst your mother and a few others are actually getting things done."

"Good works for the wrong reason," said Élodie.

"Be fair, the thought is there!" I laughed.

"Wrong thought!" Dada huffed. "Anyway, your mother is hoping to do a Spring fair. She went around to all the locals in person asking for preserves. She seems to have been promised the earth. There are lists a yard long in my study!"

"Your study, you've let mother in there?"

"I had to, Mrs George was having a seizure every time she laid out her plans. 'Can't cook. Can't bake, please milord do tell her.'" The last few words perfectly mimicked our cook and I laughed, as Élodie looked puzzled. Her face was a picture as she tried to get through her rissole. She obviously had the one made with shredded boots.

"What's it like in England?" Élodie asked after eventually swallowing.

"We aren't as badly affected as the cities. Some of our land has been ploughed up to use later. We lost some of the horses again. Food is just about adequate, but Mrs George is making so much of her own. Our garden has very few flowers now, it's strange."

"It's winter, Dada!" I laughed.

"Well, in preparation for the vegetable season..." We chattered on, finishing our food. Dada almost licked his custard from his plate. As I had said, the good cooks were on today. How could anyone destroy the same ingredients that others made taste so good? It was a complete mystery to me. We walked back to the Barn. Dada kissed Élodie on the cheek and she went inside. "It's important to stay safe my darling."

"I will Dada, I have my tie chee training." He gave me an indulgent smile.

"All the same my darling. Try not to go out alone, I know it will be difficult and do keep an eye out for anything unusual." He hugged me close and kissed my head.

"I will Dada and you be safe as well."

He strode away and I started crying. Just as I was about to go in, I saw De Freitas in the corner of my eye as he stood smoking a cigarette, but with his eyes obviously on me. I shooed him away with my hands and he laughed, then saluted and was gone. I turned towards my dearest girl and tried to smile at her.

"*Ma mie,* why so sad, it was nice, no?"

"Lovely." Then I burst into a real flood of tears. Élodie took me by the waist to our little stable and closed the blanket door behind her. Her lips found mine; she was relentless and held me tight. I had to push her away.

"I love you so much," I gasped.

"*Moi aussi ... Je n'aime que toi*" She breathed into my neck, and her lips were on mine again. We scrambled to our cots and lay facing each other. We knew it was too dangerous to make love, but my body ached for her. She held my hand on her breast and we looked into each other's eyes. I felt tears trickle down my cheek and she reached and wiped them away with her finger.

"Do not cry *Cherie*, we will be safe."

"It's not that. I am so afraid Dada will be killed, that you will be hurt." She leant forward and kissed me again, then, "We will be alright Poppee, it is in the stars." She had not used that many e's in my name for a long time and she smiled.

"We will all get home, your father, Alfie, us. We will all be safe. Maybe your mother will explode!" I snorted. "Anyway, with the debonair Captain De Freitas, who by the way is in love with you." I snorted again as Élodie laughed.

"Debonair Captain De Freitas," she repeated," who will safeguard you with his life, or at least his soldiers."

"It's probably true," I said and shuffled so that I could move my hand on to hers that touched my breast. Soon she was moving it rhythmically and I could feel my insides melting. I had to stifle a moan and realised it was too indiscreet and pushed her hand away. She looked me in the eye and returned it to the self-same spot and I was soon moaning softly again. We must have fallen asleep soon afterward. I heard Sophie come to bed and mumbled something to her. I felt a peck on the cheek and was soon asleep again.

A whistle had entered my dreams and I was jolted awake. I was looking directly at Élodie, but my hands were on my side. I hoped Sophie hadn't seen or indeed heard anything indelicate. She said nothing, too busy dressing for the alert that had been raised. Élodie didn't make a move. The whistle was not for her, so she was blocking it out and adding a few more minutes to her sleep. Lucky girl! For me the day was to begin again.

December 21st, 1917.

Darling Mother,

I didn't realise you knew Lady Greenwood! Why didn't you say? She has amazing stories to tell of your days as Debs and of your fights on the street. If you had told me she was with you, well golly I would not have believed it and I'm not sure if I should write anything the censor may pick out. Suffice to say I'm amazed you had your freedom after some of the exploits she told me about. It seems now that you rather sugar coated some of your escapades.

Your Christmas hamper was a delight. I'm sad I cannot be with you all, but duty does call. Maybe we will see you soon. I did see the old chap and he hopes he will be with you for the holidays. I really love you and miss you. I hope when I come home next you will have forgiven me for coming and that you will understand why I had to. Just think back to your fighting on the streets with Lady Greenwood! We all have our motives for doing things. What would I have done if you'd ended up in prison?

I can't remember if I told you, a Chinese worker, Chan has been instructing me in an exercise. I call it tie chee since that is what he says, but I don't know how you should pronounce it correctly, or how you write it. What it does though involves lots of deep breathing and hand movements and can also be used as a self defence system. It's wonderful and I feel so much better when I have finished. It clears the mind wonderfully and that's what you need out here.

Saw father, he was in great form and looking so well. Won't tell me what he's up to or what Alfie is doing, though he assures me the pipsqueak is also well. They are just two chaps messing about it seems to me sometimes, though it was lovely to see him.

I hope life is treating you well, be it at house or Hall. Have you closed down the house till this war is over? I can't remember what you decided. I don't expect too many bombs are falling in London, but I suppose it's best to be safe than sorry. At least we know you are all safe in Scraptoft, as no bomber could reach there. How are staffing levels? I suppose by now only Mrs George will be left, everyone else will be at the Front or doing a protected job at home. Must be strange to have gone from employing so many to having so few to employ. At least you will be able to see that women can work as hard as

men. Better probably, but I know that you know this already! It bodes well for women don't you think? At last the men can see that we are not all gentle little flowers to be protected. Indeed, one day we may get to vote! Something to look forward to I'm sure. Will you lead us into the house of Commons mother, or will it be one of your old chums?
Well I will leave on that note.

Yes, I do love you my darling Mother

Pandora

I was of course already dressed. I wasn't sure when I had last had a change of underwear or of socks, but this wasn't a time to hang about. The whistle had gone and we were off. Sophie yawned as I washed my face in freezing cold water.

"Nice to see your papa?" she asked.

"Lovely Sophie, but in uniform!"

"I know, wonder what my old pops is up to as well?"

"He didn't mention him, though he wouldn't even tell me where Alfie was."

"Did you hear any bombing last night?" Sophie asked.

"No, it was a bit quiet wasn't it, wonder what they want us for so early."

We had to evacuate a field hospital further up the line that was in danger of being overrun. The 'guests' were to come to Lapugnoy and then later on to the railhead. It was a difficult trip on roads we hadn't used before, so the ruts and shell holes were difficult to manoeuvre around. As we had had so little rain recently, there was no mud, so again no sliding, but it was hard not to avoid the small craters that pockmarked the cobbled, in places, roads. Either side of the road were steep piles of dirt, so it felt like we were almost underground.

The sky was bright and blue above, but our view ahead was limited to the back of another ambulance. We only had to worry about bumping into a pal rather than anything else, unless a German fighter decided to have a recce this morning. The only problem was the dust. It was getting in my eyes and the front of my overalls were going brown. I had some goggles, but they kept getting clagged up. The windscreen was down and to be honest if it was up it would still be a problem as the wipers would smear the dust into mud and I would be blinded. All I had to do was keep blinking and wiping my face and goggles and trust to the bus in front, hoping it wouldn't stop too suddenly or skid to the side. The nurse accompanying me, had decided to sit up front, but was fast asleep. Lucky her. I envied her the dreams she might be having even though I had only woken up little more than an hour ago. Sleep came quickly as we were tired, but it was usually fitful. Some nights bombing raids would occur and we had to decamp to the shelter, or we would be kept awake by the constant barrage from our side or the German guns. That had happened to be almost every night save for the past few days, maybe that was why we had to collect our friends from nearer the Front. The Germans may have been concentrating on this side of the Front. Who could tell? No one would, so we had to guess and that was where rumour and gossip could hold sway. I never believed anything unless I had seen it, so fanciful notions of trench taking and invasion passed me by without evidence. Our boys had held firm for months now. There seemed to be no movement at all. Whenever we travelled to the Dressing Station, it was always in the same spot, proof of the resilience of our trenches and our troops. Though as a man, you did need to be resilient with the incessant fall of bombs and incendiaries. At least no gas had been pumped this way for a while. The results of that had been too horrific for words and I had been physically sick every time I cleaned out the back of my bus. I had said that it was the screams I hated the most during my work, but the hacking, screeching coughs of those affected stayed long in my dreams as well. I wasn't sure how many miles we had travelled, but I started to hear the crump of guns laying a barrage and could see black clouds of smoke up ahead. Then the noise started to intensify as we got closer and the nurse, Ruth, awoke with a start.

"Gosh dreamt I fell off the roof," she laughed.

"Best hold tight, Ruth."

"Don't know why I'm coming really, there must be enough nurses up here to come back if they're evacuating."

"Who are we to argue?" I said. I then shivered as I heard the unmistakeable sound of planes above us. Ruth rolled the window down and put her head out to look.

"Don't!" I shouted, but it was too late. A volley of machine gun fire swept the road and Ruth slumped into the window. Her white headdress was quickly turning red as blood poured from her wound.

"Oh, for God's sake!" I screamed and slowed my ambulance down and pulled into the side. I hit the steering wheel with my fists and shook my head. I reached over to Ruth to try to find a pulse, but there was of course nothing. Elspeth banged on my door, and went around to the other side. I heard the plane again and Elspeth disappeared from sight as another hail of bullets hit the road in front of me. I jumped out and ran around the back, opened the doors, and went to the front where Elspeth was lowering the body to the floor. She didn't seem to have any marks on her, but the blood told a different story. We carried her to the back and then with the help of Elspeth's nurse we placed her in the ambulance on a stretcher. Elspeth hugged me.

"Thank God you're safe Poppy." I didn't know what to say. I looked up ahead, the leading ambulances had disappeared and there was no longer any dust in the road.

"Best be on then," I muttered and climbed aboard. Not a speck of paint missing from the old bus, yet a life had been taken. It was ridiculous. Later they moved Ruth's body to another ambulance, along with some other corpses I supposed. Then my ambulance was filled with some pretty jolly young men who had their ticket home. Two men sat in the cabin with me. Both from the ranks, both quite talkative after a fashion.

"Been quite active," one said.

"Shush, Ernest, don't talk about it in front."

"Yes, I must be a spy. I will write down your words as I drive, now what was that quite active?" I snapped. "Does that mean that my German friends are breaking through?" I turned to look at this Private and raised an eyebrow.

"Can't be," he started to mutter.

"Take no notice, Miss, Billy here, sees the worst in everyone."

"Well shall I just dump him on the roadside here and we can give himself something to moan about?"

"He doesn't mean it, miss."

"Call me Poppy." I said

"Fraulein Poppy?" asked Ernest. I laughed.

"We held on for a few days before we got reinforced by the French of all people. "Thought we'd seen the last of them." Billy said.

"Yes, mutterings of mutiny and desertions, so no good to anyone?" I asked.

"Here's us protecting them and they swan off, so it was a surprise to see them."

"So, you held out?"

"Yes, course we did, Poppy." Billy continued.

"That's why we're all getting moved. The clearing station is closing. The dressing station got overrun one night, all killed but we took it back in the morning." Ernest said grimly.

"Don't know what they're going to do about that," said Billy

"Germans are bastards! You should..." Ernest started

"We don't need to hear about them then, do we, Ernest?"

"Spose not, what's it like in Lapwotsit?"

"Lapugnoy? Just rows of tents and more tents." I replied.

"Rain?"

"Of course, but not for the past few days, Hence all this dust." I pointed ahead; we could hardly see for the clouds of dust that were being swept into my wagon. If it wasn't rain, it was dust, if not dust it was the snow. We had every weather and every manifestation of weather. Dust, mud, water, ice, goodness I sound like some scientist!

Christmas Eve 1917.

Well here it comes. Christmas is coming.
The goose is getting fat.
Doubt if we'll be getting any goose, maybe not any meat, but who could tell.

Hello Diary, how have you been?
  We need a Christmas Tree. We need some decorations for said tree. I need to wrap up the few gifts I have for my pals. We need to toast the day in. I hope it is a quiet day, but I'm sure it won't be. We are having Christmas dinner in the Mess tent. Ours is scheduled for 10.00 hours on the dot. Seems a bit early to me and leaves us with a lot of blank day ahead unless we get called out to the Front. We can't drink anything just in case. A dry Christmas indeed. But there again, one drink will be just what the doctor ordered. I don't suppose the Germans will care to be fighting tomorrow, so we can perhaps relax. Probably not have that football match that they played in 1914 I think, but maybe they will lob some Christmas gifts between trenches instead of damned grenades. I seem to remember that happening last year and a Tommy giving me a carved doll he had caught. Don't know where that is now, I should have put it on the tree. Mother sent a parcel, full of lovely things. Apparently, some of the Tommies are performing a pantomime, but I don't think I'll go. I don't want my bottom to be pinched like it was last year! I wonder what Father Christmas will be bringing us all tomorrow! I for one, can hardly wait!
  This will be my second Christmas on the Front. Last year we had a sublime time. Too many had too much to drink which was such a risk as we never knew when we would be needed.

Digging our wagons from the snow soon sobered us up and that, what with setting fires under our engines and having on at least five layers of clothing meant we had an exhausting few days. It was so difficult to walk, let alone drive, bundled up as we were. I think we made ten trips on Christmas Day. There was no truce and the German and British artillery seemed to have great fun swapping shells instead of presents ...

December 24th

Dearest Poppy old bean,
    How are you old thing? A blooming Merry Christmas to you and all the gals! Hope it is special. We will be having a special Christmas pudding says cook, but very little other fare as we are a bit busy. Though you never know, Fritz might relax as its Christmas! Can't tell you where I am of course, save to say it's muddy! And wet! And cold of course! But you must know that though we haven't had a rain for at least three days!
    A Christmas miracle to be sure!
    We are doing all right, moving forward every so often. But then moving backwards, but not so far, so progress is being made if a little slowly. Men are in good spirits, trying to keep it like that.
    Mater sent the most amazing parcel of Christmas tuck. Keeps me going, I can say. She will send gaspers. I don't know why, but it means I can give to the lads, so it works. She told me you keep stealing my socks and scarves. If you have there will be trouble. Looking forward to some leave. I saw the old man. He was in fine fettle. Up to no good again in pastures fresh. I have no idea what he is doing. Pater tells me you have had your leave so missed you again. I hope you are well. You have all my love and please keep safe. I think of you every night and send a goodnight kiss. Have a wonderful Christmas, presents when we get back to Blighty! You had better purchase me an enormous gift to match the one I have got for you. I had female advice, so you know it's a good 'un. Therefore, I deserve the maximum thought and expense.
Toodle Pip!

Alfie Your loving brother!

A letter from Alfie. That arrived today on Christmas Day. Where was he? Must be quite close looking at the date. We had found a tree. Dead as a doornail and planted it in a pot. Someone had wound bandages around it and others had made Chinese lanterns that hung from blackened branches. I had made a silver star and plonked it on top of the tree. Wonderful. Underneath was a gift for each of us from Lady Greenwood and a gift that each of us had given to a person whose name we had drawn from a tin hat. Mine was for Sophie by chance and I had got my mother to send me a collection of poems by Apollinaire, *Alcools: Poèmes (1898-1913)*, with a beautifully bound leather jacket. If I hadn't earmarked it as a gift for someone, I would have kept it myself. We had made some Christmas Cards for each other. Finding chalks and crayons had been quite a chore, but we had succeeded. Thank goodness it was the good chefs turn to present dinner, but it wasn't what we were used to at home. Especially as it was at ten hundred hours sharp! How could it be? We had some pork, though I am not sure where it came from, potatoes and cabbage, with quite a thick gravy. There was of course bread and as a special treat butter. Again, I was not sure where that had come from. For dessert a plum pudding with sauce, pots and pots of tea and beer and wine. It was a veritable feast compared to what we usually had and luckily enough it seemed that the Germans were not going to be distracted from their food today, as all guns seemed to be silent today. So, we had a session of recleaning our ambulances before we attended our own festivities in the Barn. We swopped gifts, I received a beautiful patchwork angel from Elspeth and shared some of the contents of our Christmas parcels. Mother had sent me so much, but of course it was the gaspers that everyone delighted in and they became a second Christmas gift to everyone. I might as well have smoked as the air was full of tobacco as the night progressed. We had more wine than we should have had, and

I hoped to goodness we wouldn't be called out too early in the morning.

Finally, my ambulance hosed out and clean, presents swopped, food eaten and treats exchanged. The smells of the day were long gone. All that was in the air now was the sniff of disinfectant and cordite. I had parked my bus at an angle against the remains of a wall so that when I opened up my rear door, I had a closed off triangle of space. I had taken off my overalls and navy blouse and had wiggled out of my bust band. My socks and boots were by my side and I was barefoot wearing a pair of Alfie's old cotton pyjamas with a scarf that had kept me warm this morning now wrapped around my waist. I knew I looked a sight, but there was no one to see me. It was getting dark and I could still hear the guns at the Front booming away. I settled into my *tie chee* stance and closed my eyes. Maybe Élodie was right to close hers. I thought about what Chan had told me in the early sessions we had taken together.

"Every muscle in body must be relaxed and loose." He had told me in broken English, then, "Body keep upright position no lean or tilt." I widened my feet and sank into the proper stance. "Must empty chest of air, relax shoulders, drop elbows." It was as if he was by my side. I nearly opened my eyes to check but contented myself with a smile to myself. It went on his words in my head, repeating what I had heard too many times, "Tuck in back and keep a light consciousness on crown of head." Now Chan hadn't said 'light consciousness', he had called it something else. It was only a couple of weeks later that he told me one of the officers who spoke mandarin had told him what he wanted to say. It was a surprise that an officer would speak to a coolie other than tell him what to do, but he must have been in a benevolent mood. Anyway, a light consciousness it was, that I inferred was a kind of spiritual feeling that we had to find and to be honest it was a pleasant feeling when you did reach it. Today was one of those days. As I cut my hands through the air and swept my body from side to side, I could almost hear the noise my hands made as they parted the air around me. I felt light footed and at ease with everything. I opened my eyes and then closed them again. In my private world, I felt at perfect ease. My body was doing what it had learnt to do, I had no need to force it. My memories of each movement followed on cleanly and perfectly as far as I was concerned. I may not have been as perfect a mover as one of the Chinese, but I felt the benefits and wanted only to continue into the night. I felt at peace with everything and the tiredness of the day seemed to have drained out of me. For the first time in weeks I felt as if I could face anything. That made me burst out laughing. Anyone who saw me now, bare foot and in pyjamas, seemingly catching fireflies at night would have thought me mad. But I felt wonderful. I had to find Élodie, to share this with her.

Élodie appeared at almost midnight and was soon happily unwrapping her gift from Florrie, and eating chocolate with some plum brandy from Elsie. This was heavenly. All I wanted now to make the day complete was some time with my dearest girl alone, but that was impossible. Clemmie and Sophie started to sing a carol and we all joined in before Elsie started a bawdy music hall number that although we shouldn't know, we all did and we sang on in that vein for some time before tiredness cried out to us and we fell into our cots, bodies numbed with alcohol, but full of happiness after an escapist's day.

Her news was more important. We had leave together. Élodie was to travel to England before me and I was to follow. I felt elated. A few days together in the peace of rural Leicestershire. What a treat that would be. I could put up with the cattle class of the railways if it meant seeing everyone at Loveday Hall again soon. It was almost fate that I received a rare letter from mother.

January 9th, 1918.
Dearest Pandora, My darling daughter!
So sweet to receive your letter. Father sends his love and will of course be writing soon. He is so busy in his

mysterious ways and has left us alone for some weeks recently. I can't tell you where because he won't tell even me, his wife! Oh, to be so distrusted!

We are now donating spoons to the war effort, not enough to donate you and Alfred and your father.

Here the censor had removed a great chunk. Bless mother and her unfailing ability to upset the wielder of the blue pen. Not a letter passed them by without them striking something out. It was a real pain when she decided to write on both sides of the paper as that was destroyed as well in all its innocence.

Mrs Jacobs' cottage was attacked by some malevolent. Windows smashed and everything. Her brothers all dead, as if she didn't have enough on her plate... This is the third case this month. It's all very strange. Mrs George's sister had her door painted with a red cross of all things and old Mr Gerrard had his windows smashed. Too many children avoiding school and with too much time on their hands, but the red cross, that was odd and a bit spiteful.

I do hope you are eating well. Cook has packed a hamper and that may have gotten to you already, but if not do enjoy when it arrives! I even tried to make some jam so sent you a pot. Do tell me what you think. All the ladies say its divine, but you can't trust them. It does sell well though.

Your Chinese exercises seem interesting. Perhaps you can show them to me, I am getting a bit sedentary these days. I'm not riding as much, especially as the army took all our best hunters what seems years ago now. Doubt if we'll ever have horses like that again!
Sometimes I cry at night imagining the beasts' fate. It really is a cruel thing, war. The senseless killing of animals and man. What a waste and how can all of it be replaced? We don't see many men about our village anymore and Leicester is also shorn of the male of the species, unless he is wearing a uniform and in transit across country or on the seaside train!
Alfred writes quite often. I am glad you are both safe. Father,

well you know. Glad to hear your news of leave. I am so looking forward to seeing you soon. Do bring that French girl over if she has leave with you.

Take care my darling Pandora.

Your loving mother

The train rides from the coast were as crowded as usual, soldiers mostly, all making rather rude comments and jokes about everything. They were a bedraggled bunch, on leave for who knows how long, or just moving about the country for training. As I got nearer to home there were fewer and fewer of them, until I had a compartment to myself as I travelled from Leicester to Thurnby. The smoke from the engine filled my compartment as I had the window open. I don't know why, I loved fresh air and now was being slowly poisoned by fresh smoke! I still had the letter from mother. It was odd. It was bad enough all the violence in France and beyond, but to have these strange things going on at home somehow made it all seem worse. A trap was waiting at the station and I smiled a greeting to our gardener who had driven it down. He was smoking his pipe and we talked about his son who was in France, and his daughter who had gone to work in a hospital in Leicester. He then went on to moan about how little room there was now for flowers, as most of the gardens had been made over to vegetables, but he was oh so pleased with some of those crops. We would not want for vegetables he promised. I got off the trap at the bottom of Main Street and was about to make my way up the hill to the house when the local policeman approached. I had gone to school with his younger brother, Eric, and remembered him teasing me mercilessly. He was a little different today.

"May I take your bag, Milady?" he offered.

"Well thank you, Constable Roberts, you won't throw it into the lake, will you?" He laughed, but went a little red, obviously remembering past faults.

"How are things at the Front, Milady? I'm soon to join up."

"If you really want to know," then I thought, "It is horrible Ewan, really horrible."

"Well young Eric went, and he seems happy enough."

"I think they try to show the best of it as to not upset anyone. Why not stay in the police, you're still doing your bit."

"Well Milady, people do talk so and I feel I ought."

"Not enough going on here at the moment?"

"More than enough. We've had some arson after the window smashing. Did you hear of it?"

"My mother wrote about cook's sister and Mr Gerrard, was it?"

"Yes, but Mr Clark had his front door burnt and white feathers through his window. It was lucky they didn't do it the other way around." That was awful, I remembered Mr Clark, he had always been very nice. His son worked for the government in some protected capacity or other. Again, the son was older than me, so I wasn't really sure.

"And someone else?"

"Yes, our old school mistress. Her thatch was badly burnt. She's moved to Leicester to be with her daughter. I don't know if she'll be back." I had no idea who could have hated old Mrs Beckingham that much. She had always been so wonderfully nice to us all at school. She never caned anyone, never seemed to raise her voice. What on earth was going on?

"White feathers again?"

"Yes, and another red cross on the door."

"Any thoughts?"

"None at all. Who would do it? Everyone seemed to get on so well in the village. All these lads away makes it a little less lively on a night. I have no idea. Leicester police neither." We approached the gates at Loveday Hall. Down the driveway the grand old building looked forbidding for some reason.

"Well thank you, constable." I smiled.

"It's no problem Milady. I will come to the front door.

I've got to check all is well with Mrs George." We walked in silence down the driveway. The sun was bright and there was little wind. As we neared the great front door, we paused.

"It is good to see you back in one piece, Poppy, milady," Ewan smiled blushing as he handed me my bag and made his way around to the back of the house. The front door still had its Christmas Wreath pinned on it and as it slowly opened, I could smell Christmas smells. Cinnamon and nutmeg filled my head and then there was the delicious scent of oranges as my dearest girl, Élodie, leapt into my arms and hugged me as if I was falling.

"*Ma mie*," she whispered into my ear. "It is so good to feel you again." I staggered and then regained my feet as mother appeared.

"Pandora, my darling. How are you? You look so thin." Starting as she meant to go on, always worried about my health. I disentangled myself from Élodie and hugged her and kissed her cheek. She held me close and I could also smell her perfume, the smell of my childhood, the scent I would always associate with her.

"It's so lovely to see you mother. I hope Élodie hasn't been too much trouble?"

"None at all. I have learnt so much from her. Come in, come in, let us not hover at the door."

I lay in my bath. Memories and surges from Boulogne flowed through my body. I wondered what Élodie was doing now, whether she was getting on cook's nerves or mother's. I scrubbed roughly at the grime on my feet, thinking how gentle she had been when we shared our bath. Shivers ran down my spine. There was a knock on the door and I sunk under the suds as I shouted, "Come in." It was mother. She looked all flustered. She pulled a chair over to the side of the bath.

"Do you need anything, darling?"

"Just to stay here forever," I smiled.

"Well you could if you wished."

"It's heaven mother; just the sensation of hot water!"

"I can't imagine," She smiled. No, you can't I thought.

No one could imagine, but there may be time to tell one day. This wasn't it though.

"How have you been mother?"

"Keeping busy. With you two away and now your father getting involved, I need to occupy my mind and my fingers."

"Committees?"

"Of course, it's what's expected, though it's hard as I don't believe in war."

"No, I've rather gone off it," I smiled.

"You never did support it did you darling. I can see why. The steady flow of ruined young men back into England. It's such a waste."

"But do others?" I asked.

"I'm not sure darling. The people at my meetings are all rather *gung ho*, unless it's their son who has been injured or killed. Then they go surprisingly quiet. I suppose it's all right if it's someone else's son, but when it's your own..." She paused wistfully.

"Give me your ankles, I'll get them clean for you." Even when a child, it had never been mother who had bathed me, it had always been Alice, our nanny. This was a bit of a shock, but in honesty a really nice shock. I raised my foot as she rolled up her sleeves.

"It's almost red raw where you've been scrubbing, Pandora!" she reprimanded.

"It's a few weeks of dirt I'm afraid." I felt myself going red.

"Never mind dear."

"Have you got any meetings whilst I am home?"

"I cancelled them. I want to spend time with you."

"I could have come."

"No, I don't need to show you off like some do, dragging their poor sons along to show wound stripes. I don't think anyone ever tells the truth about what's going on. No one wants to really know."

"They just have to look at the lists of fallen to know

really."

"But the numbers are so great. I don't think anyone truly understands. The village has lost so many boys. It's tragic. Our gardener's son, the blacksmith's, Mrs Jacobs lost all her brothers, Mrs Bennet has lost both her boys. I went to see her, but what can you say to them?"

"I know, mother."

"Of course, you do darling. Give me your other foot. This one's clean to the bone. Literally." She laughed. I hadn't heard her laugh for such a long time. "Then there's all this arson and window breaking I wrote to you about..."

"I know, I spoke to Constable Roberts on the way here. They have no idea who it is or why it's happening. It seems so cruel."

"It's bad enough the victims all seem to have children living away. They are all alone here. You're right, that's what makes it all so cruel."

"Well let's not talk about it, mother. What shall we do?"

"We could all go riding tomorrow, if you are well enough?"

"I'm not ill mother, just tired, but riding would be nice."

"Will your clothes fit you? You are so thin."

"I'll find something, mother. Don't fuss."

"I don't."

"I know mother. All will be well. Heard from Alfie?"

"That boy, hardly ever writes, then it's always so full of what a hoot he's having and how he'll see me soon. Last time was way before Christmas!"

"I remember. They wouldn't let any of us go. War didn't stop for Christmas."

"I don't suppose it does." She put my foot back into the water and found a towel to dry herself. "Take your time, darling. You may want to refresh the bath and lose the grime."

"I have twice already, mother. There'll be no hot water left for the rest of the house!"

We laughed. I stood up, so used to showing my body in communal showers that I surprised mother. She handed me a towel.

"You are so thin darling. Quite wasted away. Do they not feed you at all?"

"They do, but it's not always the best and then we are busy and miss meals. I do adore your parcels though."

"I am pleased. Things are short over here as well, but I can see that we will have to send more." She gave me her hand as I stepped from the bath, then pulled me towards her in a warm embrace. "I'm so happy to see you Pandora." Then she was gone. This was a different version of the angry mother who had railed against me going to France. Perhaps at last she could reconcile my behaviour. I hoped so. I didn't want my mother to be my enemy. I needed her to be my mother. I needed her and felt a rush of love for her.

January 16th, 1918.

Well Dear journal of mine,

Here I am at home and nothing seems to have changed too much on the inside of the house anyway. Outside of course lots has changed. No men in the village, fewer staff here. Women doing men's jobs as we always knew they could and hopefully will in the future. Mother is looking a little tense. I know she loves me though so can ignore any fierceness she shows, but there are a few more grey hairs. I have had the most wonderful hot bath. My whole body seems to have relaxed at last. The tenseness from my shoulders has gone and it was lovely that Mother, my mother! Actually washed my dirty ankles for me. she has never ever, ever, done that. Its why I know she really loves me. Ha ha! Looking forward to the touch of my dearest girl. It's not been long, but I do miss her so. I miss her lips; I miss her hands. Strange goings on in the village. I'm sure Élodie will have discovered much!
Well I must find a dress and then go to see the wonderful Father who is back from France as well...

Chapter 8

"I enter the world called real as one enters a mist."

I had found a day dress that more or less fitted me. I had pulled a belt around my waist, but it was so long now that I had to tuck it in and fold it behind my back. I was surprised at how much weight I had lost. It had taken an age to find something to wear. I knocked on Dada's study door and went in. He was at his desk, reading. He looked up at me and smiled broadly.

"That's better, you young ragamuffin. More like a lady."

"Not you too, Dada!" I moaned.

"No, just that you looked so disreputable. Now much tidier. How do you feel?"

"Wonderful. It's such a relief to be home. Everyone is so nice."

"I'm so proud of you, Ophelia, you are so very brave."

"I don't feel like it sometimes." I sat down on his big leather settee and he got up and sat beside me. I snuggled into his shoulder and he put his arm around me.

"We miss you, your mother especially."

"I know Dada, I miss you both, and Alfie. I still can't believe I haven't seen him for so long."

"Well it will all be over one day, one way or another. Anyway, my news is that I've been called back to work with Lord Quittenton again. You know his daughter?"

"You know Sophie, we work together. What are you doing, or is it hush hush?" He laughed.

"Yes, very! I'm meeting regularly at the Admiralty. Liaison and things. Knowing my luck, I'll be back overseas again." I sat up, shocked.

"You don't ..."

"Oh no, Ophelia, not at the Front again, that was a one off, but there's more to all this war stuff than simply fighting."

"I know that, Dada, but don't go near the Front again,

will you?"

"Not if I can help it, darling. Now tell me about France, the truth mind as it will help me when I speak to Lord Q." So, I did, and he was very quiet and very shocked.

I sat with Élodie in the drawing room. We were drinking coffee that she had smuggled over from France. She often told me she would die if she didn't have coffee. She made me laugh. Her hand brushed mine and I felt tingles run through my body.

"Mother wondered if we would go riding tomorrow, Élodie ."

"You know I hate horses! But you go. I will discover your village."

"You sure? All this way together and then you want to leave me."

"I spoke with a Mrs Beckingham yesterday. She was at the burnt house picking up some clothes. She was very frightened."

"So, you know about the fires?"

"Yes, it is strange. But I cheered her up by talking about her favourite former pupil."

"Too kind, Élodie."

"And she told me some stories."

"Enough, my love!"

"Yes, *ma Cherie*, more than enough. I think I have some power over you now." She giggled.

"I doubt it darling."

"Anyway, Mrs Beckingham had a big red cross on her door and the thatch burnt very badly. Her daughter was really upset and wants her to move away from the village."

"But she can't, she's part of the place. What is her daughter doing?"

"Office work in the city. Rarely has time to see her mother."

"But it's only a few miles."

"You know how it is. And I spoke to Mrs George's sister Mildred. I was taking her some of the gardener's potatoes for cook."

"How sweet of you," I smiled, and Élodie giggled.

"Get the cook to like you and you will never be hungry, Poppy. Mildred says it took two days of scrubbing to get rid of the cross. She wished her son had been here to do it for her."

"Is she scared?"

"No, she's like cook, a tough old girl. Her son is in Manchester, so can't come home. He sent her a telegram, but his job seems to be too important."

"Well, we don't know what a lot of people are up to do we?"

"She was telling me how Mrs Jacobs had her windows broken and is not talking to anyone anymore."

"How odd."

"She must suspect everyone."

"I remember her youngest brother, he was killed in the war. He wasn't very nice, but still."

"All of her brothers are dead and her parents, poor soul. She lives alone and must brood."

"So, who would smash her windows and why?"

"A very nasty individual. It's just luck that the fires didn't kill anyone."

We went out for some fresh air. We strolled arm in arm down the hill into the small village. Houses were dotted either side of what was really a glorified mud track. At the top of the village there was a proper road, but leaving it meant you almost stepped out of time into another world. In a way it was nice that the few men we saw, tipped their caps when they saw us, but in another, I didn't really deserve them to defer to me. I had done nothing. It was however quite idyllic, except there were no young men about. Ewan was the youngest I had seen, and he was soon to leave. The men all seemed to be in their sixties and where we would have seen the man of the house pushing a wheelbarrow, or carrying a hod, and we now saw women doing it, of course doing so very well! The tenancies in the village had I supposed always been run by the women folk, but now it was a real hands-on job for them keeping the farm or small holdings going. Every house on Main Street now seemed to be dug over for vegetables or fruit, and fields that used to be dotted with sheep or cows were now covered in different crops. Though I thought it strange that our farmers were not producing meat anymore. Perhaps feed was too expensive. There was however no shortage of chickens and Main Street and Church Hill were invaded by them as they seemed to roam free. How and where eggs would be collected was a mystery. Ducks had made our lake their home so I could expect that as a feast at any time, alongside cook's vegetable delights.

    We walked around the top of the village, ignoring the road to Leicester and to the train station at Thurnby, and made for All Saints, which was a beautifully small church and one that Alfie and I had been forced to go to when younger. For some reason I wanted to visit today, and we passed the Manse and stepped up into the churchyard and up to the porch. The silent chilled air was just as I remembered it and as I stood in the doorway, I felt Élodie shiver. She took my hand and we walked in. Impressive stained glass windows looked down on us and Élodie let go my hand and crossed herself before bobbing in front of the altar and going to sit down in the pew at the front. I nodded to a woman who was arranging flowers at the back of the church and joined Élodie. The pew was as uncomfortable as I remembered. Rock hard to focus your mind on God as you sat there during any service. It was so peaceful. I sat beside Élodie and closed my eyes. Her fingers felt for mine and I clasped them, my thumb caressing the back of her hand. Her skin surprisingly soft, though I could feel her veins clearly through the skin. We did not speak. We did not need to. We just sat there in peace and tranquillity, away from all the noise that we had experienced over the past two years, away from hatred and pain. Alone, but together. I felt happy and sad in equal measures. I felt better than I had for a long time. This was what we were fighting for, the chance to be content and happy. I was content and with Élodie by my side I was more than happy.

    Mrs Beckingham was just as I remembered her. A tiny

happy looking woman though she did have a few lines around her eyes. She smiled a greeting.

"Why Ophelia, you are a sight for sore eyes. How are you?" I hugged her. Socially it wasn't the right thing to do, but it was how I felt, and times were changing. I held her for a bit longer, then let her go.

"And you have met my dear friend, Élodie Proux."

"Madame," said Élodie, smiling broadly. "We meet again."

"I hope you didn't reveal my secrets to dear Ophelia, Mamselle Proux."

"Mum was the word, Madame Beckingham. Please do sit down." I beckoned over the waiter and soon we were drinking tea and eating hot buttered toast. It was a miracle that they had butter, so it was worth enjoying.

"You both look rather thin, girls."

"I know, it is all the fashion!" laughed Élodie .

"Food is often horrible at the Front, Mrs Beckingham, or we are too late to eat, or too tired to eat. It is a mess really."

"You poor things, and doing such important jobs."

"We just seem to get on with it. Anyway, to business. Élodie said you had no idea who could have done this terrible thing?"

"None, all of us having to suffer. It's worse for old Mrs Jacobs, she lost everyone to the war. Our children are just away from home."

"How are you filling your retirement, Mrs Beckingham?"

"Well, I have so much to do at home in the garden. But now, with this business it's ridiculous. I'm too old to drive ambulances, even if I knew how. My husband fought against the Boer in the last war, we've all done our bit so why..." Her eyes filled with tears.

"You mustn't take on, Mrs Beckingham. It will sort itself out. You'll see. You can return..."

"It's so expensive. Of course, it's one of the estate cottages, but there was such a mess."

"Well, if that's all keeping you away," I said, knowing full well it wasn't. "Élodie and I are here for a few days. We can help out."

"We are so practised, Madame Beckingham. We know what to do. Leave it to us." So that was tomorrow's exercise sorted out. We chatted amiably for the rest of the afternoon, before it was time to get the train back to Thurnby. Once again, our gardener Lovell, appeared out of the smoke of the steam engine and we trotted off back towards Loveday Hall. As we neared the village, I asked for us to be dropped off at Frank Clark's cottage. We could see what he knew. Frank Clark was a really nice man. His daughters Florence and Gertrude had been in my class. They were a year or so younger than me and both were in service now, whilst his eldest son was working away from home. It was a bit odd he should get a white feather. Everyone knew he had been an old soldier and that his son was doing something important. As with every young man who was not at the Front, I was quietly pleased that they were safe and not at risk, but then this insidious threat had appeared.

"It's not as if I hadn't done me time, Milady. It were bad enough fighting Boer, but now to have someone here fighting me. It makes no sense."

"Nor to us, Mr Clark." We sipped from our giant mugs of tea, the taste was far removed from that in France, so even Élodie was glad to drink it.

"And your son, has he been able to visit?" she asked.

"No chance, Miss, he's too important to them up north. I never see him. Nor the two girls. Transport is so difficult from London at the moment. Well you'd both know that."

"And there is no one who you can think of?"

"Not a soul. But let me catch them. I'll sort the buggers. Oh, sorry ladies."

"Mr Clark, we've heard a dashed sight worse than that in the last couple of years. We even have nurses swearing like troopers. It's undignified I know, but don't worry yourself." I laughed.

"Even so, Milady. It makes me angry, but I should

mind me manners."

It was dark when we left, and we were able to walk hand in hand up the hill towards Loveday Hall. "It's so quiet, Poppy."

"You almost forget, don't you?"

"I know. The silence of the night. It's quite beautiful, isn't it?"

"But also sinister with what's been happening."

"I think I can see what it is though, Poppy. Can't you?"

"I think so, but we can talk about it later. Let's just enjoy the silence."

We stepped through a gap in the giant hedge that protected part of our grounds. This allowed us to reach the lake. Any other time of year I think I would have jumped in as Alfie and I had done so often during our childhood before mother demanded a little more decorum from us. Dada would always laugh when he saw us standing like drowned rats hiding from mother if she happened to be out as we were trying to creep back into the house. Mrs George used to really whack us with a wooden spoon if she caught us in her kitchen dripping onto her always immaculate slate floor. I laughed to myself at the memory.

"What is it, *Cherie?*" A puzzled Élodie asked and I explained and within seconds she was in her underskirt and was making towards the water.

"No, Élodie! We might be seen! It's much too cold!" I shouted as I had my skirt around my ankles and soon, we were splashing in the water, shivering and giggling like the two hysterical children we were. Élodie didn't know the half of it. I loved to swim, and I adored doing so in our lake. In the summer it could be as warm as taking a bath and though it was a little more bracing now, I soon warmed up and was able to luxuriate in its arms as I cruised from side to side, with Élodie cutting a swathe alongside me. It was too cold once we had got out, so we hurried into the house, tip toeing upstairs so as not to be discovered in soaking underwear and with chattering teeth.

The door creaked open and a shadow entered my bedroom. Seconds later the naked body of Élodie was pressed against mine and my sigh was long and heartfelt. I wrapped my arms around her and kissed her as if I never wanted to let her go. Which was the truth to be honest. It felt doubly thrilling to have to be so secretive in my own house and so difficult not to make any noise as we made love together. Sated we lay wrapped together.

"It seems simple really, Élodie."

"I know, everyone else appears to have done nothing, to have made no sacrifice, whilst she ... will you confront them?"

"I don't know, we have no evidence, just our feelings."

"We know how strong our feelings can be," she giggled.

"In every sense." She kissed my lips hungrily.

"I have to go, *ma mie*"

"No, please stay."

"I cannot. We might fall asleep and then what would be said? It is safer like this."

She slipped out of the bed and I could see her put on her dressing gown in silhouette.

"I do love you, Poppy. You are my world."

She leant over and kissed me on the lips again. I pulled her down on top of me and for a moment she struggled against me then relaxed and the kiss became longer and deeper. Finally, when we needed to breathe, she pushed herself away and gasped.

"Good night, my love."

"I love you." I whispered.

The door slid open, the hall light shone in and then it was dark again. I turned over onto my side. My body aching for Élodie. I felt tears trickle down my cheeks. This secrecy was horrible. Why couldn't we be open about our love. I didn't feel ashamed. I loved Élodie so much. I wanted her here, by my side, in my bed. What was wrong with this world.

Next morning I found Élodie sitting at the huge kitchen

table chopping vegetables as Mrs George pottered about chatting, washing up, mixing and stirring. She seemed very happy. Élodie was glowing and gave me one of her smiles. She seemed in heaven. She pointed a carrot at me.

"Missed breakfast, Poppy. Mrs George is very disappointed in you."

"Miss, that's not ..." Mrs George started. Then she saw the look on Élodie's face. "Don't try to cause trouble young lady!"

"How many more carrots, *Madam la chef*?" Élodie laughed.

"A few more. Mildred said she would come over tonight. She loves her carrots."

"Is she all right after the painting on her door?"

"Yes, she's always been a tough old bird. It's just being on her own that's the problem."

"It's strange, isn't it," I said

"Here in the village where everyone knows everyone that people are suddenly alone and scared."

"Luckily, everyone who has been attacked has someone who could help, save for old Mrs Jacobs," said Mrs George.

I looked at Élodie. She gave me a knowing look.

"Well ..." I started then grabbed a carrot and took a bite.

"You need a proper breakfast, Miss Pandora!" Mrs George snorted.

"I'll have a big lunch."

"You need to feed up young lady, you're all skin and bones!"

"Not quite," I protested.

"You are correct, *Madam la chef*! She needs to eat up."

"And you are little better young lady. You both need to put on a little."

"We will, when all this is over," I smiled.

"At the moment we don't have time, but when the war has finished, we will come back to you and you can feed us up as much as you like!"

"Well if rationing ever finishes I will; though I do make a wonderful vegetable soup. If I say so myself."

I took another bite of the carrot, winked at Élodie and left through the outer door. The sun was coming to its height. I had slept so late. Élodie had been right, if we had slept together, we would have been found out as the maid came to clean. I shivered though it was not particularly cold and made for the rear of our building, over the lawn into the small coppice. The icehouse was closed up and I followed the path alongside one of our tenant farmers fields. It used to be full of cattle I seemed to remember and now was waving with some crop or another. I followed the track until I got to the road that linked our village to others to the East and headed towards her house.

Mrs Jacobs couldn't help herself. Her bitterness seeped from her mouth with every word she spoke. "I hated me brothers, but they were me own flesh n blood. They got taken away. Why should I suffer like that? When they got Jeremy, he was the final straw, drove me mother to an early grave so there I was alone. No family. No one to help in my old age.

"But your windows were smashed."

"That was me. No one thought of me. No one ever does. Henry was the worst. He was a bully. Me mother doted on him. He could do nowt wrong."

"I remember Henry. He was at school with me."

"Right evil thing, but me mother ..." She paused and looked into the flames of the fire.

"I still don't understand," I said.

"They didn't bother with their protected jobs, their special status," she spat.

"Who?" I started, but she just went on, her voice clipped and angry.

"Never in any danger. Soft jobs, in cities away from bombs and mud. Jeremy told me about the mud. All those children safe and sound and my brothers six feet under."

"They all had important..."

"Pah, they hid from the war."

"The white feathers?"

"The least they deserved. I should have just burnt them all down. Got rid of the lot. Then they'd know how it felt."

She was quite mad. Her grief had turned into a mania. It was lucky that no one had yet died, but what was I to do? I was trapped here. She fingered the pistol. Her eyes staring, her hand shaking. I was afraid it would go off. She held it up in front of her face, I winced as she shook it towards me.

"This was Henry's. It's German. He left it here last time he had leave."

"I've seen them. Do you know how to use it?"

"Course I bloody do!"

I sat and watched her. I thought of Élodie and saw her face in my mind's eye. I concentrated on her face. Her beautiful face with her sparkling emerald eyes. 'Come and help me' I said to her, get me out of this mess my darling Élodie. I tried to envisage where she was, could she hear me calling her name. I briefly closed my eyes and felt my lips twitch.

"Why are you smiling, nosey parker Loveday?"

"Because I am full of happiness, Mrs Jacobs." She snorted.

"What would your mother say?" I asked.

"Pah, my mother wouldn't care two jots. She loved those boys. She barely put up with me. But she'd want them to be seen right."

"So, the burning, what would have been next?"

"Dunno, something would have happened. Bloody Beckingham woman. She'd have got it again."

'Élodie, please come and help me.' I said to myself again, seeing her in my head, looking around my tiny village. Where was she? Why didn't she come. 'Please, Élodie,' I mouthed. 'Please.'

"What's that you say, missy?"

"Nothing, I haven't really got anything to say to you."

"I loved me mother. Don't think she ever loved me, but I did love her. Me brothers though."

"You didn't like them."

"Hated them, bullies all three. But what do they say? Blood thicker than water. I want me revenge."

"So, how do I come into this?"

"Well, what's your father doing? Your snooty brother may be in France, but your father? Then your mother lording it about all over the village. She deserves to know what it feels like."

"She knows about the horrible thing that war is, Mrs Jacobs. She worries every day that Alfie and I are away, as for my father..." I bit my lip. Whatever he was doing it was a secret and why should I explain anything to this mad woman?

"I'm leaving, Mrs Jacobs." I stood up. She again raised the gun shakily.

"Sit down, Lady Loveday," she sneered. I stood there and looked at her. A shrivelled up sad old woman racked by hatred for her own people. Not for the Germans. She hated her own and for what? Brothers who bullied her, a mother who never loved her. I turned my back on her.

"Come back!" she screeched. I started towards the door. Then nearly jumped out of my skin at the sound of a smashing glass behind me. I turned to see Mrs Jacobs staring out of the window. Her gun hand limp at her side.

"But that wasn't me." she whispered. "I didn't break that. Who would do such a thing?"

The kitchen door burst open and Constable Roberts came in, truncheon in his hand. He was swiftly overtaken by Élodie, who suddenly leapt at the old woman who had started to raise the pistol again. I put my hand up to my face but could see Élodie crash into her. The gun went spinning and Élodie swung her fist and punched her full in the face. I winced, but then saw the gun and I stepped across and picked it up. Ewan Roberts lifted Élodie from her victim who sat on the filthy floor sobbing.

"Who'd break my window. What did I do to anyone? Where's mother. I'll have to clear up before she gets home. Where's the brush?"

I gave the gun to Ewan. He broke it open and started to

remove the bullets. I knelt beside Mrs Jacobs. "Come on now, we'll get you to the doctors." I said and held out my hand. She took it and got to her feet.

"Come along now, Mrs Jacobs, let's get ourselves sorted out." Roberts took her by the arm, tipped his forehead and left the cottage. I looked at Élodie .

"Thank you my darling."

"I heard you calling, *ma mie*. You were so loud."

"But..."

"I knew where you were. You didn't need to call me, but I heard you anyway."

No, I had called her. In my head I'd called out to her and here she was. What had happened I didn't know, but here she was. My dearest girl. Here she was.

March 1st, 1917.

Dearest, darling Alfred,

Actually, I can't remember the last time I called you Alfred. Was it when you pulled my pigtail because I wouldn't get out of the tractor seat quickly enough? Maybe you should have pulled harder and forbidden me to drive, then I wouldn't be here! No, you pulled it just enough! How silly to suddenly remember that, I wonder why? Anyway, I hope this finds you well, wherever you are. I really miss you and hope you are safe. I haven't got enough hair to pull anymore as I had it attacked and keep it cut short to keep away the lice! Horrid isn't it, I suppose you have the same problem unless you are working in a cushy office with you know who! All is as well as it can be.

We have had such exciting times at the Hall! I will have to tell you when I see you or when mother is indiscreet enough to mention it to you in one of her letters. I don't think the censor will allow it so who knows when you will find out! Exciting, no? Mind you, I suppose you will see Dada soon enough and he can fill you in. What on earth do you two get up to? I wish I had your job whatever it is. Just so that I could see Dada really!

I am back to work. I am not sure if I am happy or sad. It is a strange existence isn't it? I know I am doing a worthwhile job, but I do so miss you and our family. I have though made some great friends. I would never have met them if I hadn't been here so that is a real plus. All the girls continue to be very chummy. Sophie said to give you her love, though I'm surprised she has any to offer as she is besotted with her beau. I hope to goodness that he comes out in one piece as she loves him so much. Mind you my darling, I pray every night that you are in one piece. It would be awful if anything happened. Silly to think like that. Of course, it would be awful. Keep seeing you know who. He pops over for things that I know nothing of. He says he sometimes runs into you. It's so strange isn't it, none of us really knowing what the other is doing, or where they are. At least we all know where mother is! Well you know my job, but you and papa. You are so mysterious.
Love you and miss you. Do take care
Poppy your loving sister

Chapter 9

"Keep your face to the sun and you will never see the shadows."

I had parked my bus by the ambulance train and was waiting for it to be unloaded. It was a rare respite. I looked towards the track and saw lumps of coal lying there. Too good to miss. I grabbed my gas mask and went about collecting and loading pieces of coal into the bag from the cabin of my lorry. This was one of the great perks of the job. Come to think about it, this was the only benefit of the job and if I wasn't driving ambulances here, I wouldn't need this perk at all. I could collect a good half hundredweight of coal in a week and this all helped keep us warm in the Barn. I was always careful to give Lady Greenwood some when she came to my ambulance. Just to keep her sweet, but she wasn't like some of the ambulance commandants we heard about. She was a decent woman, who seemed to actually care about us. We heard tales of right harridans who would almost torture their drivers with roll calls at all hours and drills, followed by punishments if they fell foul of them. We didn't need to be ruled by an iron fist. We did our job and we did it well. I sat back in my cabin and heard the wagon's back-door slam closed. A private came to my window grinning and waved me off. I got on the road to camp wondering which direction I would now be sent off to. Guns still roared in front of me as the Germans seemed to be trying it on. What a lark it all was. At least no shells were coming this far. I spotted Sophie's bus in front of me and flashed my headlights. She waved from her window and we convoyed together. The sun was trying to creep out from behind clouds. In front of me I could see black puffs of smoke in the air as shells exploded. Probably shooting at planes, ours, or theirs I wondered. I glanced to the side and saw a couple of our flyers. The roundels clear on their fuselages.

Suddenly I could hear them. They made such an odd

growling spluttering noise. The gunner in the rear waved and I smiled and waved. They were brave boys, so exposed to it all. They didn't spend too much time aloft on each sortie, but it must have felt like forever if they came under attack. They swooped off towards the black puffs and I saw another two follow them. Would I ever want to fly, I wondered? Perhaps to go to some far away land instead of sailing one day. To America or India. Somewhere exotic would be nice. But there again perhaps it would be better to be pampered on a cruise to India, living the life of a queen in a fashionable cabin, waited on hand and foot. A loud crumping noise brought me back to the present and I saw that one of the planes was now a fireball in the sky and that some smaller aircraft were coming towards us. As Sophie turned a corner in her ambulance another loud bang went off and mud and stones were thrown towards my windscreen as a bomb exploded at the side of the road. I heard gun fire as a machine gun chattered away. I turned the corner and saw that Sophie had pulled to the side of the road. I wasn't sure that that was safe but stopped myself. The machine gunning went on and I realised it was up in the air as the planes fought against each other. I grabbed my gas mask and got out of my cabin and ran towards Sophie. She was just jumping down as I got to her.

"Poppy, you're bleeding!" She cried out grabbing my hand and dragging me towards the ditch at the side of the road. I jumped down and I put my hand to my forehead and felt blood, but no pain. I pulled off my beret and moved my hand to a cut before pressing my hat back against the wound.

"Just a scratch!" I smiled, "Get your head down, Sophie." We lay against the side of the ditch, our feet in water. Most uncomfortable while above us the dogfight persisted. Every so often a bomb would explode on the road and I dared not look towards our ambulances. The chatter of machine guns continued, and another loud explosion filled the air. I looked up and this time it was a German aircraft going down, corkscrewing with flames into the field next to us. There was no sign of the pilot. I closed my eyes and shivered. We lay there for what seemed hours as the planes howled overhead.

"What must they think?" I said quietly.

"They can't think, they have to stay alive," said Sophie. "No time to think, they just act on instinct and hope to God they are right."

"The instinct to keep alive is very strong, look at us two now." I almost laughed.

"We'll be all right, Poppy. We're as safe as houses." Sophie did laugh, but grabbed my hand as another crump filled the air.

"They'd better miss my bus or there will be trouble!" I laughed with her. "Just keep your head down." We kept our heads down as the battle exploded high in the sky. We didn't look up until there was quiet. It had almost crept up on us, one minute the chattering machine guns and growl of the planes' engines were above our heads, the next it was silent save for the dull thud of the guns at the Front. I looked up into the blue sky, spotted now with white fluffy clouds. A gorgeous blue that shone beautifully overhead. I sighed and wondered how nature could endure all this. How long before the Earth would turn against the fighters and reclaim itself for the good people, those who decried war and just wanted to live together in peace and quiet. Would the Earth fight back or would it leave it to man to decide? I pulled myself from the ditch and gave Sophie my hand and heaved her up.

"We'll be getting trench foot if we're not careful!" Sophie smiled.

"Had it!" I laughed.

"Nothing can harm me. I'm invincible!"

"Let's hope you are darling. Now back to base."

Another perfect end to a perfect day.

Élodie mirrored me perfectly. We had both been trying *tie chee* for a while. It relaxed us and helped me to remember the movements. Élodie always worked with her eyes closed as if concentrating so hard demanded it. The tip of her tongue would show and made me smile. I would move close and peck her on the cheek or mouth if company permitted and would feel myself dissolve inside as I did so, but giggle as she jumped in surprise. We finally made our way to the showers and doused each other with the cold water. Élodie made me laugh every time as she hopped up and down, shrieking at the top of her voice.

"You are so weak!" I laughed as I handed her a towel. I wrapped mine around me. It was warm for the time of year, I thought, and sat on a bench by the side of the tent. I rubbed my hair with another towel. This was one of the benefits of having such short hair, it didn't take so long to dry as when it flowed over my shoulders. It also didn't harbour any nasty nit lice, so it had its pleasures. Élodie sat down beside me and I started to rub her auburn hair. She again squealed like a baby and I had to laugh.

"For goodness sake, Élodie!"

"I can't help it, Poppy, you are too rough."

"I need to be rough to get your hair dry, you silly goat!"

"Silly, am I? A goat, am I?" She pushed me and I dramatically fell from the bench to the ground and Élodie changed moods immediately as she begged forgiveness before she saw I was laughing, fit to burst.

"You torture me, Poppy! It is not fair." I pulled her down to the floor and kissed her quickly on the lips.

"You torture me again, Poppy Loveday." She returned my kiss and for a brief moment we held each other close. But it couldn't last. We didn't want to be sent home for disorderly conduct. I got up and helped Élodie to her feet and we again sat on the bench.

"Love is a torture, Élodie."

"At the moment, it is, but soon we will find somewhere we can spend our time and show love."

"I am frightened that that will never happen. This war seems to have no end."

"But we are safe, Élodie, we won't be going anywhere. I know we will have a long life together."

"How can you be so sure? I am scared of this life every day. When there is an explosion, I think it will be me that is caught. No matter how far away it is."

"But Élodie..."

"No, Poppy I cannot help it. I fear for my life, your life. I fear for everyone. What if we are blown to pieces one day?"

"Then we can but hope that our bodies will mix together, and we will be one in death." I smiled, knowing this was nonsense and that it would be awful. It didn't bear thinking about and to be honest that is why I didn't entertain such thoughts. I blanked it all out. If death came, it came as far as I was concerned, so there was no need to worry about it. Maybe it was because Élodie was a Catholic and that's why she worried so much about life and death. I asked if this was so.

"I think I worry about going to Heaven. Sometimes I think there must be a Heaven and that I will go there, but then I think of things I have done wrong in life and so may not be able to go there. If I was to die before I was ready, before I had prepared to meet God, then it would be awful."

"But you do believe in Heaven and Hell?"

"I do, but after the Canadian I think I may spend a long time in purgatory."

"I don't think you will my love." I put my arm around her naked shoulders and felt the familiar feeling in my stomach. She was so utterly desirable, and it was so hard to not want to kiss and touch her.

"Is it not so, that to come to God and be saved, you need to repent, have faith, and be baptized?" I asked.

"Yes, but If you commit mortal sin, you need to repent, and I haven't been to confession for so long."

"But do you pray my love?"

"I try. I sometimes find no time. I know I should, but time just flies. It is no excuse…"

"Of course, it is darling. There is a reason for everything and if you have your faith, then God will understand. Does he know you have repented?

"I have told him in my prayers that I repent. I need to tell a priest."

"But God knows that you have repented. Me, I think

that you have no need to repent. Would God have wished you to be raped or to be murdered. Would he want that for you?" I looked into her eyes. They were full of tears. "Élodie, my sweet, God loves you. He has kept you alive so far. He knows that you did the right thing. He understands that you had to do what you did, He loves you."

"How can you be sure, Poppy?"

"Me and Alfie spent every Sunday listening, did you not listen to your priest?"

"I did, but I still find it so hard to understand. Look my love, here we are in a field in the middle of a war. Naked except for a towel, waiting for an air raid or a call to the hospital tent or to the ambulances. We live in such abnormal times and to think that God has not got more important things to think about than me, then is to be very selfish."

"I thought that God knew everyone and understood everyone. No one is ever left alone. We are his children. I don't have the same faith as you do, Élodie , but I do understand that God does love us all. He loves you. He won't let you go to Hell. He won't let you waft about in purgatory. You are such a Good person. You will be there. Having repented, he knows. You don't need last rites. You have God's love."

It was confirmed, Élodie and I had our leave together. A full ten days. It was hard to believe. We first arranged to visit the orphanage in Béthune to see Jacinth and Raoul. They were both lovely children. Raoul stood by his sister's side as she sat with Élodie. He was like a guard at the gate protecting his sister, but she was holding his hand, so she obviously wanted his care.

"And school Raoul?"

"We are both working well, Mamselle Poppy. We read and we write. I am top of my class. Jacinth of hers. I help younger children to read."

"I am also dancing with one of the nuns. It is like being in heaven," she giggled.

"You are eating well?" Élodie asked.

"We are both twice the size we were when we first met

you, Loveday. It is plain, but it is plenty," said Jacinth.

"We grow so much of our own vegetables. We work in the gardens, or we feed the pigs in the yard. We all have our jobs before or after school lessons."

"And the nuns are kind."

"Oh yes, Loveday. They are very kind," smiled Jacinth.

"It is not like home, it is different. But they look after us," Raoul said quietly. He wasn't twice the size, but at least he wasn't the skeletal creature we had met in the ruins only a few months ago. However, Jacinth looked taller and fuller. She was growing as she should be and was developing into a pretty young girl. We left the orphanage and felt reassured that they were in safe hands. The nuns did seem kind and the children seemed happy. What we would do in the future was undecided. But we felt a duty of care towards them both. After all they had saved us from a fate that was not worth thinking about in the cellars of Lozinghem.

We had cadged a lift on a lorry going to Paris to pick up supplies. It was little worse than travelling in my ambulance, but at least it kept us out of a smoky train carriage and crushes of people. The driver was an engaging man from Pontefract, missing his wife and children, stuck over here without leave for nearly two years. Élodie cheered him up though and it was a pleasant enough journey with not a sight of a German plane, nor the sound of bombs and shelling. Once dropped off we seemed to spend ages finding our Paris hotel. There was not a taxi to be seen and the metro was non-existent this evening, so it was late when we finally signed in. With promises of bowls of hot water, in an instant we collapsed onto the bed. I looked at Élodie and smiled. She lay, elbow on the bed and head in her hand looking down at me.

"You are so beautiful, Poppy. I cannot understand how I have lived ..."

"Shush, Élodie." We made love. It was so beautiful. We fell into a deep sleep. I dreamt of nothing but Élodie.

Élodie grabbed my hand and we stepped into 20, Rue Jacob. It was quite dark, but Élodie tripped along, knowing her way.

"Do not be shy, *Cherie*. She is formidable, but..."

"I know, I know, you told me. I'll do my best!"

Élodie laughed, then stifled it as we went into a large parlour. The walls covered in gilt paper, a little faded, but still showing their beauty. The windows were shaded by lace, but I could feel the warm spring sun flooding through. An oldish looking woman sat in what could only be described as a throne and waved Élodie over.

"So good to see you again, *petite*, it has been too long, and this is?" She beckoned me over and I kissed both her cheeks.

"Ophelia Loveday, Madame Barney, but you can call me Poppy if you wish."

"Welcome, Poppy. Welcome, Élodie. Your clothes are through the door." She pointed ahead. I looked at Élodie and with her lips turned down, her eyebrows raised she grabbed my hand again and almost yanked me away.

"Charades," she hissed.

"You didn't warn me."

"I didn't think she would."

The door opened onto a scene from Dante or some other writer. The room was full of squealing young women in various stages of undress. The common theme though was flowers in the hair and almost see-through shifts that many were pulling on or rearranging with help from each other.

"Ah, our final nymphs." A voice from the throng shouted and two flimsy pieces of material were thrown our way. Élodie caught them.

"Flowers in the vases or on the bed?"

Dozens of flowers and the scent suddenly hit me. After the barren wasteland of the North, the colour and scents were beautiful. I looked at Élodie. She already had her dress off and was pulling off her stockings. Seeing her half naked like this shocked me, but she always did have a different attitude. No one in the room cared. I just wanted to be in a corner somewhere.

"Come along, Poppy!" Élodie hurried.

"Undo my dress then." I hissed.

"I'll do it!" A voice volunteered and before I knew it my dress was being slipped from my shoulders. I felt myself blushing and muttered a thank you. The nymph floated away, and I quickly pulled the shift over my head. I looked at Élodie and smiled and then saw her naked body beneath the shift. I looked down at my figure and then at the other women and decided I had to remove everything or look really odd. Élodie came over and started plaiting flowers in my hair and kissed my lips as every flower was placed. The sun started to shine through the shuttered windows, and someone flung them open, and the room was flooded with natural light. I looked over Élodie's shoulder. It was a scene of beautiful chaos. Flowers were strewn everywhere, women were laughing and showing off their dresses, and it had to be said their bodies. You could see some women with very greedy eyes in the room. One made contact with my eyes, but I quickly gathered some flowers and started to weave them into Élodie's beautiful auburn hair. It was obvious to us who were ladies of leisure in this room. Our hair was not pampered and precious like theirs, but short and shaggy. The flowers made us look like shepherdesses from old paintings. But I suddenly felt so happy away from the horror of the Front, amongst beautiful things and beautiful people. I stepped back and admired my work. Élodie brushed a hair from my cheek. Her touch was electric, and her eyes smiled.

"You are so beautiful, *Cherie*."

"As are you." I whispered leaning forward to kiss her. I felt no embarrassment here. It just seemed so natural, so right. Just as it should be. Élodie took my hand and barefoot we returned to the parlour. I couldn't really concentrate on what was being said, but soon we were outdoors in the sun and on the lush lawn. I looked towards where Élodie stood. A statue in a tableau of Barney's design. The unusual shimmering warmth of this March day weighed heavy as we tried to hold our poses. It was our turn to be nymphs at the court of Ariadne and I was aware that Natalie Barney watched from an upstairs window, as other scantily clad young women flitted across the lawn paying homage to their mistress. Élodie pointed out Dolly Wilde as she danced amongst them, her gossamer tunic almost a second skin, looking so beautiful, dark hair cascading over her striking face, glistening with perspiration. I wasn't sure whether she was intoxicated by the dance or by something she had taken, in all honesty I had never spoken to Dolly, and Élodie had told me that when she had met her in Paris before she always seemed to be affected by some drug or drink. I thought Dolly looked like a goddess though, and as she whirled past my dearest girl, she gave Élodie her most winning smile. A smile that had broken many hearts, and I could see why so many men and women had fallen under her spell. A beautiful girl danced alone pretending to play her lyre whilst more scantily clad dancers appeared bare foot on the swiftly drying grass, slipping and spinning between each other in some exotic, erotic pattern. A pale dancer weaved by and as I inhaled her musky scent and without looking, I knew it was my own true love Élodie who was breathless as she looked into my eyes and I breathed her in. I had had enough of dancing. It was hot and I felt sticky. I needed a bath and a kiss from my darling girl. I took her hand and led her away from her shrine.

"At last, Poppy, you rescue me."

"I kidnap you. I want you for myself. I see how Dolly and Natalie look at you," I smiled. She leaned into me and kissed my lips. Despite the heat a shiver ran through my body and my tummy turned to honey.

"Indeed, I see how all the nymphs and fauns look at you. Their eyes grab you and gobble you up. You are their captive and I must fight to set you free." Élodie laughed and pulled me closer. I felt the warmth of her body permeating into mine. We might both as well been naked, my arousal was almost unbearable.

"I am yours and yours alone, *ma Cherie*."

"I know. I tease, but let's finds somewhere we can cool down."

We sat in the shade of an arbour and drank champagne from

the flutes presented to us from another nymph with a tray. This was heaven, or Arcadia, or what was the Greek? I had lost my thread. It was starting to chill, not too much, but soon we would have to go indoors. For now, it was just a delight to sit next to my love, almost skin to skin as the sun dipped low in the sky. Here we both were at the court of Natalie Barney.

Élodie had been invited, her reputation as an artist going before her. She seemed to know everyone. I hadn't realised her popularity. Indeed, I knew very little of her past. She had never really spoken about it. I knew she had studied art at University, but that was about the limit. She never spoke of home or her parents. She was a mystery to be honest, but that was part of the magic of her. Music started to play again. This time it was from a real lyre player and flutes, though we couldn't see where they were. More half-dressed dancers appeared and threw rose petals as they weaved in and out of each other making patterns with their bodies as if floating on air. To one side the nymphet Dolly Wilde stood, serene and now naked as masked fauns and centaurs paid homage to her.

The music carried gently on the air, fluttering like the women's costumes as they seemed to be choreographed into surrounding Dolly. Then all became silent as Natalie strode to stand beside the naked goddess. She opened a large book and began to read her latest work, words floating breathlessly out into the warm Spring air, bewitching us with their sensual emphasis and erotic meaning. She seemed to shine, to glory at the rapt attention she was being given and indeed it did seem to be wondrous as her words took us to places unimagined and stirred feelings some did not know they had. Élodie leant her head on my shoulder whispering sweet nothings to me as I watched the audience of flimsy cobweb clothed women nodding and absorbing the gentle cadence of her fervid words. No man was present today to articulate any dissent. Here was all one Sapphic pleasure, a treatise to woman, a glorification in words, music and dance of her part in this society behind the walled gardens of Rue Jacob. Élodie leant up towards my face and kissed my lips again, then lay down on the bench, her head in my lap. I twisted her short hair, curling threads between my fingers and she smiled and closed her eyes.

"I have to admit, it is trying that Natalie always seems to devour me with her eyes," she said, a smile on her lips.

"Not just you my love, every woman it seems and that Dolly too. I see how she looks at you."

"I know. I could be embarrassed, but I know she understands me."

"In what way?" I asked.

"I met her when I was in Paris once."

"Do go on," I smiled.

"I was in Montparnasse, when I was on leave you remember. I wrote that I met her here at Natalie Barney's, then later I was just making my way home. I had on my nurse's uniform as that was my smartest set of clothes and I passed a café where there were lots of American ambulance drivers."

"Well we know how they used to behave." I laughed.

"I know. They had obviously been drinking all day and waved me in when they saw my uniform. It was a happy time. The fighting was almost forgotten, or at least ignored for the time of their leave. No one cared a bit about anything. They had to make up for a lot of missed time."

"We all do. We could have just wallowed in the past, or move on. I think we do rather well, don't you?"

"I know. I still get the odd feeling and loud noises you know."

"I do my darling."

Every time there was a thunderstorm Élodie would retreat into herself, reliving memories of the Front and the cannon fire. If there was ever a loud bang, she would be the same. It meant tears and shivers and more nightmares. She had not fully recovered from the sights and sounds she had experienced, perhaps never would.

"I think I had too much absinthe that night. Such an evil drink!" she laughed.

"I missed my train and realised that as I sat there laughing and joking and drinking that everyone was so happy, and I wanted to be part of it. When I realised I had to find somewhere to stay, the bar owner said I could have a room upstairs. She didn't want payment, which was a change, as lots of people tried to make profits during this time, but I think she had lost a son, or had a wounded son, so was grateful. Anyway, I went upstairs and collapsed on the bed. Didn't take my clothes off as I was, you know, not quite myself and must have fallen straight to sleep."

I brushed away a wisp of auburn hair from her forehead and she opened her eyes and smiled at me. Her emerald eyes seemed to draw me inside her and I leant down and kissed her.

"Do go on, my darling," I said.

"Sometime during the night, I woke up and there was Dolly standing in my room. Naked and so beautiful. You have seen her, but it was a shock to me. I've never known anything like that to happen before and didn't know what to do. It was silly. My first thought was what would Poppy do? I don't know why. I had no interest in her, I love only you so was a bit embarrassed. Well actually, I was totally embarrassed, so closed my eyes quickly. She got into bed and I didn't dare move or breathe. She pushed herself into me and I could smell her scent. She took my hand and placed it on her breast and held it there. I was still in shock I suppose, so still, I did nothing."

"Well what could you do my darling?" I laughed. I tried to imagine the scene, but it only made me giggle.

"Well, I fell asleep again, the absinthe I expect, and, in the morning, she was gone."

"Did you speak again?"

"Again? No words had ever passed between us until now."

"What happened?"

"I told her I had dreamt she came into my bed."

"Did she deny it?"

"Far from it, she smiled and said she had to, but that I was asleep, so she did not disturb me."

"How odd."

"Then I had to explain that I was deeply in love with another."

"How did she take it?" I smiled and kissed her hand.

"She understood. To be honest I thought whether to mention it at all, as I had pretended to be asleep, but I felt I had to be true to myself and especially true to you."

"You are so sweet."

"But it was so embarrassing. I had no idea that people could behave like that."

"Well you can see today that they are quite free with their bodies."

"And we know they all seem to have a certain reputation."

"I know, but just think if they were men would anyone say anything? It just shows how the world sees us," I said.

"The one thing I love is that behind these walls we can be who we really are. It seems like such freedom."

"I know, I know. This is what I dream about. But I don't want to be behind walls to show my love for you."

Clouds were starting to pass overhead and there was a sudden chill in the air. I shivered, not surprisingly as I was wearing so little. It would soon be time to go. We both had purses full of cards and invites to some of the notable women of the day, especially from Romaine Brookes, Barney's some time partner and long-term lover. She had seemed very keen to meet us. I hoped it would not provoke a scene as she was very much in love with Natalie it seemed.

"You French!" I laughed.

"But she is *une Americaine*!" squealed Élodie in delight.

"I know, but only here in France can we be... Ourselves!"

"Tonight, we go dancing, then tomorrow the Eiffel tower and Romaine, then…" Élodie clapped her hands like a small child.

"We finish by seeing the sights again, but let's get back

to the hotel. I need a bath."

We bade farewell to our hostess, with promises of return visits and invitations to meet in several European cities and were on our way. As the gate to Rue Jacob closed, Élodie skipped into the middle of the road. "I need more champagne, I am so excited!" squealed Élodie, grabbing my hand. But this was too much for an old gentleman who grunted as we flew past him towards a night club recommended by one of today's fauns. We laughed, it didn't matter what he thought, not here, not at this moment. We were so in love and didn't need anyone's approval. The salon we had entered, the Lunettes Club, was in subdued lighting, but we could see the luxuriant fittings and even more luxuriant guests. It was early, but there were a few customers scattered about the large room. An elegant man approached us. Élodie waved him away. I looked at her and smiled. She would not dance with anyone. She was a strange girl. She loved to dance, but it would only be with me or on her own. The man looked disappointed, so I decided to humour him.

"I will dance with monsieur, but I am not interested in monsieur," I said, smiling.

"*C'est vrai.* That is enough, Mamselle, I am not interested in women. My partner is not inclined to dance with me today." He nodded towards the bar. A small man raised his glass to me, I dipped my head then turned to my dance partner, a tall elegant man with striking looks in a wonderful white tuxedo. He led me to the floor. He was a superb dancer, I felt as if I were floating under his guidance. The music from the small orchestra was a delight, filling the room with rhythm and suggestion. It was easy to get intoxicated by its movement. The air rushed by as I twisted and turned, my head high, my smile wide, floating as if on a cloud.

"You dance beautifully," I said.

"I know, it is a gift." He smiled but he was not bragging, just stating a fact. As we whirled around the floor, I caught sight of Élodie, who was now sitting at a table laughing with Natalie Barney who had her hand on hers. Élodie made no move to remove it and sat as if entranced. I knew of Natalie's reputation for picking up and leaving lovers and a slight chill ran through me, but only for an instant. I knew our love was unbreakable. I span away, my head held high, safe in the arms of this elegant man who danced like a dream. The music finished, our dance ended, and my partner bowed, handed me his card and led me back to Élodie, who stood and kissed me.

"*Merci, Monsieur le Comte,*" I said. He flourished, then he too floated away to be met by a kiss from his partner at the bar.

"*Superbe,* Poppy," Natalie said, clapping her hands together, "You dance like a dream."

Natalie Barney and a lady friend sat at our table. I didn't recognise her friend from today's soiree. It wasn't Romaine, she was obviously on the prowl again. I wondered what effect this had on Romaine if she was in love with Natalie. How must she feel to see her paramour constantly, moving from woman to woman, partner to partner? It would drive me insane if I had to share Élodie with anyone, but Natalie did this by choice. Did Romaine? Had they followed us? I did not care, but I felt myself blushing as Natalie turned her attention towards me, doubtless rebuffed by Élodie who sat smiling sweetly. I laughed on the outside and scowled on the inside. Élodie took my hand and kissed it before standing motioning to le Comte, who met her at the dance floor and took her in his arms, before sweeping her away in a cloud of white. I knew she was doing this to torment Natalie, to show her what she could never have. I shivered with delight and pride. Proud that I had Élodie as my love, my lover, my partner.

Élodie was mesmeric, lithe and erotic. She danced like no other, in a world of her own using her partner as a prop rather than a lead. Her movements were like that of some creature, untamed yet smooth as silk. As I watched I felt herself being drawn into her and recognised the warm feeling in my stomach as one of need for my lover's touch. Natalie was trying her best to engage me, but I had eyes only for Élodie. My mind was on my dearest girl, I wanted to be with her alone.

I turned slightly at a movement besides me as Natalie left the table. She was not used to being ignored and I watched as she selected a new quarry then turned to regard Élodie once more. She was being escorted back to her seat. She leant down and kissed me hard on the mouth, slightly biting my lip as she did so, I winced but kissed her back harder. Without saying a word, she took my hand and led me to the dance floor. She put her hands around me, one in the small of my back, the other on my shoulder and pulled me towards her. There was nothing between us save for the cloth of our dresses and I felt the warmth of her body and inhaled the beautiful orange blossom aroma of her scent. Her face was next to my neck and as one we glided around the floor. I was not sure if I was being pulled or led around, but I felt myself floating across the dance floor. Her breathing was fast and her body heat rising. I felt my insides in turmoil, my stomach seemed to be melting into that honeyed goo that came when she was inside me. I could hardly bear it, but the tightness of her hold meant that there was no escape. We whirled and span as one to the music and I felt as if I would scream in pleasure and delight. As the music ended, we were miraculously by our table and I collapsed exhausted into my chair. Champagne followed and added to my light-headed dizziness. This was what love felt like.

"Let's dance again, Élodie."

"It would be a pleasure, *cherie*." I took her hand and led her to the dance floor, but she took the lead and I followed. The strings of the tiny orchestra rose and fell and we swept along to their pattern, our feet in time and together, we breezed across the floor and I felt Élodie tighten her grip on me and our bodies became one, melded together in movement. Her warmth seemed to percolate into me, and I became breathless. I ached between my thighs as her face became closer. Any nearer and she would be inside me. I shivered and she let me go and spun me around. It was as if I was a puppet and she was leading me, I knew whatever movement I needed to take and if I was unsure Élodie seemed to feel it and led me in the right direction. As the music faded, she swept me back towards our table. Natalie had returned to her friend and she clapped her hands delightedly, rising to kiss first Élodie, then me on the lips. She had no shame. I dropped into my chair breathless and drained as if I had just made love to my dearest girl. By the look in Élodie's eyes I could see she felt the same. She moved her chair nearer to mine, excluding all from our world. She kissed me. More warmth spread through my body, I wanted to get back to the hotel room, but Élodie was distracted, she wanted to do more. We were both exhilarated by our dancing and the tolerance we found at the Lunettes Club. We chose to walk back to our hotel. Hand in hand, side by side, comfortable in each other's company. Paris was dark and damp, but we both felt only warmth and light.

"We should live here, Élodie." I said.

"To leave your family?"

"You left yours for me."

"I moved away long ago. You are so close to yours."

"But I'm closer to you."

"It would be a big step. I am not sure," Élodie said.

"We should think. I adore it here. I adore that I can show my love for you in the open."

"But only at night. It is not always so convivial."

"But we would not have to hide."

"We shall talk, Cherie. Now wasn't le Comte a wonderful dancer?"

"You made him look like a lamp post, Élodie!" She sniggered, "Poppee, do not be cruel, he moved very well with you."

"And so did Natalie when she knew she was out of luck!"

"A predator, she tried with you?"

I blushed unseen in the darkness, "I'm not sure, I didn't honestly listen to her I had eyes only for you."

"Jealous?"

"She was. I would be if I thought I needed to be."

"You never will."

Montmartre was still busy way after midnight. It had

come alive with music from bars and cafes and groups jostling on the pavements and in the road. A few had drunk too much, but were merry, not aggressive. Beautiful and not so beautiful women plied their trade and we stepped around beggars and children out looking for money. We strolled back to our hotel holding hands, easy in each other's company. Content with each other, looking forward to what the rest of the night would bring. I felt my heart beating faster, but every time I looked across at my dearest girl it seemed to skip a beat.

Poppy Flowers at the Front

Chapter 10

"Be like a flower and turn your face to the sun."

We had been summoned to Romaine Brookes' studio. It was an invitation we could not decline. I was fascinated by her, but Élodie was entranced by her. Not as a woman, but as an artist. Élodie delighted in the images that Romaine produced, life-like, sad, dark, exquisite. Romaine was a wonderful painter. Almost as talented as my dearest girl I thought to myself! The long-time lover of Natalie had written that she wished to paint us. Élodie had shrugged, I had demurred, but Élodie turned her shrug into a pout so we had taken a cab to the studio in the beautiful sixteenth arrondissement, all sweeping boulevards and low hanging trees. Élodie enthused about her work and by the time we had got to the door, I was excited. Romaine answered the door herself, a tall angular, but beautiful woman who seemed to have slightly haunted sad eyes below her bob.

"Please stand as you are." We did as we were instructed, and Romaine stepped back. The sun was shining, and it was a beautiful day. Romaine looked at us both, her sad eyes piercing.

"Please come in." She opened up her arm and guided us in. We followed her. "I am Romaine Brookes, Natalie said you were too beautiful to miss, I would like to paint you."

"*Pas de problem, Mademoiselle* Brookes," said Élodie.

"Please call me Romaine, Élodie." They had met before, Élodie took my hand and presented it to Romaine.

"So, you must be Poppee?" she sounded like Élodie, with all the ees.

"Romaine." We kissed cheeks.

"Please, the changing room is there, if you could undress?

"Naked?" I was surprised.

"*Pas de problem.*" Élodie took control and pushed me into the room.

"I didn't think we would have to undress."

"Be bold, *Cherie*, she is a genius."

"I know, but..." Élodie was almost naked and tugged at my top playfully. She didn't seem to have a care in the world. Of course, being an artist, she was used to all this, but me? I shivered as she pulled at my blouse. I disrobed slowly and we went into the studio. It was brilliantly lit with easels and half-finished paintings all over the place. On the walls were some rather austere paintings of women. I recognised one from yesterday's soiree but could not put a name to her. I stood behind Élodie, a hand across my breasts and the other between my legs, I didn't like to be so exposed. It was strange.

"Please sit here." Romaine showed us to a dais covered in purple velvet. Élodie took my hand and led me there.

"Please relax, Poppee, I will not bite. Now, Élodie, if you would lay here, like so and Poppee here." She proceeded to move us about on the velvet, it felt luxuriant to the touch. She pulled at our legs and wrapped our arms until we were tied in a naked erotic knot, bodies clamped to each other. I felt surges through my body. The only time we were ever this close and naked was when we made love. I could look into Élodie's eyes. They sparkled with pleasure, I recognised that look. It seemed like pure lust.

"Now if your lips can just touch..."

It was too much for me. I jumped up and ran to the changing rooms.

"*Un moment...*" I heard Élodie say.

I quivered, "We are too close. I want you so much, she is a devil!"

"I know, it is a pure pleasure, but you need to relax my love, just imagine we are
alone."

"I cannot, so close to you, nothing between us. It is torture..."

"Come back my love, we will survive, then we have the painting for our memory..." She led me back into the studio.

"*Desole,* Romaine, I had the cramp. It will be all right

from now." I lied. Moulded again into the required shape, I looked at Élodie with a half-smile and could still feel the erotically charged tingles between us.

"The kiss?" Romaine asked and our lips brushed, this time I started to count in my head, trying to think of other things.

"That look, Poppy, is perfect, please hold your positions." She proceeded to sketch onto various pads. Her hands moving so fast at times it seemed to be a blur in the corner of my eyes. She would walk around us, drawing shapes from different angles. At times she would be so close we could feel her breath as she stared at us trying to get the right position, at other times she would move as far back in the studio as she could and sketch something down before moving swiftly on to find another vantage point. I felt my body tightening as my muscles ached and strained in the unusual position I was in, I wanted to move, but didn't dare. I was still counting, every so often my body would tremble, and I would say numbers aloud trying to distance myself from the sensual position I was in.

As we returned to our hotel Élodie skipped like a schoolgirl along the wide pavement. Few cars travelled the boulevards and few people were out and about. I wondered if the strikes we had read about were taking a hold, or whether Paris had just emptied of people. A bus rolled past us, the female conductor hanging on for grim death as it turned a sweeping corner. I took Élodie's hand and pulled her closer. Her smile was radiant. The rays of the setting sun were speckling through the trees that lined the road. There was more greenery here than on the Front. Élodie swung her parasol and smiled.

"This is almost heaven, *ma mie*. If we didn't have to return it would be."

"Well at least we know it cannot go on forever. No more bombs on Paris, for a week or so. Perhaps they have given up on that idea."

"We can but hope, but I am sure there will be more

twists and turns before the end."

"Be sure there will be. Does the sun inspire you on an evening like this?"

"To paint? The light is so different, the shadows so obscure. It does make you think about what you paint. I will be so happy to sit down and draw something when there are no bombs flying around my ears."

"I would rather you kept your head down than paint when bombs are falling my darling. But where would you choose to paint?" I laughed.

"Florence for the light of course, and the scents and the tastes. And that would just be you." She giggled. "I would have gone to Germany earlier as things were so exciting over there, but who knows what it will be like when the war ends. What if the Germans actually win? Would we be allowed to travel there, or would they bar us?"

"Germany will not win, Élodie, I am convinced of that. We have God on our side."

"Are you so sure? I feel that God has left us to get on with it. He doesn't seem to care one way or the other. There has been no great religious sign has there?"

"I suppose not Élodie. Well, if not Florence or Germany?"

"I will certainly come to study here in Paris and I will learn a great deal. I want to be successful. I want to be the best I can be."

"Well I have faith in you my darling. I know you will achieve so much." Élodie pulled me closer and kissed my cheek.

"You are my biggest supporter. But you have seen so little of my work."

"Indeed, my darling. Where is it all?"

"At home, safe and secure. In my notebooks which are not so safe or secure if a bomb falls on them." She laughed. "If a bomb drops on them, the odds are that we will be under that bomb!"

"Well, let us hurry, Élodie. I want a bath and I want my

bed."

"You don't want to eat?"

"Yes, that as well. So much to do and so little time. Let's hurry."

March 13th, 1918.

Darling Dada,

I pray this letter finds you well. I got a chum of Alfie's to post it for me.
He said that Alfie was in "fine fettle," to quote him, whatever fettle is! He did say to send regards to you both, though if he hadn't I would for him!

We recently spent time in Paris. It was divine, I will tell you more when I next see you. It never seems to change, though there aren't many people about!

We have had so many gassed cases at present, who appeared this past week. There are tens in each ward. It was horrible to see them lined up on stretchers outside the operating theatre tent, though there is nothing much that can be done with them. Driving them in my ambulance is bad enough as every bump jolts their lungs, and the sound of coughing is horrible. I then have to wash out my ambulance which is full of the most revolting stuff. Don't tell mother, she will only complain again about me being here!

I'm not sure what they write in the papers at home as we haven't seen one for a while, but if it's about the glory of war, well you know as well as I do that there's very little glory over here. I wish those people, those glory boys, could see our own boys, burnt and blistered all over with great mustard coloured blisters, and with blinded eyes, sometimes temporarily, thank God, but usually permanently. They go all sticky and shut. Then there's the lungs the noise they make as they breath, they can't speak, don't have enough breath to and so their last few hours on earth are really pathetic. Can't see, can't speak, only pain.

I'm glad all I do is drive them from the Front. Élodie sees the worst of it and she is working all the hours God sent.

I drive whilst it is light or once an offensive has started as you know. Sometimes I feel I am driving whilst asleep. I can't remember how I got to a destination. That's quite frightening.

We do see more planes in the sky. Watching them fight each other is quite exciting but also tragic. We rarely see a parachute. The planes explode in balls of fire or just float slowly to the ground. If the pilot's not dead, then what a fate. But I suppose he knows that before he goes up. I haven't transported one pilot, friend or foe, since I started which tells you a lot.

We do have Germans in the back of the van, along with all sorts Africans from so many of our colonies and other countries, Canadians, Americans, the odd Russian, and they are odd. They never complain, but always seem so grateful. The Aussies and Kiwis, well I know it's across the world, but they are like from a different world. They never seem to salute anyone, especially their own officers. They laugh at our officers. To their faces sometimes, they are really, what is the word Dada? Irreverent! That's it. they are truly irreverent!

The censor should leave that long list of allies in. Any German who reads that will be so scared and will know that their day will soon be over. We have the world on our side and Germany can't continue for much longer. They are alone and we will triumph. It is incredulous to me that the German High Command doesn't recognise this fact and surrender.
All my love as always,

Ophelia

We were drinking génépi in the hotel lounge. It was an unusual taste, another new thing that my Élodie had introduced me to. We had looked at bottles of a few digestif and this was the one that had caught my eye. It now caught my throat, but in a smooth warming way, and I was pleasantly surprised by its unusual taste. I thought that we would be able to enjoy the rest of the day alone when a messenger arrived. I was really surprised. "A man calling himself Sophie's father would like to see you." He said quietly.

"Send him in," I said. Sophie's father, Lord Quittenton, what on earth could he want? Had something happened to Sophie? I felt a shiver going through my body, but as I rose to greet him, I was somewhat reassured by the look on his face.

"Lady Loveday."

"Lord Quittenton, is Sophie all right?"

"Oh yes, my dear, she's as right as rain." Relief surged through my body. I sighed deeply.

"Please let me introduce my companion, Élodie Proux."

"Mademoiselle Proux, Sophie has told me so much about you."

"Then I am a little worried, Lord Quittenton."

"No need, my dear. All is good." With one hand, he beckoned a waiter over. "Would you like a top-up ladies?"

"That would be nice, Milord," Élodie smiled.

"Brandy and what the two ladies were drinking, please." He remained silent until our drinks arrived. I sipped mine and again the warmth flooded down my throat and made my chest tingle.

"What brings you to Paris?" I asked.

"Now that's the thing. I'm not really here."

"So, you are here on War Office business?"

"No longer than I need to be. I would like your help. I hear from your father that you have indeed been very helpful and so wondered ..." He paused. As if not sure to continue, then he took a swallow of brandy and started again. "We have a contact in Paris who we need to debrief. He is a rather strange man and has not been responding to our messages, so we are not sure what his position is. If he has been discovered, he could well be dead. Most of our other contacts in Paris are known to the Germans, so we needed to find some fresh blood so to speak."

"Fresh blood?" Élodie asked.

"People not known to the enemy. I heard from Sophie that you were in town so wondered if ..."

"We would love to help!" Élodie said, smiling broadly.

I nodded my head and smiled as well.

"Our contact, Claude Nougé, has information that we need. Can you collect ..." When he had finished his instructions, Lord Quittenton left and I sat across from Élodie with raised eyebrows.

"What first my love?"

"Clean ourselves up and then off to see Monsieur Nougé. The sooner that is done, the sooner we can start our own adventures.

"A bath, shall we have a Boulogne-sur-Mer bath?" Élodie grinned.

"Is there any other my darling?"

Claude Nougé lived on the side of the Seine on the Ile de cite. You could just see Notre Dame every so often as the houses were high and blanked out all but small portions of the sky. But you could hear the bells and every so often their beautiful tolling would fill the air. Echoing between the tightly packed houses of the Ile. I slipped my hand into Élodie's as we walked the uneven, rather foul smelling, cobbled streets. We eventually found the apartment of Nougé. It was of course dark and looked in need of repair as befitted his seedy reputation. We battered the door and waited as a series of locks were undone. I smiled at Élodie, who raised her eyebrows. Monsieur Nogue was as decrepit and seedy looking as the building. He looked us up and down, assessing whether to condescend to speak to us. His unshaven face was battered and bruised. A cut on his forehead was still oozing blood under a makeshift bandage. How could this be Nougé, the intelligent, clever man that Lord Q had described?

"*Monsieur...*" started Élodie.

"What do you want?" He demanded in guttural French.

"You are hurt?"

"What's it to you?"

"Lord Quittenton sent us." At that he stepped out from the doorway, looked up and down the narrow street then ushered us indoors. As he closed the thick door, I noticed the thick cudgel he was carrying.

"Won't be caught off guard again. Quittenton you say..." He rebolted the door and turned the key in the lock. We followed him up the narrow stone stairs and were shown into a dark room. The shutters were closed, and the only light source was a flickering candle.

"Why did you let us in?"

"You are only women." Élodie and I exchanged glances but ignored the slight.

"Quittenton sent us. He needs some information. We were to warn you of other interests, but it seems we are too late."

"This?" He pointed to his face, "It's nothing, a disagreement over a woman. What is this warning? Who would threaten me?"

"Quittenton said you are the only one who can help us, but he knows that it comes with a risk."

"If the pay is good enough, I can deal with the risk." he grinned, "Now what is it you wish to know?"

"Normal terms, a payment into your account?"

"Agreed." Nougé grunted. The room seemed to close in on us. It was humid, I felt perspiration trickle down my spine, but despite this I shivered. Élodie briefly touched my hand in reassurance. She too was feeling the heat. The darkness didn't help. It was oppressive. Nougé hunched up and sat on a stool pointing us to the damaged sofa that must have doubled as a bed as there was little other furniture in the room. "Tell me what Quittenton wants."

"He wants the information you have gathered over the last three weeks. He doesn't know why you have not kept your side of the bargain and reported in the usual way. He needs to know how reliable you really are." Élodie spoke clearly in French.

"Pah, it's not been safe to go outside. This woman's husband... Anyway, suffice to say he's been sorted now. Tell Quittenton I will drop off the information in the usual place by the end of the week."

"Lord Quittenton wants the information now." I said

coldly.

"Does he indeed. Well..." We could see the cogs in his head winding over and over.

"Well I don't have it here with me. I put it in a safe place. I will have to collect it."

"Shall we wait here?" Élodie asked.

"No, come back in a couple of hours. It's not close by. I don't want people here when I'm out. Come back at five." And we were dismissed.

We arrived back at Nougés after strolling along the Seine. Fishermen peppered both sides of the grey murky water and didn't seem to be having much luck. They were all old men, the young were all away of course. Women and children gambolled along the edge. Who would have thought the Germans were so close? I was irritated as Nougé did not answer the door when I rapped upon it.

"Maybe he is out, spying," Élodie laughed.

"Should be here," I snorted, then pushed the door which opened.

As we entered the building, we started up the stairs. The familiar smell hit our nostrils as we reached the head of the stairs and there was Nougé lying on the floor, his face a pulped mess and his lifeblood emptied onto the dirty carpet that lay underneath him. Flies buzzed and I felt sick.

"Who?"

"We have so many enemies, Élodie, who knows?"

"Shall we look around?"

"I don't think so, he was going to collect something. We won't get that from him. He's not going to have written it in blood or anything else, has he?" I said calmly.

"People don't do that," Élodie said.

"Not by the looks of it. Trouble is that this is real life, not a film-show or a theatrical or the penny dreadfuls."

"And they also die rather nasty deaths. Let's get away before les flics arrive."

"Let's just have a quick look. He may have put it somewhere, whatever it was."

The room had almost been destroyed. The cushions had been cut open, the drawers emptied. There was not a book in the bookcase anymore, they lay torn and ruined all over the floor. The place had been searched. Had they found anything? It would be impossible to know. Élodie looked down at the body. He was laying at such a strange angle. His right hand was open against his chest. His left hand closed by his side. It was as if he had been warding off blows with only one hand. Élodie reached and tried to unclench his left hand. Rigor mortis had already started to set in, but eventually it opened and Élodie cried out.

"*Une clef!*"

All we had to do now was find where the key fitted. Élodie pulled at my hand and we hurried down the stairs. Having found a bar, we sat with coffee and brandy to soothe our nerves. The key was on the table between us. The number large and the writing small but clear. "3792 *Gare de L'Est,*" I read.

"Most of the soldiers use that very station to make their merry way to the Front," Élodie said.

"Well that's simple enough. We go there and find the locker."

"Do you think he was killed before he went to the locker or as he returned?"

"Well if he returned, he wouldn't have the key."

"No, I suppose not. So that would mean people were watching," Élodie said. Outside away from the stifling air of the apartment, we glanced around us, but who could be watching? The two old men with their dogs, the young soldier in uniform but lacking an arm, or perhaps the three young women giggling loudly at the table next to us. It was hopeless. I sipped my brandy,

"Let's get it over with, we can get to the station and then the British Embassy by evening time. Then back to the hotel." We finished our drinks. Looking down the road, we couldn't see any taxis so walked. Élodie, as ever was sure of her directions and we made our way to the station. As we got closer, we saw more and more soldiers, so if they weren't mutineers, they were off to another Front. The huge edifice of *Gare De L'Est* loomed above us, but it was the sight of rows of wounded soldiers that of course attracted our eyes. Men laid out on stretchers, with blood-soaked bandages. Colonial troops were tending to them as were many nurses and doctors. A row of motorised ambulances lined up to collect them. It was not chaotic, but shambolic. Why were these men being displayed like this, I thought? Where is the dignity? They were on show and this couldn't possibly help morale. This and the two nights of recent bombings couldn't be helping anyone. Élodie had told me of rumours about dozens being killed in a metro station as they took refuge from the air raid. There was no safe place for anyone.

I remembered what I had written to Dada. There was really no point in wondering if a bullet or bomb had your name on it. Death would come when it chose to. The nurse killed whilst sitting next to me in my ambulance was an obvious example. It could have been me if the shot was just a yard to the right. There surely but for the grace of God. Élodie pulled my arm.

"Over here, *Cherie*, be quick." We hurried over to the bank of lockers that stood against a long wall. Many were open and battered. We found ours and quickly turned the key. Inside was a package covered in sacking. It wasn't very big but was heavy. I pushed it inside my bag and turned. Straight into a large man with a dark coat and a darker looking face.

"*Deuxième Bureau, Mademoiselle*. The package please." He held out his hand. Élodie was to one side of me, her eyes became fierce.

She shouted, "Run! *Allez! Vite!*" Remembering all of Chans instructions, I hitched up my skirt in a most unladylike way and performed a perfect Snake Creeps Down Leg Kick and the man went down hard onto the floor as my foot connected with his head. I had only just been able to perform the manoeuvre before ripping my skirt. I don't know why, but we took the stairs down, towards the metro. Was it even running, I wondered? I hadn't heard its swishing rattling noise, but then I hadn't been listening for it. Why was I having all these thoughts, my mind was a whirl. I didn't know who the man was, why he wanted the package, especially if he was supposed to be on our side. I hitched up my skirts and saw Élodie do the same as we careered along the long corridor, going ever deeper underground. There was a shout behind us, I didn't dare look. I saw Élodie glancing over her shoulder.

"Split up!" She called and disappeared to the left, so I went along the corridor to my right. Ahead were some turnstiles. I hoisted myself over them in the most unladylike manner and was on the metro platform. It was empty. I could hear the noise of running behind me and turned. There was no one there at the moment, but I could hear shouting. Then the unmistakeable sound of a gunshot started to echo about the station. What in God's name? I thought, and started towards the entrance to the platform, but then thought how stupid. If he was *Deuxième Bureau,* was he working for or against us. I couldn't take the chance. I ran to the platform edge and then manoeuvred myself down onto the track. I stepped over the rails carefully. The signs *'Ne pas descendre sur la voie. Danger de mort'* were clear. I was in danger of death, and not from any trains. I ran towards the darkness of the tunnel and suddenly went flying as I tripped on some obstruction or another. My head landed with a clunk on the concrete sleepers holding up the rail, my face perilously close to what could have been a live rail. I had no idea what was on and what was off, which rail was electrified if any. I shuddered and held my cheek. That really hurt. All I could see were little starlight flashes on the ground in front of me. Rats! That slowed me down but increased my heart rate.

The lights disappeared as pitch blackness seemed to envelope me. I put my hands out and felt my way to the wall. It was slimy, yet dry, a really strange sensation to my fingertips. I came to a gap and I eased myself in, just as I saw a flashlight embrace the darkness from where I'd run. There was more shouting and scrambling sounds. French swear words littered the air as the men came nearer. I held my breath. One. Two, three went past me. I slowly exhaled, glad I did this silently as a fourth man passed within inches of me. I tried to disappear into the wall. I felt rats scuttling over my feet and hoped my shuddering would not alert the men to my presence. Another gunshot echoed from far away and the men returned. This time walking rather than running. Was the gunshot a signal or had they shot my dearest girl? I felt tears prick my eyes. What on earth was I doing here in the soot and the filth of the metro, when I should be cruising around the beautiful city of Paris? Why had we agreed to run this errand for Quittenton? As a result both our lives were at risk. It was bad enough trying to escape the bombs and shrapnel at the Front, without coming to a city and appearing to play out an act in a new theatre of war. Tears streamed down my cheeks. I watched as torch light danced about the walls and the chuntering men disappeared from whence they had come, and all was silent, except for the squeak and the rustle of the Metro rats. After what seemed an age, I decided to move. My legs were wracked with pins and needles. I made my way slowly back to the platform and peeked above the edge. It was empty. How stupid I thought. I would have left someone on guard.

  I smelt the acrid smoke of a cigarette and the guard was given away. He was hiding by the entrance to the platform but was too stupid to hide correctly. I carefully crossed to the other side and keeping in the darkness made my way along to where I hoped there would be a gap to another tunnel, and sure enough there it was. I squeezed through to the other track and again with great caution stepped over the tracks. I didn't know if they were live or not, but *Danger de mort* were my by-words! Heaving myself up onto the platform was no mean feat and I staggered when I got there. I looked down at my skirt, thank goodness I had worn my navy blue one, but it was still filthy, and I could feel dirt on my face and my hands were black. There was no way I wouldn't attract attention. Just then I heard the sound of sirens in the streets, and a few moments later people started to come onto the platform. An air raid!

That was all I needed, now at least I was now camouflaged to some degree. What I wouldn't give for a lie down though, my heart was racing, and I thought it would explode along with any bombs the German Gothas might drop. I pushed a hair from my face and just then another hand appeared and brushed away another. Élodie! Not shot, not hurt in any way, just my Élodie. I hugged her and would not let her go until she eased me away gently, her face lit up by her beautiful smile. Her eyes sparkling, as if she had just attended a party, or had played a game.

"Where have you been, *ma Cherie*?"

"Hiding in the bowels of the earth. I thought they'd shot you."

"Yes, I see your tears on your dirty face," she smiled. "Here, let me try to wipe it clean." She produced a handkerchief and dabbed at my face. She put it to her mouth and then wiped some more. I winced as she caught my sore cheek, her gentle lips kissed away my pain. This process continued for a while until she stepped back.

"Ah, *ma mie,* a little bit more presentable."

"The shots?" I enquired.

"At rats I think, they were nowhere near me. You still have the package?"

"In my bag."

"Let me have it, just in case they see you again, though I think we will be well hidden now. We must split up when we leave. Try to find a charming man at the station exit to take your arm and protect you." She raised an eyebrow, then smirked.

"I know, *Cherie,* we do not need help, but it will confuse these so-called allies of ours."

"Maybe they are allies and were trying to help."

"I do not think so. I hear that the war is not so good in Paris all of a sudden, and that the place is crawling with spies."

"Where do you find all this out, Élodie?"

"I just listen, and I see. You observe the beauty of Paris, I observe the gutter!" She laughed, but there was no humour in it.

"Still, we are safe. We have the messages. We have each other." She turned to the wall and pushed the package down the front of her blouse and quickly did up the buttons of her jacket. She smoothed it down. I pushed her hair back into place and as I finished, she took my hand and kissed it.

"Je t'adore," she whispered, and my insides melted. We sat on the floor, snuggled up together. We loved the warmth of each other's body and the satisfaction that this closeness gave it. In this subterranean world rules no longer seemed to apply, and we could act as we wished. All around us were old people and children. Young women and older women. There was an absence of young men, just as there was in Britain. We knew where they all were. Stacked up outside or dying at the various Fronts. Were we going to lose the war? The Germans were now much closer to Paris than they had been for a while and two nights of Gotha attacks didn't make me feel very secure. The French were notoriously fragile, and we had both heard of the mutinies that had occurred in various places. They had tried to keep them quiet, but rumour as well as fact spread quickly along the grapevine that was the trench network on the Western Front. Fresh air slapped against my face. I thanked the old man whose arm I had taken, but I had seen no one watching for us. Élodie joined me and we hurried along towards the Gare de Nord. At last we saw a taxi. Élodie hailed it and it stopped alongside us.

"The British Embassy, Monsieur, 35 Rue du Faubourg Saint-Honoré," I asked as I collapsed into the leather seat. Élodie sat close and rested her head on my shoulder, I squeezed my arm around her back and pulled her a little closer. I just needed the reassurance of her body against mine. Rather, I needed her.

Later safe in the official building of our government in Paris, a rather pretentious man in a red and gold uniform said loudly, "The Earl of Derby will see you now." We followed him. Little did he know.

"Uncle Edward!" I ran towards him, and he hugged me

tight.

"Why Pandora!" He grinned. "How lovely to see you, but what a state you are in. Where have you been, and this is..."

"Élodie Proux, *Monsieur Le ambassador*," said Élodie, "I am a friend of your niece?"

"Oh no, we just always acted as uncle and aunt to the Loveday children. No blood relations, just friends with her mater. How is the old battle-axe?"

"Gosh, Uncle Edward, you can't call her that!" I laughed. "Though to be honest... No, she is very well. Just tired of the war, as everyone is."

"But what brings you here?"

"Lord Quittenton had us run an errand for him. Turned out a little trickier than we had thought." Élodie had retrieved the documents from her blouse.

"We were chased by someone who said he was from the *Deuxième Bureau*..."

"Oh, those bounders, can't trust them, you were right to run off. They didn't hurt you, did they?"

"Couldn't catch us." I laughed.

"Though we had to take to the metro tunnels to escape them," Élodie added. Uncle Edward opened up the package. He skimmed over its contents, part of which was a model of a cannon. A pretty toy for a boy soldier, I thought.

"In code my dears, but this is an interesting little trinket." He handed the little gun to Élodie.

"I think my grandson will like this!" Élodie handed it back. "Now young ladies, I'll tell her ladyship you are here, and I think a bath apiece will be in order. Then some clothes, then a good dinner. What do you think?"

March 10th, 1918.

Dearest Journal

Well we escaped with our skins intact! I have no idea how we get into such situations. Well part of it is of course our own fault, we accept these offers of work and go gallivanting along without a thought of fear in our heads. It must be some kind of disease when we are involved.

I get so intoxicated. I seem to enjoy it so much then when it is over. I realise how close we came to calamity. I have no idea why I do love it so much. My dearest girl too, she is so clear headed and, can I say it, clear eyed. She is devoted to any task we have. Sleuthing she calls it. I giggle when I hear her using that term. Sleuthing indeed. We are such detectives that we get into such straits!

There is such evil in the world, and we are seeing it close up. But where does this evil come from? I have no idea and these people, how do they live their lives? Do they know they are wrong? I suppose not, to fight for your country is admirable. We are doing it. Even to kill for your country is right, I am sure of that. But the senseless killing, that is the thing. The death of Nougé for example. He was a spy, he played both sides perhaps, but should he have paid with his life in such a brutal way? I don't think so. Would we face that fate if we were in his position. A metaphorical shiver has shuddered across my body, I don't want to think about it. Perhaps we will be safer at Lapugnoy. I hope so ...

Chapter 11

"You cannot kill a breeze, a wind, a fragrance; you cannot kill a dream or an ambition."

Lapugnoy hadn't changed, if anything it was even busier. It was almost like a small town. There were streets which had hospital tents on either side of them, huge tents for operating and recovery. The Barn was in what could be called a suburb, a short trip from the roads that networked across our region, most leading to only two places, the Front and a hospital, or other medical outfit. Rows of stretchers were laid out by the main operating tents. Orderlies were being told where to lay each man. Those with wounds that could be helped were nearest, those who had no hope were further away. Another ever growing line was ready for the mortuary tent which was a lot bigger than we had had back at the Barn. It sickened me that as we were getting closer to victory that more young boys were dying. We had heard tales of the Germans starving back in their homeland and a mutiny at one of their ports. We had to win now, but still it seemed they could not stop killing each other. Amongst our dead and wounded were many grey uniformed Germans, as well as men of different colours and nationalities. It was as if the world was here in this small corner of Northern France, intent on wiping itself out in pursuit of a victory that would be meaningless to so many. I saw Élodie moving up and down the rows, stopping to talk to patients from all sides. She spoke German and was able to reassure some of the young men she dealt with. It must have been nice for them to hear a recognisable accent, as they lay there begging for their mother or wife. She could act as a surrogate just as I had so many times for our own boys. Just when I thought it could not get any worse, I was proved sadly wrong.

The Germans were attacking on all Fronts and breaking through on many. They had bombed Paris and were said to be less than forty-five miles from the city, with huge guns. God knows what damage would be done to the beautiful city. At our clearing station we were exhausted. The ambulance was groaning under the efforts it was making, as was I. The feelings that ran through my body each morning were ones of utter dejection. I hated all this. I wanted to go home. All we did was to patch up these boys and send them either back to fight, or to England to live a ruined life. Was that what they were fighting for. At each stop, be it dressing station or clearing station, I was surrounded by death and blood. I closed my eyes and that was all I could see.

The long drives in the rain, or the brilliant sunshine sometimes disorientated me. At times with fatigue, I felt I was back home, driving down country lanes. There was no green grass or waving cornfields here though, all was stark and grey. With black trees easily picked out on the horizon, as there were so few of them, a crump from a gun would bring me back from my daydreams, and often I thought I must have been asleep at the wheel, driving by some kind of remote control. Nurses may sit in the front or the back and their inane chatter would keep me awake most of the time. They would talk and talk, never of what they were doing in the wards, but of love affairs or parties at home, anything that wasn't about death and destruction. But it was just talk to me and of very little consequence. Of course, I would answer politely and try to be part of the conversation, but more often it was easier to let them drone on and keep happy thinking of better times. I would stare out at the muddy or dusty road ahead, trying so hard to focus on what I was doing, before drifting off to some place where all the terror and despair was coming to a head. When this happened, I would suddenly jerk into reality, and like a wet dog shake it all out and start again. I had to go on. We all had to go on, whatever choice did we all have? We could give up I know, give in to the Germans and their demands, or we could fight. But who had right on their side and what was right anyway?

Poppy Flowers at the Front

March 28th, 1918

Dear Diary

It's been a while since we spoke. Lots has happened. I am not the same girl that started writing back in October. I have seen so much and seen too much. I have found love and love has found me. it is a secret love and only you and I know of it, but it is a beautiful love and makes me feel so good. I know now that if the worst was to happen, that I had found true love and true happiness, if only for a few short months. Why has it to be with a backdrop of such inhumanity to man? I have all I want, except I suppose the freedom to show the world my love, but at least I have love.

It is her birthday today, and I am sitting here on my cot deciding whether to wake her from her sleep, or to let her dream on. She is so beautiful when asleep. Her eyelids flutter and she smiles a lot. She no longer has as many nightmares as she used to, which is a good sign. I do love her so. I heard yesterday that there had been more bombings in Paris, but that they didn't think it was from the Gothas. I don't know what that means. Could they have a cannon that fires shells that far? I hope to goodness not, because how could they stop them. It was all very fragile in Paris when we were there, but it seems so long ago now. Time does pass so quickly as does the course of the war. We feel we are on top and then we lose ground. We gain ground again and think all is well, then another train load of our boys is shipped back to England and my ambulance needs rinsing out again. I hate it. I hate it!

"Happy Birthday my darling." I whispered into my dearest girl's ear. She opened her eyes full of sleep and smiled.

"What time is it?"

"Time that the birthday girl was up and about. Look I have gifts for you." I looked around, no one was about, so kissed her on the lips. She pulled me down onto her, and giggling I fell to the floor between the two beds. "You pig!' I squealed.

"To taste your lips drives me mad. Was that my birthday gift?"

"It could be, or here are more practical things." I handed her a package. Not as delicately wrapped as I would have wished, but needs must.

"Narcisse Noir! Thank you so much, *ma mie!*" My travails around Paris had not been in vain, though it had been hard to find a perfumery in the city that had some stock of her favourite scent.

"Then this." I handed her another package. She opened it greedily and brushes and pencils were scattered over her cot.

"Oh, my darling, where did you find all this?"

"It was difficult, *Cherie,* but for you I would search to the end of the earth." She pulled me towards her again and this time the kiss was a little longer and a little gentler.

"I love you so, Poppy. All I needed for my birthday would be you."

"So, you have a little extra. This your final gift, but I expect you to share."

"Oh, *mon dieu! Nougat de Montélimar,* where is this from if not heaven!" She laughed almost hysterically as she ripped off its covering and broke a piece off. She pushed it into my mouth, then took a piece for herself. I got up from between the cots and pulled mine closer to hers and lay down. All was silent as we sucked the sugary sweet, at peace and so happy in each other's company.

They had talked about the Americans coming to help for so long, that I was fed up with waiting. I could not understand why they hadn't come to defend us sooner. We thought the same way, or perhaps I was wrong. We had seen the odd soldier over here who had joined up with one group or another, but I now knew they were here because of the increased number I was carrying in my ambulance and the appearance of so many American Red Cross ambulances at our station. There had of course been the massive German offensives, probably because they were worried about the Americans finally arriving and trying to gain footholds before they did, but as the German offensive seemed to be petering out, the arrival of or threat of America had had its effect. I don't know though, maybe it was the Americans who brought over the next thing to hurt us, and that was the epidemic of Spanish flu. If it wasn't the bullet or the bomb that could trip us up at any moment, we now faced an even more effective killer that didn't care what uniform you were wearing and where you wore it. The flu was raging across our battlefields and across towns and cities as well. Hundreds were dying and I was now transporting men with no wounds, but terrible fevers across the wastelands to the train stations. I had never really thought about being blown up or shot, but I was suddenly quite scared about catching the flu. It seemed that once it got hold of you, that was that. It seemed that those affected would just appear to have normal flu symptoms, though the feelings of lethargy and fever were common most of the time along with aching muscles and sickness. But then it would get worse and would be so quick.

    We VADs on the ambulances had taken to wearing surgical masks as we drove and as we moved men in stretchers from ambulance to train or ambulance to tent, though I had started to try to avoid doing this and leaving it to orderlies. It was the speed of the flu that was so terrifying. Once contracted it seemed there was very little chance of recovery. It was frightening. Aches and diarrhoea would follow fever and nausea. Many then developed severe pneumonia attacks. It was horrible. Dark spots would appear on their cheeks and patients would turn blue, suffocating from a lack of oxygen as their lungs filled with a frothy, bloody substance. It was almost as if they had suffered from a gas attack, their very own invisible gas attack. But it seemed such a horrifying way to die, as if bullets and shrapnel were not enough. We now had this. It seemed that all the nurses were now wearing masks to offer some protection, and on calm or rainless days the sides of the hospital tents had been lifted as if to beg the wind to blow away the germs that were causing the flu.

    Élodie was washing her hands more as if that would be

some safeguard. I felt it couldn't hurt, and my sore chilblained hands were now even more red from scrubbing after each journey. Every little thing that would help I expect. I didn't know where the illness was coming from and the doctors didn't seem to know what to do to stop it. It was a case of cross your fingers, I supposed, but this all scared me more than the bullets. This was perhaps the first time I had felt real fear since I had come over here. I had to resolve to get on with life and not succumb. Leave beckoned and I could hardly wait, anything to distract me from reality.

That evening we attended a song and dance event at the mess hall. The officers were so young, perhaps even younger than they had once appeared. It couldn't be because we were getting older, as I was still but a slip of a girl! Were we running out of men at home? It seemed we might be. It was heart-breaking to think that some wouldn't be seeing out the year, maybe even the month. They disappeared like flies in winter. Swept up by all manner of killing machines. We both danced with whoever asked us to. I liked to dance and was happy to do this. Élodie on the other hand was quite odd when it came to dancing with men and tried to avoid it. She loved to dance alone, but here she made a special effort for these boys. Red faced she sat beside me and handed me a cup of punch. Goodness knows what was in it. There was a fruity alcoholic taste, even though we had been told there would be no alcohol to be had.

"The boy at the counter gave me a big wink when he handed it to me, so I suspect something fishy is in it," Élodie said straight faced.

"Fishy? My darling if it were fish I would not be able ..." She gently thumped my shoulder.

"Do not make fun of me, Poppeee. You know what I mean."

"I know my darling. I was trying to make a bad joke."

"*Desole, ma mie.*" She was shamefaced, then asked, "Have we not had enough of this? I need to go to bed."

"Yes, a short walk in the moonlight and then bed.

Perfect."

She took my punch cup away and placed it on our table and helped me to my feet. Electricity shot through me as she touched me, and I shivered.

"Cold, my love?"

"In love." I smiled at her. Her emerald eyes sparkled as she blew me a little kiss.

Outside it was cold, and we pulled our coats tight. The barn was off in the distance and we made to take a short cut through tents to make our way home.

"The stars shine down on us, Poppy."

"Yes, they are our biggest supporters. They see everything and accept everything. In their eyes we can do no wrong."

"But here on earth another matter, *cherie*."

"I know, perhaps we should shoot out to the moon or the stars to find happiness."

"I am happy, *cherie*. I've never been happier." She put her arm through mine and I pulled her closer with my elbow. I heard a faint cry in front of us and immediately thought of the poor soldiers, who had not been able to dance.

"That was a woman, Poppy!" Élodie said.

There was the cry again and some muffled noises between two tents in front of us. Élodie pointed me to go one way as she made to the left. All hell broke loose. As I turned at the end of the tent, I was faced by a scene almost from a farce. Élodie was almost riding on the shoulders of a soldier who had hold of a nurse. She was flailing at him and kicking out at another soldier in front of her. Élodie started screaming at the top of her voice and the soldier let go of the other nurse as Élodie shifted her grip and went for his eyes. I ran and kicked at the soldier in front, catching him on the knee. He also let go of the nurse.

"Run!" I shouted. From somewhere the soldier produced a knife.

"Don't be stupid..." I started, but he made towards me. I could run and leave Élodie, or stay and face this thug. The thoughts flashed through my head. Chan. Remember what Chan said. I steadied myself and lowered myself into the stance we had rehearsed so many times.

"Been watching those chinky bastards have you, love," he sneered. I stared at him. Élodie's cries in my ears. My mind raced, then I stopped it racing, stopped it dead. Calmness was a mantra of Chan's. I had to be calm. Sink low. I swayed as he lunged at me and smelt his sweat as he flashed past me completely off balance.

"Bastard!" he hissed and stabbed at me again. It was so easy to move away from his clumsy thrusts. Everything seemed to have slowed down. No longer could I hear Élodie's cries, no longer could I see the starlit sky. All I could see were his eyes. They moved closer. I raised my hands, palms facing me and moved them slowly in the rotations Chan had shown me. I dropped my left leg back and sank lower. He came at me again. Deeper I sank then as he was about a yard away, I exploded up. Golden Cock, Chan had called it. My right foot hit him square on the temple and he collapsed onto the muddy ground. I turned to see Élodie, still struggling on the other man's shoulders. He was grabbing at her but couldn't reach her. It would have been comical if on a film, but this was all too real. He didn't see me, but he felt me as I kicked him hard in the stomach. He too crumpled onto the floor, Élodie rolled off him and ran to me, hugging me tightly.

"*Mon dieu,* Poppy. What is happening?" Several soldiers suddenly appeared; a Provost looked at the scene of carnage. The young nurse with another soldier by her side pointing at the two objects on the ground.

"Well ladies, seems we're too late," he smiled, as his men dragged the two inebriated men to their feet.

"Stinking drunk, though no excuse. Take them to the guard room."

"Well Élodie, take me to my bedroom," I smiled, and linking arms we made our way to our cots.

I wasn't sure how many times I had shown my pass, but at last I was on the ferry for my leave. I was to meet my parents at Dover, and we were to drive home for a glorious week. I didn't have Élodie with me, which was a real sadness to me, but I was so looking forward to getting home after months away that it almost didn't seem to matter. Though as I looked out at the calm sea, I felt tears slipping down my cheeks. It had only been five hours and I was missing her dreadfully already. A young man in a snow-white uniform came and asked if I wanted a cabin for the crossing, but I assured him I would be fine on deck. He was probably worried about me mixing with soldiers and walking wounded. It was always nice to have your virtue cared about. I sat at the bow end looking towards England, expecting at any time to see those white cliffs. It was not yet midday and I felt confident we would not be hit from a U Boat, or a mine, and that I would see my parents soon. I recognised a nurse from our clearing station, and we settled down for a chat and the time flashed by as we were able to joke about where we had come from. Of course, it wasn't really a laughing matter, but the good old British stiff upper lip still survived it all and we could make fun of many of those we left behind. The channel seemed to be full of ships of all sizes. I was sure most were carrying troops though where they had got more soldiers from, I had no idea. There were also many merchant vessels, black smoke smearing the sky, transporting foodstuffs and the essentials of living to the continent. Hospital boats with huge red crosses painted on their sides chugged back and forth. They seemed to have the shortest stop-over period as they would arrive in port, disembark and turn around almost before they were empty. Many was the time I was almost dizzy in the act of delivering wounded soldiers and then returning to France. I would have to be quick to leave this boat and meet Dada. I didn't want to return to France without having a taste of Leicestershire fresh air, and a mother's love.

  It was so wonderful to see Dada on the quayside, standing tall and looking out to sea. I waved wildly and he caught my eye and waved just as wildly back. I ran to disembark, grabbing my bag and ready to show my pass and all the other paraphernalia that went along with getting back into the country, but was waved through by the same young officer who had asked if I wanted a cabin. We had reached Dover and decorum to one side I jumped into Dadas arms and he hugged me tightly and swung me around off my feet like he had when I was small. "So good to see you, darling." his voice cracked.

"You too, Dada." I kissed his cheek, he took my bag and put his arm through mine.

"Your mother is in the car. Be prepared."

"Ever was Dada!" I laughed. Mother couldn't hide her obvious shock at the sight of me. Luckily, I had kept my beret on or I would have had to again explain my short cropped convict-like hair. But I was too thin, too pale, too dirty, everything was too much. How could they treat me so badly? It wasn't until Dada put a stop to her that I was able to sleep in the back seat.

As if by magic I woke as the car manoeuvred its way through the gates at Loveday Hall and down the drive. I had been asleep for hours lulled into comfortable unconsciousness by the warmth of the car and the gentle hum of its engine. How different from France with the noise and the bouncing on the rutted cobblestone roads. It had been like a magic carpet ride home. It was also magical that George, our butler was there waiting with his wife Mrs George. They were magicians. He took my bag whilst his wife fussed and cooed. It was so nice to get back to normality, and though in the past I hadn't liked to be treated like the landed gentry, it was all of a sudden so nice to be welcomed in such a way.

Dada was in his study. Mother's books and charts were piled high in a corner. He had almost got his room back!

"Well Ophelia, it seems that the German danger is passing. High Command think they have shot their bolt."

"Does that mean we are winning?" I asked.

"Not really sure my dear. They are being pushed back. The Americans are making a difference, but you know it is all so fragile. We make an error in a sector and they could all pour through again, and we would be back at square one."

"Any news of Alfie?" We hadn't spoken of him for a

while. I knew that Dada knew what he was up to and where he was, but he kept it close to his chest. Even from his own family.

"Alfred is safe at the moment Ophelia, so rest assured. Young colt has been posted to another position."

"Did you get him moved?"

"Never, he'd not forgive me if I ever interfered. Just as you wouldn't if I had hauled you back from France."

"I'd like to have seen you try, Dada." He suddenly looked serious.

"My darling Ophelia, if I had wanted to, I would have had you sent back in an instant. You were under-age, I knew that. I only had to inform your commandant. Your mother begged me to, and I had to dissuade her from doing so herself. You were our first and only real argument we've had in over twenty years of marriage."

"Why didn't you?" I wondered, feeling a little crestfallen.

"Because for one thing I knew you needed to be there. You had to do your bit. Not for you jam making, or committee running. You had to be there."

"And the other reason?"

"I was so proud of you."

"Oh, Dada!" I exclaimed and hugged him as my tears began to flow.

"It's a damn awful thing, Ophelia, to be proud of the most important things to me in the world for putting their lives at risk for others. But it's so true. You and Alfie are so special and so brave, one day your mother will understand."

"I think she does now, Dada, she's just too proud to admit it."

"I know," he huffed. He knew his wife too well.

"She has moved on from her protesting days, into a woman who feels she has to present a different style of life. She could do more for her suffragette friends, but at the moment she is lying low. Perhaps when the war is over, she will reconvene all her old comrades. Then we shall see."

"Indeed, we shall!" I laughed. That was how my visit

continued, one of happiness and laughter, as Mother and Dada fussed and coddled me along, with cook trying to build me up by filling me to bursting with as much food as rations allowed. My chilblained hands were clearing up and my aching shoulders were at last loose and free. I felt a new woman as I returned across the Channel.

    At last, back on French soil, after months at the Barn, it seemed that we were having such success against the Germans that we were told that we were striking camp and moving our base to be nearer to the Front that had moved substantially forward. Before we had settled at the Barn, at what now seemed to be years ago, we had led a very nomadic life, moving backwards and forwards to new camp or old, as we had success or failure. This now meant sustained success. We had broken through the German Front line and were moving nearer to Belgium. We would lose our brick walled billet for now, unless we were really lucky finding a new one, and move into a canvas home. Living in tents was always cold and damp. Even when the sun was out it was either moist or too hot inside, and not very pleasant. As we got to our new base, we found German POWs, and some of our own fitter patients, laying duckboards and sprinkling cinders on the ground. Others were digging drainage trenches and still more latrines. I was tired out.

    We had moved all our patients to the rail ambulance in a very short time, and then we had to shift an influx of patients to another clearing station before we loaded up our ambulances and some twenty lorries with our equipment. This could become a regular occurrence if we had more success, but that would be no bad thing. Breaking camp and moving further North, chasing away the Germans, collecting more invalids. It would mean great disruption and sleepless nights, but if it meant we were going to win the war it was a tiny price to pay. Sophie and I carried our bags into our allotted tent and found Élodie already there. In the corner, our trunks were stacked neatly. How they had got there, and not to a far-flung part of Belgium unknown to us, would forever be a mystery.

"How do you do it, Élodie?" asked Sophie.

"I know the right people," she smiled.

"The kettle is on and we can have tea." From somewhere she had found a small primus and kettle. We had all the mod cons.

"I even have coffee. I made exchanges for it with a Tommy. Which would you prefer?"

"Coffee might help us stay awake. We may be busy soon," I smiled. And of course, we were. Soon my ambulance was winding its way through a new place in France, though to be honest, it didn't look too different from any other place in northern France that we had been in over the last two years. The road was sunken and a mixture of potholes, shell holes and dried mud. Every so often we would hit a cobbled stretch, but that was more than likely more difficult to drive on. We would see armies of coolies repairing roads and digging embankments. I wondered where Chan had gotten to, we had been split up for a while now and I missed his smile. I had of course continued when I could with the patterns of movement that made up Tie Chee and felt refreshed whenever I had finished. It really did clear my mind.

All around black cadaverous trees dotted the landscape. We could once again hear the crumping sound of heavy guns in the distance, that we drove towards and the sky ahead seemed dark with foreboding. We were to drive to the Dressing Station this morning, always a little more unnerving as it was closer to the fighting, and then take the wounded to the new Casualty Clearing Station. From there we would reload. There I am talking as if it were parcels or packages! We would have the treated wounded placed in the ambulance and take them on to our base, or to the train line whichever was needed. It was hard to get into any sort of rhythm when driving, as every trip was different, every collection of boys in the rear having their own needs. Sometimes many were on the point of death, and other times they had been lucky enough to have slighter wounds, though we had all got used to hearing how infection had caused so much death and amputations. Then there was the flu and all of us trying to avoid the invisible infection, a hopeless task I know! Sometimes, the boys could be soothed by the nurse who sat with them, other times nothing could stop the screams of agony, the sound I hated so much.

That night of course it rained. The canvas of our tent protected us, but the noise of the rain rattling above our heads for some reason was magnified. Sophie slept peacefully at one end of the tent, and Clemmie snored softly next to her. Élodie sat, her arms folded across her chest in the middle of the tent, and as the rain became heavier, I found myself supporting myself on my elbow looking at my dearest girl. The oil lamp flickered on her cheeks and I was intoxicated by her face. She seemed so peaceful and so beautiful. It all seemed so wrong, such beauty and at this moment peace here in northern France, just a few miles away from carnage and destruction. We may be advancing slowly, but what were our boys marching into? It seemed the more success we had, the more died. It was maddening, we were told we were winning, but the dead bodies didn't seem to agree with that.

Mind you, we were having so many German boys coming through to our lines and into our hospital trains. They seemed so young and vulnerable. Vulnerable because they had such wounds and injuries, young because they were but boys. Was Germany running out of men to fight, or had the young all been intoxicated into fighting for the Fatherland? Who would have thought? The nearer they came to defeat, the younger they got. I concentrated back on my Élodie and wondered where we would finish up. We had not really spoken about a future, save to say we would like to be together. Of course, I wanted to be together, but how would all of that work? Where would we live? What would we do? Could we stay together, or would society demand we part and live out our lives in a way only acceptable to its norms? What norms I scoffed to myself? Where man destroys man, yet a woman could not love another woman? What world were we creating? A man's world in all probability. A world my mother had once tried so hard to change. Would I be the one to try and make a worthwhile change or would I accept what was the status quo? The sight of my darling girl confirmed that I would not accept what we were all expected to live with. I wanted a different world. The only problem was how to achieve it. Would it be open or a secret? Why was love so difficult? It had happened so quickly!

After years of pushing inches backwards and forwards it was decided that we were doing enough in our sector to come home.

May 23rd, 1918.

Well dear diary

Here I am indeed! Three weeks before I am to be demobbed, I am based here in sunny Norfolk as an aide in a hospital for our soldiers. Mother and Dada have visited, and I am champing at the bit to get home. Mother was her usual self, commenting on how my hair was still too short, and when was I to start looking like a young lady again, and that I was still too thin, and that Mrs George would need to fatten me up depending upon when rations were lifted. As if I had had any control over that. Dada, of course, was still in his immensely proud mood. Alfie was now in Belgium somewhere. Still doing his bit, but not getting shot at thank goodness. Dada was now officially back on the retired list. Well for the moment anyway, as he tapped his nose when mother wasn't looking. I wonder what that means, is my papa a spy? I still had no inkling as to what he had been up to on those visits to France when I'd seen him. The joy that he had given me on each appearance could never be described. Élodie is unfortunately still in France. We had been apart for almost a month and it really is agony. It almost hurts physically. No Diary, it does hurt physically, like a pain where my heart is and a big stone in my stomach. A stone made of ice that is never going to melt until I see her again, and what if something happens to her. The flu is still raging across the continent. She is in the worst possible place. Anywhere away from me is the worst possible place. Well come on diary, tell me something to cheer me up! There is nothing, is there? She writes, but mail now was worse than it had been for a long time. I long for news from her but haven't heard anything for two weeks. My duties at the hospital are the general dogsbody type, running errands, greeting visitors, cleaning. At least I had a bed indoors, not in a tent and I was gloriously warm in that bed. No more fleas or freezing rain for me ...

I had finished my shift and was too tired to go to the canteen to eat. I climbed up the steep stairs to my room. I yawned as I turned the corner at the top and that yawn turned into a squeal at the sight I saw. Sitting on a trunk outside my door was Élodie. I felt spasms of delight flow through my body, and we almost knocked each other over as we ran towards each other and hugged,

"Where?" I started.

"Your room, let's go inside your room," Élodie breathed. I didn't want to let her go. Still holding her tight, I struggled for my key and somehow opened the door and went inside. I kicked the door shut behind me and her lips were on mine, devouring me in their passion. I ran my fingers through her hair and held her close.

"I've missed you so much." I gasped.

"Me you, *ma mie*. I have not lived since we parted."

We fell onto the bed and our lips met again. I breathed in her musky orange blossom scent and felt my head swimming with desire. I had missed her so much. She pulled at my clothes and I at hers, and soon we were naked on top of my bed, entwined in a passionate embrace. I could not get my fill of her body, nor she of mine. I had not felt like this for so long. I abandoned everything into her body, and we were soon as one, skin to skin, heartbeat to heartbeat, as close to her as I could possibly get. So young and so in love, a mad passionate love. I don't know how long it was, but finally we lay together sated. A sheen of perspiration was all that was between us. She lay tightly against me. I felt her warm body slowly breathing in time with my own.

"How did you get in here?" I asked.

"With what you call a sob story. Penniless nurse from France wanting to visit war-time colleague. The man at the desk just waved me through. He obviously likes you."

"Very lax!" I scoffed.

"Do you not want them to be lax with me, my sweet?"

"Of course!" I kissed her lips. "I was to go into town. Will you come?"

"I have come this far. I do not want to leave you again, not for a second. But first my gift."

Gift? Making love was the gift, and we spent another hour renewing contact with each other's body. I had been so alone without her, and now I could not get enough of her. Her naked body next to mine was so enticing, but I had to get up. I kissed her cheek, her neck, her mouth. I pulled her towards me.

"I cannot get enough of you, Élodie, I want you all, all for myself." She returned my kisses with even more passion, but I had to push her away.

"I need to wash my love, then we must eat. Where shall we go?"

"Stroll in the park, or a walk along the seafront?"

"The front would be nice. The wind is getting up and the tide is coming in."

"Then that's what we shall do."

"Yes, perhaps we could eat at the Hotel."

"That would be nice, do you have money?"

"I have my stamps."

Washed and refreshed, I passed Élodie her coat and found mine. We tucked each other's hair under our berets. Élodie produced some bright red lipstick and carefully smoothed it onto my lips sending chills through my body yet again. I took it and did the same for her.

"Presentable?" I asked.

"More than, *ma mie.*"

We went into town and onto the front to find the Paris Hotel. The buildings looked drab and uncared for. Paint was flaking and there was an air of tiredness about the place. The only thing that seemed alive was the sea. The tide was in and the sun was starting to sink on the horizon. It was now a calm and peaceful evening; the wind had dropped. One could almost think we had come to the seaside for a holiday, not to endure the last few months of a war that now seemed to be going our way. A warm breeze was running off the sea. We strolled arm in arm, parasols twirling.

"I met with Raoul and Jacinth in Béthune before I left."

"How are they?"

"Very well, Jacinth has grown so much. But Raoul is still very protective of her."

"You gave them my love?"

"Of course. Jacinth says for me to hug and kiss Loveday for her, and to tell Loveday she misses her and cannot wait to see her in the Hall that bears her name."

"She said that?" I laughed.

"Indeed. She is very impressed. She is a beautiful young girl. She will break hearts."

"And Raoul?"

"Still a little small for his age. He does not seem to thrive, but he is a happy boy. He is working hard and wants to be a gendarme, or an engineer. He cannot make up his mind."

"My word. How proud we shall be of them both."

"Jacinth dances. She dances as much as she can. The nuns frown upon it but let her have her head. One of them, Sister Boniface, was in a corps de ballet before she joined the convent and took holy orders and is teaching her."

"Goodness, so young..."

"But so very determined. She will win that one."

We entered the Paris Hotel and ordered some tea and cake. Luckily, they had both. We sat looking out towards the sea as we waited. There was a slight sting in the air as the wind caught the sea and carried tiny drops in the air onto the coast. We could smell the brine and for some reason this made me feel so alive.

"This is wonderful."

"Indeed, *cherie*. I am so happy we are here together,"

"Together? What plans do we have? What shall we do?

"Make love, that is all I want."

"You are so shallow, Élodie !"

"You want me to lie, to tell you of my grand plans when all I want is your naked body next to mine?" Warmth flooded through my thighs at the very thought and I felt my face flush.

"And by your cheeks I know you want me."

"I want my cake!" I laughed.

"But we need to think," Élodie paused, "I would like to finish at my university."

My heart jumped and dropped. Would we be apart?

"Where, in France?" I asked.

"Yes, it would not be for long. But you too need to study, to go to university."

"But to be apart." I hated this idea.

"We would meet for holidays."

"Oh, Élodie, I could not bear it."

"We will have to bear it, *ma cherie*. We need to do what is right."

"But..." I felt tears in my eyes. Élodie took my hand and squeezed it gently.

"You know I am right. You want to teach. You need to go to university. I need to finish my degree. It was so rudely interrupted!" She laughed, but she was not happy. "I have thought of this as I waited in France to see you. The missing you is so awful, but the meeting again is so beautiful. My heart leaps at the thought of seeing you after a gap. My love has not diminished."

"Nor mine, my love has grown. I have missed you so much."

"I think the worst part was not knowing when I would see you. At least we can tick off the days. You in your journal. We would know when we would see each other again."

The tea arrived and we spoke of other things.

May 26th, 1918.

Dear journal of mine.

I am heartbroken but I know Élodie is right, so I start the countdown to our next meeting! She is to study in Paris. I had thought about going to Oxford. Lady Greenwood had recommended her old college. I would like to teach, but for some reason I thought I would always be with Élodie. I am so selfish! I know she has to find her own way in life and cannot be ruled by me. I wonder if mother will agree with plans to go to university. Well she will have to agree. I am not going to become some kind of adornment to be taken out to various houses and parties. I know that in a few years I will need to be presented at court, my debutante fate cannot be escaped, but in the meantime, I will do as I wish. This is going to be so hard though. I have found my love with my dearest girl. If our love is strong enough, we will be able to go on. We have enough to put up with society's whims not to allow that to upset us. Being apart will be a torture. I will have to bear it. I will bear it. My love cannot be taken away. Distance will get closer as we pass our time apart. Going to university was my dream. Élodie knows this and she is right to encourage me. Likewise, I knew she wanted to finish her studies. So, I will bear it all. My love will endure. Our love will endure ...

It had always seemed strange to have German patients, in Lapugnoy it was a matter of convenience, I suppose. We could hardly leave them rotting on the battlefield, though some would have. But here in Cromer it seemed even stranger, to actually make the effort to transport them over the channel, and then to ferry them around English hospitals was bizarre.. Our soldiers were trying to kill them, and we would patch up any that survived. We had always cared for them if we found them at the Front, but here in England. Well we did what was right. We took the higher ground. I had no idea as to how our boys had been treated at the Western Front. Of course, we heard tales of atrocities and had to decide whether to believe them or not.

I preferred to believe that our boys were treated as well as we treated theirs. I was mopping out a room where there were two of them. A guard sat at the end of the corridor, but I think they were on parole. Anyway, one was so weak he wasn't going anywhere, the other was a heavily red bearded man, wearing thick pebble glasses who just seemed to sulk. Well who could blame him. Things weren't going right for his country and he was a POW. He should be unhappy. I looked out of their window and saw the expanse of the central quadrangle. Small figures were shuffling about, most led by a nurse or an orderly as they tried to get some movement back into shattered limbs. The gardens in the middle of the buildings were being tended to by soldiers who were using it as a way of recuperating. Maybe that would be a job some of them could do in the future if anyone would be willing to pay them. I wondered what jobs they would be going back to. So many women were doing the jobs men had done. They wouldn't dare to take the jobs from women to give back to men, would they? That would be monstrous. Men would have to apply again, and we could see everyone appointed on merit, rather than on their sex. I was brought back to reality when the weaker patient spoke to me for the first time when he thanked me.

"How do you feel?" I asked in my fractured German. He laughed and coughed. I recognised the cough. He had been victim to gas and wasn't looking too good. His face was grey, and his eyes a little glazed.

"As well as can be expected, *Fräulein*," he said in English.

"You speak well," I said, impressed.

"Being forced to fight against a country you love is a handicap, *Fräulein*," he said, and half smiled. This was an educated man.

"You must have lived here once?"

"Before the war I was at university in Durham. My friends did not understand my English accent when I returned to Heidelberg."

"Did you study there as well?"

"I did." Then his body was racked by coughing and he grasped for a handkerchief to hold to his mouth. Exhausted he sank into the pillows. The other patient made some comment in German that I didn't understand and left the room.

"He called me a traitor for speaking English," he laughed. "I think it is because he is ignorant and doesn't speak English himself."

"But he does have an impressive beard," I laughed, as did the patient before coughing took over again.

"What is your name?" I asked when he finally calmed down.

"Ewald Gruber, and you, *Fräulein*?"

"Call me Poppy. What was his name?"

"He told me Jaeger, but I am not so sure."

"I've never been to Germany. We were so close when I drove ambulances, but it seemed so far away."

"It is beautiful, though now…who knows what will become of us. Heidelberg is a wonderful town, full of what you would call Gothic architecture, I think. The spectacular Heiliggeistkirche church looming over the café lined Marktplatz, a grand old town square in the Altstadt. You look up and see the red-sandstone ruins of the Castle, like what you say, a fairy tale, I think you would enjoy it." Ewald smiled wistfully as he shared his memories and his face seemed to relax and take on a brighter colour.

"And what do you intend to do when you return?"

He laughed and then started the awful cough again. When he had wiped his lips, he said, "If I return, I will teach English. The irony of it all. What do you think?"

"I think it is a wonderful idea. Now I must get on. Do you want me to raise your pillows?"

"No, I will sleep now. I feel quite weak. Thankyou though, *Fräulein* Poppy. Thank you for your kindness."

As I left the room, I wondered how he had been treated before. I wasn't being kind, I was just being normal. Not like Jaeger, who seemed to deliberately barge into me as he returned. What an unpleasant man, I thought. I wonder why he is so angry; I'd have thought anyone who had fought in France would be grateful that their war was almost over. Still, the war did strange things to people. He was probably one of the fanatical few left over.

There was a call for a special meeting with Matron. Wonderful, probably a new cleaning rota. There had to be more to life than this! "We are so lucky," Matron started as she surveyed us all, "Her Majesty, The Queen Mary will grace us with her presence tomorrow. The hospital must be spotless. Everyone will be working to that end. You will also be spotless. Uniforms tidied up. Haircut. You know what is expected of you all. We will need to be busy."

'We,' I thought, that sounded a bit rich. So, I hadn't been far wrong. All I had done since leaving France was to clean. To scrub and to wipe. To brush and polish. My hands had just about recovered from the chilblains of France and now they were getting the hand equivalent of trench foot. All I could smell was disinfectant. At least I wasn't smelling of mud, or blood, or death.

"We will have a talk from an equerry tomorrow morning at eight and then she will be here at ten, prompt. We are so lucky, and you should all be so proud. Some of you may even be lucky enough to meet her."

Lucky indeed, mother and I had spoken with her many times in the past. She was a lovely woman. She and mother had secrets that I couldn't hope to discover. Maybe she was a secret suffragette. I snorted aloud at the thought. Faces span my way, Matron roared, "And Loveday, you will not be one of them!"

Suitably chastised I left to find Élodie. We spent a few moments together before I had to attend to my duties. This all seemed so pointless after what we had been put through in the last two years. We had the mud and the blood, and now at home we had to clean. Cleaning out my ambulance after every trip whilst in France was necessary. But cleaning a spotless hospital seemed so utterly absurd. And all for a guest.

"So, your Queen is to visit, *Fräulein* Poppy?" asked Ewald.

"Yes, but how did you know?"

"That misery Jaeger mentioned it. He heard it from a nurse. Was it a secret?"

"I'm not sure, if it was it was badly kept, but what does it matter?"

"Muttered some choice words when he told me. He has a dark soul, whoever he is." Coughing interrupted him again. A horrid sound. He might not be dying, but he wasn't well at all.

"Have you seen the doctor today?" I asked as I raised his pillows for him.

"I did and the good news is that I am to be sent to the country. I will be glad. Jaeger is to be sent to the local Camp. I am pleased with that as well."

"What was the prognosis?"

"A long hard recovery, perhaps never complete, but then so many are dead. So many are scarred. I am lucky I suppose."

"Did they say where in the country?"

"By York I think, somewhere in the hills. I shouldn't really know, but the nurse was kind like you. It will be peaceful. Then it will be back to Germany one day. Perhaps even home to Heidelberg, but who knows."

As we talked, I polished the taps and cleaned the sink. Washed the windows and finally mopped the floor. At least I could take the load off the hardworking nurses. Thinking of which, I wondered where my nurse was. She had shown her papers to Matron and she was contemplating letting her work here. It should be all hands to the pump, so I don't know why there was any issue. Red tape was always a constraint though. As I left the room, Jaeger pushed past me. His red beard could be said to be bristling, his eyes hidden by the pebble glasses. He still seemed so angry, positively seething. I don't know what a prisoner of war is supposed to behave like, so perhaps I should not be surprised.

Élodie waved as I approached her seated in the canteen.

"Success my love, I will be here for a week."

"That's good news. We can maybe demob together."

"Perhaps we can and then onto freedom."

"Are you to work tonight?" I picked at my breakfast. It looked unappetising and I was not disappointed when I ate. At least it was warm, so I decided to finish it. Waste not, want not as Mrs George would have said. There again her cooking was a delight, so not much chance of putting her grub in the bin. Grub? Where on earth did that come from, what a common little madam I am becoming. Need to revisit my linguistic training. Mother would have kittens if she heard me speaking like that, especially at any social event she would be holding. I almost choked on what was supposed to be porridge, as Élodie smiled at me quizzically.

"And tomorrow morning. A long shift of work. Did you hear, a soldier has been killed in the town?"

"Murdered? No, not a peep. When was this?"

"No one knows, he was killed, and his rifle stolen. Perhaps the Irish?"

"Who knows. Maybe a gangster."

"There are no gangsters here ... are there?"

"No more than normal my love."

Élodie sipped from her glass of water and I drank my tea. At least that wasn't stewed, and I thought back to the chemically tasting tea we had endured in France. I wondered what they had put in it. Rumours abounded that they had tried to reduce the Tommy's sex drive by adding something to it. In my experience they weren't affected in the least. And we had to drink the same muck. Oh well.

"Like in the films?"

"Maybe, speaking of which, maybe we should go to see a film. We haven't for so long. Buster Keaton in the what was it ... *The Bellboy*, or Charlie blooming Chaplin in something ..."

"Now we've won the war perhaps we can watch *Hearts of the World*, with Lillian Gish she is so beautiful."

"And her sister Dorothy, she is as well."

Élodie sighed, she looked and sounded so tired. We all needed a rest. Hopefully that would come and we would see real peace and quiet."

"Perhaps, *Cherie*, but I am frazzled. All this travelling and then running about here. It is exhausting. I'm so tired." I squeezed her hand as I left the table.

Time waited for no man or woman here in the hospital and of course there was much to do. The Queen would be here soon. Was I to rewash the floors, I wondered? Would another layer of polish keep the dreaded flu away? I wondered where the guard was who had slouched at the end of the corridor, probably painting kerb stones white. I almost made myself laugh; I was so funny.

I entered the German prisoners' room. It seemed unusually quiet. No coughing or wheezing, no greeting, nothing to hear, but what a sight I encountered, so terrible. Ewald lay on his bed, his throat gashed and the sheets bloody. His eyes were lifeless, vacant. My heart sank, falling as if into emptiness. I looked wildly around the room; it was empty. Something caught my eye by the mirror above the sink. In the bowl, once spotless after my hard work were the remains of a red beard. The person who had shaved hadn't taken much care. In the bowl were the thick spectacles that Jaeger had worn. It became clear, it was a disguise. Who was this Jaeger? I turned towards the door to go for help when I suddenly saw stars as something hit me on the back of the head, and I went spinning towards the floor. I grabbed at the end of the bed to stop myself falling. As I started to fully regain my senses and my footing, I saw him. A far-off memory from France reappearing in front of me like the devil incarnate. Kunz looked at me through his narrow, spiteful eyes.

"So, here we are again. Interfering seems to be your middle name." He held the rifle at his midriff, but his finger was on the trigger and it was pointing straight at me, unerring in its aim.

"Sit down, please." His voice was cold and heartless. I obeyed him; I didn't really have any option. I didn't think he would shoot me, but once he got near to me, it was a different matter. My head was spinning and I felt as if I was going to be sick. What on earth to do?

"I'll scream," I said

"I'll kill you, if you do."

"But they will be warned."

"There is too much noise. Anyway, people always scream in a hospital. It is a place of pain and terror."

"But why kill Ewald?"

"He was weak. He had given in, no longer willing to fight our enemy."

"But the war is over, surely …"

"Not while I still breathe and survive. I will always be at war until the day I am told to stand down."

"But he had fought for Germany, he was on your side."

"There you go again. Who is on what side? Do you even really know what side I am on?"

"The wrong side whatever!" I snapped.

"To you perhaps. But whilst we still exist, we will fight you British. You will never be in complete control. We will always be there, niggling at you, biting you, until we are once again powerful enough to destroy you."

"What are you planning this time, Kunz?"

"A simple task. I have my rifle. Ewald would not promise to stay silent so he had to go. You I hope will be more sensible."

"But what, Kunz?"

"It is pleasing you remember the name, not that it is mine anymore. Today I am Jaeger, tomorrow when I finish here, I will be … no I will not tell you."

"So, you won't kill me then?"

"Perhaps I will kill you, but not with the rifle. And now you are here, perhaps I can use you." He started towards me. I was suddenly terrified. I remembered how he had shot at my feet in France, how he had seemed to be responsible for so many deaths at Lapugnoy, and how now in Cromer he was infecting us with his evil again.

"Roll over onto your front and put your hands behind

you." I obeyed. What else could I do? He ripped a sheet and the long strip used like a rope bit into my wrists as he pulled it tight and made me wince. He was simply a swine. He yanked my head back and stuffed something into my mouth before binding something around my face. Then he stood up and kicked me in the side. The air seemed to burst out of me, and pain shot through my ribs. I felt tears well up and sniffed hard. The bastard would not succeed. But how could I stop him? And where was Élodie, I wondered. Safe, I hoped.

Élodie looked across at the rank of nurses facing her in the courtyard. Alongside her was another row. All sparkling clean in newly pressed, starched and ironed uniforms. Most were in light blue, but she and a few wore the grey of French nurses. She smiled at one who stood almost directly across from her. What a world she thought, all dressed up and on show when only a few weeks ago we were ploughing through the mud of Northern France with uniforms cloyed with dirt and filth. She remembered how blood never seemed to be red, but always black as it stained her clothes, often going through to her underclothes. How she would shiver with distaste as she washed it from her dress. How times had changed indeed, though she wondered if royalty had come to the front would they have had to change into a clean uniform to save their feelings. She was a world away when Matron appeared in front of her and she stepped forward and curtsied before the Queen and moved back into line. The Queen smiled and asked how she was. Élodie thought, 'I am exhausted and feel so dirty,' but said aloud, "I am very well, ma'am."

"'You are not English?"

"I am French, ma'am. After my time at the Western Front, I am over here visiting my good friend, Lady Loveday."

"Pandora Loveday? She is here? How delightful. Matron, where is she?" Matron looked blank.

"I have no idea, ma'am."

"Do find her, we have much to catch up on. Nurse you must join me for tea when I have finished my inspection. I hope Pandora will be able to come as well, Matron?"

"I am sure we can find her ma'am. Perhaps, Nurse Proux?" She raised her eyebrows in an unspoken request.

"Of course, Matron. I will find her." Élodie smiled at the irony. She hurried off, walking not running, but keen to find her dearest girl, and give her the good news. Once out of the courtyard she ran towards the nurse's wing and raced up the stairs toward her room, and for some reason her heart was beating faster. She pushed open the door, but the room was empty. She thought, where could she be? A sense of panic overwhelmed her, not knowing what could have happened to her friend. Suddenly, she remembered the German prisoner; Poppy had been keeping him company. Élodie hurried back down the stairs and along the disinfectant reeking corridor. The floor was glistening with polish just in case the Queen might inspect a ward or two. So highly polished Élodie thought she caught her reflection as she ran. It was like a great labyrinth. They never seemed to end, and she was worried that she would turn the wrong way. She started to call her dearest girl's name, which echoed along the corridor, the repetition mirroring her confusion.

My wrists were bound by the torn strips of sheet with an agonising tightness, cutting into the flesh, and my stomach hurt like hell. Looking towards Kunz through tear-veiled eyes, I was bereft. He stood at the window, looking out onto the quadrangle of garden that must have been slowly filling up with dignitaries. A band started to play. For God's sake I thought. Just when you needed silence. I heard Kunz laugh to himself.

"You English are so predictable. When I heard that her majesty was to appear, I knew it was my chance. She was bound to be out in the open for a while. All I needed was a rifle. As you can imagine, I am a crack shot."

My mouth felt awful, full of cloth, making it hard to breathe. My hands were numb, all feeling seemed to have drained away. But my pain was nothing compared to what this animal Kunz could bring. I shuffled my feet up towards my body and rolled onto my side. It was so uncomfortable. I didn't know what to do. All of a sudden I heard her, she shouted my name, the tone of anguish and desperation.

"Poppeee! Poppeee!" She must have been at the end of the corridor. Kunz looked at me, and back toward the door. He slowly opened it and carefully looked out, his rifle leading the way. He slowly drew the rifle back into the room and faced the door waiting. He had taken his eyes from me. Now, I realized in an instant, was my chance. I struggled onto my knees as quietly as I could, my arms numb, my body stiff from the radiating pain. The door burst open and that seemed to shock Kunz. I scrambled onto my feet just as Élodie appeared suddenly in the room, through the swinging entry, the half-doors. She looked at Kunz and me, and then at Ewald. Next she screamed at the top of her voice and stooping low, she ran at Kunz. I ran at him as well and we both hit him simultaneously. The rifle went off and we heard the bullet zing around the room. My head had buried itself in his stomach. I heard Élodie groan as he struck out at her, but felt her hitting him around his body, unbowed. I grovelled my way to my feet and kicked out at him, at his head, at the rifle, at anything I could reach without being able to use my hands, whilst Élodie was still flailing at Kunz like a machine. I could now see her and that most of her blows were hitting him around the face. I ran at him again like a bull attacking a toreador, my head sank into his stomach once again and he made a strange noise as air rushed from him. He lashed out in his frenzy and caught me again on the side of my head, but I felt nothing. Élodie was on his back, hands around his neck, frantically, he tried to shake her off. Élodie was continuing to scream. Why couldn't anyone hear? The sound of the band came through the window and I realised we were all alone. I moved closer to him again and he seemed transfixed, though I was also unsure what to do. I looked at him considering my next move when he suddenly dropped the rifle which by now he had only held by its barrel and he seemed to be overwhelmed by panic, attempting to flee. He stepped forward and pushed me away and tried to shake off Élodie, who was fighting like a wildcat. She tore at his face and though he tried to defend himself, he was failing. A hell cat more than a wildcat, Élodie was unstoppable. One hand up to protect his bleeding face, he prised himself away from her with the other and shook her off to the floor. He made for the door. I ran forward again and rammed myself into the back of his knees and he went flying face first along my beautifully polished floor. Behind me in the doorway, I heard the bolt of the rifle being drawn back.

"Get up, you *bâtard*!" I heard Élodie snarl. Kunz scrambled to his feet and looked past me. His face bloodied, but white, his eyes glinting. I turned and saw Élodie holding the rifle to her shoulder. I was mesmerised by the awful tableau, full of hate on both sides, a version of my Élodie that I never thought I'd see. Her eyes stared at him, her normal emerald green now almost steel-like in their fixation upon Kunz.

"You won't shoot an unarmed man, *Fraulein*. You English and your ridiculous sense of fair play," Kunz sneered, his face now ugly and bleeding even more profusely. He turned away and I thought this was the end of it, jumping as the gun exploded with a flash. I stared wide eyed as Kunz grabbed at the back of his thigh and fell to the floor, screaming in painful anguish, whining with self-pity and pain.

"But you forget, *monsieur*, I am not *Engleesh*, but French," Élodie muttered under her breath. I felt Élodie's hands at my gag and as she struggled to loosen it, I spat out the cloth. Next she carefully untied my wrists and rubbed them both to get some feeling back into my numbed limbs. I smiled, a tear on my cheek.

"What about..." I nodded towards Kunz.

"I don't care; look at your poor face," Élodie said.

"It's my tummy that hurts most." I paused and asked a moment later, "Why on earth did you shoot him?"

"Oh, Poppeee, because of Nurse Sloan in France, because of Nougé, because he was going to get away, and because he had hurt you, which should never happen. And I did it because he frightened me when we were in France, and more because he killed your German friend. And well, simply because he was horrible."

"Is that all?" I replied, laughing. "Just that?"

"No, that was not all. And did I say, because the monster had the temerity to try and get in the way of our appointment *a deux* to meet the Queen of England for tea!"

Poppy Flowers at the Front

Poppy Flowers at the Front

Poppy Flowers at the Front

Poppy Flowers at the Front